HOTEL LIAISON

Visit us at www.boldstrokesbooks.com

Acclaim for JLee Meyer's Fiction

Forever Found

"… succeeds in giving the reader a thoroughly enjoyable romance filled with tension and longing from the first pages. I highly recommend this first effort from this talented new author." – *Just About Write*

"…neatly combines hot sex scenes, humor, engaging characters, and an exciting story." – *MegaScene*

First Instinct

"Meyer does a terrific job at developing the espionage storyline and keeping the reader wondering where the next plot twist will lead. Well-developed characters and swift storytelling make this a wonderful read; I couldn't stop turning the pages." – *Lambda Book Report*

"Meyer's heroines are quirky, funny, and so very good together that you can't visualize them apart. Between the multi-dimensional characters with their genuine virtues and flaws, a plot you won't have figured out from the beginning, and a most satisfying conclusion, *First Instinct* leaves readers sated but anxious for more." – *Midwest Book Review*

Rising Storm

"Meyer has given her readers an exciting roller coaster of a ride. Her descriptions of the by-ways of California's northern coast are wonderful, as is her description of the off-beat characters that inhabit the area. This is a book readers will not be able to put down. Be sure to leave a solid block of time with no interruptions!" – *Just About Write*

"The saga of *First Instinct* continues for Conn, a secret operative, and her lover, Leigh. Hiding away, they are safe from Conn's world. When their cover is blown, they are forced into action. But they never forget to get it on between harrowing escape scenes." – *Curve Magazine*

By the Author

Forever Found
First Instinct
Rising Storm
Hotel Liaison

HOTEL LIAISON

by

JLee Meyer

2008

HOTEL LIAISON

ISBN 10: 1-60282-017-1
ISBN 13: 978-1-60282-017-3

THIS TRADE PAPERBACK ORIGINAL IS PUBLISHED BY
BOLD STROKES BOOKS, INC.
NEW YORK, USA

FIRST EDITION: JUNE 2008

CREDITS
EDITORS: JENNIFER KNIGHT AND STACIA SEAMAN
PRODUCTION DESIGN: STACIA SEAMAN
COVER DESIGN BY SHERI (GRAPHICARTIST2020@HOTMAIL.COM)

Acknowledgments

Tamara: A special thank-you for your time and memories of some very special women. I bow to you.

Susie, Rachel Spangler's partner: thank you for your help navigating the world of academia.

Sage Amante: for invaluable assistance with legalese and plot possibilities. Thank you, my friend.

Cheryl: For the gift of ideas and patience when answering the question, "Hon, what's another word for…"

Jennifer Knight: A gifted teacher as well as editor. I thank you for your insight and humor. Most of all, thank you for shaping *Hotel Liaison* into the book I am proud to offer to our readers.

Stacia Seaman: You do your magic in sometimes very tight time frames and we always manage to meet deadline. You are much appreciated by this author.

Len Barot: Your vision and dedication to teaching the craft have created something unique in Bold Strokes Books. It's an honor to be part of it.

Sheri: Your covers always draw the eye of the reader. Thank you for your talent and dedication to create just the right tone for this book and all the others.

Proofreaders, webmistresses, media liaison, everyone behind the scenes—a great big thank-you hug.

Dedication

"For it was not into my ear you whispered, but into my heart.
It was not my lips you kissed, but my soul."
—Judy Garland

For Cheryl, keeper of my heart and soul.

CHAPTER ONE

G et *out!*"
Those words, followed by a loud crash, sent Denny Phelps and her mother, Sika, scrambling toward Stefanie's office. They arrived just as the door was flung open and a large thirtysomething man stumbled out and rushed past them, not looking back.

Stefanie Beresford, red-faced with fury, appeared in the doorway, shouting, "And *stay* out!"

Her chest was still heaving when she finally noticed Denny and Sika standing frozen in place. Denny shot a pleading glance to her mother and Sika reached out and placed a hand gently on Stef's arm.

"What happened, dear? Did Kevin hurt you?"

Stef felt herself deflate, the anger being replaced by dejection. "No, not physically." She motioned her business partners, also dear friends, into the room. "Might as well have a seat. This involves all of us."

Having a seat necessitated Denny's putting chairs upright for herself and her mother. She chose to ignore the remnants of a broken vase that were scattered on the floor.

Once they were settled, Stef leaned her elbows heavily on her desk and said, "Our construction budget is gone."

"What?" Denny blurted out. "That's impossible. We had everything figured out to the penny. Even for overages."

Sika quietly said, "Let Stef tell us, Denny. Be patient."

Denny never ignored her mother's requests.

Sighing, Stef said, "Seems Kevin has a drug problem. Our money has been steadily disappearing up his nose."

She resisted sweeping everything off her desk to land with a satisfying crash on the age-darkened wood floor. She'd hired that Irish blowhard on her brother George's recommendation. Kevin was supposedly a font of knowledge about commercial construction. This and his claimed connections with smaller contractors in the Bay Area and San Francisco building inspectors had swayed her. She'd been a naïve fool.

"What about the subcontractors?" Denny's almond-shaped deep brown eyes were glazed with concern. "Did he pay them?"

"Not recently, and our suppliers will probably be next to knock on our door, asking for their money. Shit. Sorry, Mamaka." Sika didn't curse, and Stef always felt bad when she did so around her.

Mother and daughter sat back heavily in their chairs. Although Denny was a few inches taller than Sika and her skin was a lighter color, they shared the same high cheekbones and regal bone structure, the legacy of Sika's West African heritage.

"Don't apologize," Sika said, "I feel like swearing myself. Is *all* the money gone?"

Stef calculated. "No. Luckily, one of the subcontractors called me directly and complained about not being paid. I did a quick inventory and stopped Kevin's access to that account. We have enough to get us about halfway finished. That's if we cut back where we can and immediately find a new contractor who won't rob us blind."

She was heartsick, and struggled to not just get up and lay her head in Sika's lap and cry. Her mind was blank. Not exactly dynamic CEO material.

In a move that usually signaled deep thought, Denny unconsciously patted her black, closely cropped hair. Suddenly brightening, she said, "Hey, remember Jock Reynolds from my basketball team?"

Stef stared dully at her best friend, trying to understand why she would bring up Jocelyn Reynolds. *Speaking of blowhards.* Cautiously, she said, "Yeah, I remember her."

"Well, she's a general contractor now, has her own business right here in San Francisco." The look on Denny's face told Stef that she thought she'd come up with a solution. Denny always had a glass-half-full take on life.

Stef still wanted to weep. Instead, she tried to suck it up. "Denny, Jock Reynolds did nothing but tease me about being 'vertically challenged' when we were in college. She slept with any woman she could charm into her bed and barely made her grades to continue playing and graduate. What makes you think she'd be any more reliable than that worthless idiot I just threw out of here?"

Sika arrested Denny's response with a small hand gesture. "I've read about several of her projects in the city. They speak well of her company. It's mostly female workers and she doesn't try to hide the fact that she's a lesbian. I think we could at least get a bid. Perhaps she's grown up since those days, Stef. People change."

Denny gave her mother a grateful smile. When Sika spoke, debate often ended swiftly. If she wanted something to happen, it was usually a done deal. Stef worshipped her, having been taken under her wing when she and Denny were college roommates. The Beresfords had tossed Stef out of the house when she came out to them, so she'd stayed with Denny and Sika during all holidays and breaks. She was used to being outflanked and outnumbered by the Phelps women.

Resigning herself to the inevitable, she said, "Okay, but we get two other bids as well. And we check references and talk to one of the building inspectors we trust, *not* the ones that vouched for Kevin. Denny, please get on it right away. We need to have someone in place and working by next week."

"You got it."

"I'll start calling the subcontractors and trying to put them off or negotiate payments or come up with something that works," Stef continued. "And I'll try to scare up more cash. Looks like I'll be living in the hotel during the construction. Oh well, what's a little dust?" She tried to sound positive but couldn't stop beating herself up for being such a bad judge of character.

"Why not move in with us?" Sika offered.

"You and Denny only have a one-bedroom apartment as it is, thanks to this project. We have a whole hotel that was residential in its most recent, seedy incarnation. Maybe I'll move next door to Mrs. Castic on the third floor. She seems to be tolerating the renovations well enough."

"I worry about her." Sika frowned. "She's got to be in her seventies. It can't be healthy for her to be around the noise and dust. It will be bad enough for you."

Denny said, "She's a tough old bird. She gets herself up and out almost every day, walker and all. Even in the rain. Told me she likes to go sit in Union Square and watch tourists dodge pigeons."

They all took a moment to appreciate that.

"You know, I think she comes from royalty or something, back in her home country." Stef couldn't recall all the details. They'd chatted recently when she stopped by to fix a light switch. "Somewhere in Eastern Europe, I think. One of those countries that's been renamed a lot. The Nazis ran her whole family out, and her father died in a concentration camp. She's been through a lot."

"How long has she lived in the hotel?" Denny asked. She was playing with her phone, probably trying to find Jock's number.

"I'll have to ask her." Now that they would be neighbors, it wouldn't take long to hear the woman's life story, no doubt. "Well, we'd better get back to work. Mamaka, your gourmet commercial kitchen might have to be scaled back a bit. But one day, we'll put your Cordon Bleu training to work, I promise."

Sika smiled. "Don't worry about that. Maybe we'll just have a light fare for our guests until we're more established. Concentrate on getting the main part of the hotel open and I'll get the old kitchen cleaned up and running with a minimum of fuss and a lot of bleach."

As Denny and Sika left her office, Stef stared after them with a mixture of gratitude and trepidation. She was thankful every day to have such good friends, but she'd gotten them all into this venture and she had to figure a way to get them out and make it a success. She *had* to.

Her family would get a good laugh to find out about her bad

judgment. Being banished for being a lesbian had lasted two years, and they had never cut off funding for her college tuition, room and board. Denny had gotten her a job. They both worked as part-time housepainters. Stef was proud of that.

When she graduated, her stepmother and father actually attended the ceremony and took her, Denny, and Sika out to a sumptuous feast to celebrate. Stef had often wondered if Sika had something to do with that, but she never asked. Perhaps she didn't want to know.

Things were still far from smooth with her family, eight years later. When she said she wanted to work in the family business, her father's response was tepid at best. He wanted her two brothers to take over the company when he retired. He never talked about her being a lesbian, but made his disappointment in her clear. She was expected to marry a man who could work for the family, and have children who would form part of a new generation who would keep the Beresford hotel empire expanding.

Stef bit the bullet and worked in the administrative offices of Beresford Hoteliers in the acquisition section, thinking she could prove her worth. Her younger brother Jason worked in all of the divisions, ostensibly to move up in management and become a senior executive. He was a good guy and had been her closest ally since childhood. But he wanted their father's approval so much, he had developed little self-confidence and always seemed to mess things up. Their older brother, George, put up with Jason's failings and even tried to cover his ass, probably because he saw no threat to his own position as heir apparent. But he was more than willing to see Stef fail and was also the first to take credit for her hard work.

After only a few months, she'd realized that no matter what she accomplished, she would never be the boss and her father would never acknowledge her value. She would be treated as an unwelcome interloper by both him and George, regardless.

While Stef was discovering just how irrational and sexist her male family members could be, Denny had graduated in hotel and restaurant management and started a career in another large chain of hotels.

One night after work, when Stef was having dinner with Sika

and Denny, she admitted how disenchanted she felt. She'd reached the conclusion that she would have to run a business of her own if she ever hoped for any satisfaction in her work. She was fed up and had hatched a plan to buy and rehab an old hotel. To her surprise, Denny and Sika hadn't just supported the idea, they'd offered to partner with her in the business if she went ahead.

Their vote of confidence was a real boost. For the first time since she'd graduated, Stef felt truly in charge of her future. They developed a plan to create a boutique hotel primarily for women travelers; something safe, high tech, and customized for their needs. They searched for over a year until they located the right property, one of many decaying hotels that were rushed to completion after the 1906 San Francisco earthquake and before the 1915 Panama-Pacific International Exposition. The property had eighty-five rooms and, reportedly, a ghost. Its structure and layout were well done, with a good architect and solid construction. Puzzlingly, though, in the seventies, the owners had hastily and cheaply converted it to residential accommodations, and then seemed to forget it. Now it was run down, mostly unoccupied, and barely worth the land it sat on. Perfect, in other words.

The hotel was held in a family estate trust controlled by a Mrs. Seraphina Drake Holloway, who seemed completely taken with their idea and relieved to be able to unload the hotel to them rather than one of the developers who'd already made bids well below market price. None of them had been willing to agree to her sole caveat, that one of the longtime residents, Mrs. Irina Castic, could not be evicted, ever. Stef had readily agreed, figuring they could work around a solitary resident. And, besides, it wasn't an option to toss an old lady in the street anyway. Mrs. Castic had turned out to be a charming and quiet, uncomplaining tenant.

Most of the money for the down payment came from Stef, through inheritance and savings. She was the chief executive officer, in charge of securing funding and executing the overall plan of the rehabilitation. Denny would be the hotel manager and Sika the chef and manager at the restaurant when it opened. Their half ownership would mostly take the form of sweat equity, but they had sunk their life savings into the project, too. Stef usually drew the line at using her family name to get a break, but she had no such qualms when it came to financing the balance they needed. Banks were more than willing to throw money at her and didn't seem concerned by her novice credentials. Everything had worked out nicely, until Kevin-the-Cokehead.

Stef studied the project calendar grimly. Margins were already razor thin; there was no time for stopping and starting, and no extra money to compensate for her first big management mistake. Fuck, what else could go wrong?

CHAPTER TWO

Ember Lanier was twiddling her toes. Or would have been if she were barefoot. But lounging on a bench in Union Square in the heart of downtown San Francisco wasn't exactly the place to be without shoes. Too much pigeon poop and too many tourists feeding them. Rats with feathers, that's what some famous San Francisco dude had said, and she now believed it. The lice-infested buggers were everywhere. Her boots stayed on.

As she looked around, she saw familiar faces. That she was starting to recognize a few of the denizens of Union Square did nothing to help keep the panic down. She'd been on her own for a while now and there wasn't a day that she didn't consider crawling home, tail between her legs, begging to be taken back. She'd left six months earlier with five thousand in cash, convinced that was enough money to support herself until a good job came along. She was going to prove everyone wrong about her, especially her father and Heather, one of her cadre of nannies. The only one who had mattered. She'd walked out that door and slammed it, leaving her Mercedes roadster behind. She missed that damned car, too. Not that she could afford to even put gas in it.

Sure that her father would try to track her through her credit cards, she'd cut them up. What was she thinking? And to top it all off, she blew fifteen hundred dollars on fake identification papers. New social security number, the works. She'd been astounded at how easy it was to get them and how authentic they looked. She had definitely watched too much television and read too many blogs. Ironically, that was the only thing they had prepared her for. She hadn't been ready for being treated as though she were invisible, being groped by horrible-smelling supervisors who thought they had that right, or being fired from some shit job just for defending herself. She hadn't expected to care about the legions of others who shared her situation.

No matter, that was all behind her now and here she was, at the ripe old age of eighteen, getting ready to spend her third night on the streets as a homeless person. She indulged in another wistful thought about her soft bed at home in Atherton, her favorite foods that their cook would make, and a hot bath. She lingered on the hot bath fantasy for several minutes. The large spa tub would be filled with wonderfully hot water and bubbles that carried a subtle scent of wood resins; amber and sandalwood were her favorites. Heather would indulge Ember's love of candles and light several, but in her mind they became hundreds, and for once, Heather would stay and talk to her while she felt the water sluice around her, the jets drumming on her body until she was completely relaxed. And she would be completely, *completely*, safe from harm.

A flock of pigeons noisily took flight as a kid charged them, pulling Ember from her reverie. Checking a clock on one of the buildings surrounding the square, she saw there were still a few more hours until Glide Church put out the food for the homeless at five o'clock. One meal a day was all she really needed. She tried to keep to the bare minimum, knowing there were families that needed more for their children and some folks who really couldn't fend for themselves. Her friends from Atherton would have approved of the weight she'd lost, the prominence of her ribs. They wouldn't have approved of the way she got there.

She'd spent a precious dollar on a paper, to look for a job and then use for warmth and camouflage later. She'd paid close attention to how street living was done and so far, so good. A young woman on the streets was a target, and not just for other homeless people. Ember had used her wits to avoid most of the pitfalls, but spending entire nights on her own was dangerous and exhausting. She felt ashamed when she thought about the genuinely poor people sharing the lonely streets with her. If they had her options, they wouldn't be here. The trouble was, she just couldn't face going home in disgrace. She kept thinking if she could just get another chance at a job, everything would change. She owed it to Heather to learn about the real world.

She'd had a few jobs but lost them because she was clueless. She didn't know how to be a maid, or wait a table, how to even bus a table. Of course her snotty attitude didn't go over really big with the dirtbags who hired her for minimum wage and constantly tried to cop a feel. What little she'd earned, she spent, along with the rest of her money, mostly on food and a room. She was flush with cash when she first arrived, so she'd thought nothing of buying extras—a magazine, a movie, popcorn. The freedom was amazing. No curfew. No nanny. No one to keep an eye on her. That lasted about two weeks before it dawned on her that the money would soon run out and minimum wage wouldn't replace it. She would have to go home and tell Daddy he was right, she was too spoiled and naïve to make it on her own. And she'd be damned if she'd do that.

The rooms got consistently cheaper and shabbier, and the jobs paid even less until here she was, on the streets. She'd even tried a few shelters, but those could be worse than the streets and the better ones were full of mothers and children. She couldn't convince herself to take a place they needed.

A commotion off to her right served to tear Ember away from her morose thoughts. A kid she'd met, really her only friend in her new world, Joey G, had just snatched an old lady's purse and was tearing across the square on a direct path past her bench. He was a nice enough guy, but a heroin addict and probably desperate for a fix. She didn't need any enemies right now. But, damn, an old lady. She stuck her boot out as he ran by and sent him flying.

Once he was down, she stuck her knee into his spine and grabbed the purse.

"Hey, that's mine. E? What are you doing?" He twisted around to glare at her. "Get your own."

"Joey, not an old lady." Thinking quickly, Ember said, "Besides, she's local, she could identify you. Find a tourist. Better protection for you." She helped him up and, careful to keep the purse away from his grasp, dusted him off.

He gave her a wary look. "You taking it?"

"No. I'm giving it back. I promise." Strange to be bargaining with an addict about stolen property, but he looked pretty strung out. "Why don't you go to the free clinic, Joey? They can help. Maybe get you cleaned up."

"I only need fifty, E, lemme just take fifty. Please?"

He grabbed again for the purse and she held him off. She doubted there was even ten in the damned thing. He was going to take a swing at her any minute and then they'd both have a problem. Digging in a pocket of her pants, she pulled out her last twenty and shoved it at him.

He stared at it a moment, then gave her a grin that surprised her with the straight, even teeth. "Thanks, I'll pay you back." Spying something behind her, he bolted like a rabbit.

Ember didn't even have time to spot the old lady before a pair of huge hands clamped down on her shoulders and spun her around. "You're under arrest," said one of the police officers she'd spent the past few days avoiding.

One minute later she was handcuffed and marched over to where the elderly woman was standing, using a walker for support. She looked angry, and Ember had a sinking feeling her good deed was going to be punished severely.

"We got her, lady. Here's your purse." The cop was big and beefy, and his grip was like a vise.

The woman stared hard at him for a moment. "It was a man who took my purse, officer. This young woman got it back for me. You must release her and apologize."

Pondering for a moment, the cop took a long look at Ember and then the old woman. "You sure? These street kids look alike and sometimes they work in pairs or in gangs."

"She did me a kindness, sir, and you would be doing a kindness to remove the shackles from her hands." Her voice was rich and cultured, strong with authority and some kind of accent.

The cop fumbled the key into the cuffs and popped the locks, setting Ember free. He gave the woman her purse, then seemed to lose interest in them.

Rubbing her wrists, Ember muttered her thanks and started to leave, wondering what in hell she was going to do now. Well, she needed to retrieve her paper, that was for sure. She glanced across the square. So far no one had taken it.

The woman's voice drew her attention. "I must thank you properly. I will reward you."

She seemed to wobble a bit and Ember placed a hand under her elbow to steady her. "No need. That kid's just a junkie, he didn't mean to hurt you. Let me help you to the bench."

The woman accepted the assistance, then indicated Ember should sit, too. "My name is Irina Castic." She offered her hand. "What is yours? I've seen you around here before, recently." Her eyes were bright blue with no trace of age or infirmity, just sharp intelligence.

Ember politely took her hand, surprised anyone would have noticed her in her current condition. A lifetime ago, when she was a spoiled rich kid, lots of people noticed her. It was strange to realize they never really saw her at all. She was only visible while she had money. Before she could edit herself, she blurted out her real name. "Ember Lanier. Pleased to meet you Mrs. Castic."

The woman smiled warmly. "Ember. An unusual name. Didn't you run the sausage stand in front of Macy's a few weeks ago? I think you tried to give me a hot dog one day."

Laughing, Ember admitted, "That was me. I'm afraid I gave more away than I sold and I ended up being fired. But there were a lot of folks that, you know, didn't have the money."

Too late, Ember realized she'd just shown she thought the old lady was penniless. Mrs. Castic didn't miss her blunder.

"And you thought I might need a sausage, too, didn't you?" She placed her hand gently on Ember's arm.

Startled, Ember consciously worked to not pull away, it had been so long since she had been touched in a friendly way. She could feel the heat in her face as she tried to think of an excuse.

"Well, it looked good and I appreciated your offer. I just wasn't hungry then."

They sat for a moment, enjoying the sparkling clear day of which San Francisco had so many. The ever-present coastal fog kept the air and buildings washed clean in this lovely city. That same fog made it cold at night and hid a lot of dangers around corners and down alleys. Ember involuntarily shivered.

Mrs. Castic asked, "Where do you live, Ember?"

Not able to suppress a sigh, Ember replied, "Here and there." She looked across the square once more. Her paper had vanished. It was crazy to be upset about losing a stupid newspaper, but she could feel tears prickling and she didn't want to cry in front of Mrs. Castic. Pretending to know what time it was, she said, "Well, I have to go. Glide Kitchen will open soon."

Clear blue eyes met hers. "Do you take all of your meals there, child?"

Suddenly defensive, Ember snapped, "I don't *take* any meals there." Immediately contrite, she added, "I mean, I earn them. I serve and bus tables and feed kids if the moms have babies. I help wash dishes. I even tutor some of the homeless who are in school. So I'm not a beggar. I help."

Embarrassed over raising her voice to this nice woman, she felt her face heat again. She lowered her head and studied her no-longer-manicured nails. The woman was silent for a moment, then opened her purse and took out a piece of paper and a pencil. She scribbled something and handed the note to Ember.

"What's this?" Suspicion must have been evident in her voice because Mrs. Castic smiled reassuringly.

"Not a message from God, I assure you. It's my address. I live only a few blocks from here and I have a perfectly good couch you could sleep on tonight and a small but adequate shower you could use. It's all I can offer, but please let me repay you for your kindness."

"You don't have to…" But Ember knew she sounded half-hearted. She almost hugged the woman.

Holding up a hand, Mrs. Castic said, "You just be there. Only for tonight, and then we talk. Now, would you be so kind as to help me up and walk me home so you know where you are going?"

"Sure, I guess I've got the time before I report to the kitchen." Ember suspected they both knew her "job" was as a volunteer, in exchange for a meal, but it made her feel good to assure the woman that she earned her keep.

❖

Laurel Hoffman graded another test paper and neatly placed it on the stack. She stretched, glad to be in her sweats relaxing in her home office. She reached for the last paper, thankful that she would finish before eight o'clock. Her partner, Rochelle, always grumbled that she should pay less attention to the papers and more attention to her, especially after working hours. Spoken like a woman whose teaching days were mostly behind her.

Rochelle Jacobs was chair of the department of women's studies and was tenured. They'd met when Laurel was a graduate student. Rochelle had swept her off her feet, insisting they move in together after only a month. Flattered to be pursued by the older, tall and handsome professor with the commanding style, Laurel had soaked up the attention like a sponge.

She was the middle child in her family and had never quite broken out of the quiet, unassuming role that had served her when growing up. Her older brother did whatever he pleased, and her younger sister placed all kinds of emotional demands on their parents. Laurel had learned to go her own way unobtrusively. Her parents had always seemed glad to have one child who left them alone and didn't cause a problem.

Laurel suspected she was a secret disappointment to them, not because she was gay, although they'd refused to believe that until she introduced them to Rochelle, but because she was content to teach in a university. She had a feeling they wanted her to make a name for herself by writing a bestseller or being a movie star, like her younger sister Kate.

Three years after moving into Rochelle's bungalow, Laurel

was an assistant professor working toward tenure and teaching non-stop. She always got rave reviews from the students, so the other associates were more than happy to dump the least favorite courses on her. Those were the undergraduate courses with large numbers of students and the most work. Laurel didn't mind except at the end of the quarter, when papers and exams were due. But Rochelle clearly resented the time she spent with her students.

A booming voice close to her ear startled her from her thoughts. "Aren't you through yet? Some of the faculty are meeting at Le Jeune and I said we'd be there. You can finish later. I want one of their martinis. It's been a long day."

Laurel didn't reply instantly. She'd learned to count to ten before saying what was on her mind. She knew Rochelle had already started relieving the pressure of her "long day" because she'd offered Laurel a martini she didn't want about a half hour before. That was Rochelle's rather tiring drinking strategy—complaining about her long and difficult days chairing meetings and flirting with graduate students. If Laurel put her off any longer she would make another drink and then dinner would be forgotten. An argument was sure to follow and Laurel had learned long ago not to argue with Rochelle, drunk or sober. Her partner used cheap shots and a raised voice to make herself right, and the hurt went straight to Laurel's heart.

The sad truth was, she had stopped loving Rochelle but felt she was in a state of limbo, marking time in their relationship, somehow unable to do any more than get through each day. She tried to absent herself as much as possible, which only made Rochelle more resentful. They rarely made love, and actually, Laurel had started wondering if they'd ever *made love*. They had sex, and she couldn't even remember how long it had been since their last perfunctory bedroom encounter. Six months? Did she even miss it?

A part of her did, the part that yearned for intimacy beyond the physical. For true love, whatever that meant. With a sigh, she got to her feet. She didn't want to think about that forlorn inner self.

Rochelle was leaning against the door, looking her up and down with a frown. "Tell me you aren't wearing that."

Laurel glanced automatically at her deep navy blue sweatshirt and jeans. The combination flattered her slender curves and her fair hair and pale skin. "I didn't realize Le Jeune was formal," she said without expression. "I can change if you think it's necessary." In Berkeley, wearing something other than cutoffs and flip-flops was considered formal.

"You could at least think about how your appearance reflects on me."

Laurel was surprised Rochelle had even noticed her appearance. She could walk around naked and she doubted she would get a reaction. But of course, she was supposed to look good when they were with colleagues. She could still recall a faculty party soon after they got together, an evening full of cocktails and one-upmanship. Rochelle had bragged about nailing the prettiest girl in the class, meaning Laurel. At least the other faculty members had the good grace to look embarrassed that she'd overheard the boast. Later, Rochelle couldn't figure out why Laurel was sleeping in the other bedroom, but she was too drunk to care.

The next day she told Laurel that she should feel complimented. Rochelle pointed out that she could have her pick of anyone but she'd chosen Laurel. She also warned that she didn't like Laurel's attitude and she could still have her choice if Laurel didn't appreciate all the favors and opportunities Rochelle provided her.

Her words wounded, and Laurel had chosen to shut up. That day, and many similar occasions over the past several years, had closed a door in her heart, one she would make sure did not open again for a very long time, if ever. She might not know what to do next, but she knew she needed to figure something out. Whatever she planned, love was not in the equation.

Sighing, Laurel resolved to get up early tomorrow to finish her work. Rochelle usually slept late anyway, and now was not the time to protest.

CHAPTER THREE

Jock Reynolds paced in the outer office of SDS Enterprises, pissed that she had to take time from the job only to be kept waiting for fifteen minutes. She'd been up until two a.m. yesterday preparing the damned bid and dropped it off before she went to work. Denny said they needed a rush job, so why keep her waiting? She was about to get on her cell phone and complain when the door opened and a beautiful dark-skinned woman smiled at her, making her anger dissolve.

"You must be Jocelyn. I apologize for keeping you. My daughters are waiting for you."

Two things: Jock would normally throttle anyone who used her given name. And she would definitely snigger at the comment that "two daughters were waiting" for her. She didn't do either. She meekly followed the woman, mesmerized by her presence and convinced they'd met before.

As soon as the door closed and she could tear her eyes away, she knew why the woman seemed familiar. Denny Phelps was standing three feet from her, a taller, lighter version of her mother. She was grinning.

"You never stop looking, do you, Jock. That's my mama. You keep your eyes to yourself, girl."

Jock knew she was probably blushing and was grateful the others were laughing. With one exception. A humorless woman with long chestnut hair and gorgeous brown eyes was staring daggers at her, which could only mean they'd met before. Maybe a former date?

"I apologize. I just thought you were so attractive and looked familiar. Now I know why." She turned to Denny. "How are you? Haven't seen you in years." She shook Denny's hand and they hugged briefly, then she offered her hand to Denny's mother. "Nice to meet you, Mrs. Phelps."

"My name is Sika, and I'm happy to meet you, Jocelyn. We never met when you and Denny played basketball together, but I saw you play very well at the games I could attend."

"Just call me Jock, please. Denny always talked about her mama, but I had no idea how lovely you were…are."

A snort from the woman who had been glaring at her made all of them turn.

Jock had never been one for diplomacy. "Have we met? You look like you want to shoot me."

Bristling, the woman retorted, "Can we just get down to business? This useless chitchat is costing us time and money. We got your bid for the renovation work. We've called your references. Why are you cheaper than the others? We will check constantly that you are paying your subcontractors and using the materials we want. You cannot cut corners."

Her pretty face seemed set in stone. And it, too, was a face she'd seen before. But where? Jock mentally shrugged, hoping that if she got the job she wouldn't have to work with this woman very much. Maybe Denny could handle liaison.

"My bid is a fair one. I haven't padded the crap out of it, that's all," Jock said without annoyance. She was used to having to explain that she preferred not to rip off her clients. "I have an all-woman crew and we don't stand around and smoke and try to supervise each other. We earn our money by the project, not the hour. And if you'll read the entire bid, if we finish early we get a bonus, prorated for how far ahead of deadline we finish. The bonus is where most of the profit is."

Jock watched as the woman seemed to reread the last two paragraphs of the bid in front of her on her desk. She was kind of cute in her large white shirt covering what Jock suspected was a nice chest. And Jock was pretty sure her lips would be full and sensual if she ever unpursed them. She had a sprinkle of freckles over her cheeks and nose. A very attractive package, all told. She ran a slender finger over the document and demanded, "Define 'finished.'"

Lusty musings dissolved and Jock sighed in frustration. "Finished, as in passing the building inspection. Satisfied?" She was getting sick of the attitude. "Look, if you don't want to do this, just let me go back to work." Enough of this bullshit.

The woman stood, revealing a smashing figure, jeans hugging wonderful curves, and full breasts under her loose-fitting shirt. "When can you start? We need it right away, yesterday."

She was a lot shorter than Denny or her mother, or Jock, who came in at 6'2". Shorter. "Stumpy? Is that you? Stef the Stump. You look great." The words were out before she could stop them. Seeing those drown-in-them eyes narrow dangerously told Jock that not only was she correct, she'd just discovered why the woman was so hostile. *Uh-oh.* "I mean, Stefanie, I didn't recognize you. You look…different."

Digging a hole, that was her specialty. The more attractive the woman, the deeper the hole. Why not bury herself completely? She was thankful when Denny interrupted.

"Okay, that's decided. When can you start, Jock? We can have the contract ready in a day. We really need to get going because our other contractor…didn't work out."

Jock shook her head and said, "Yeah, I heard. I didn't know it was you, though. We just hear according to address, ya know?" She thought better of telling them that Kevin was a known screwup. It just didn't seem like the time.

Stefanie's voice cut like a knife. "When. Can. You. Start?"

"I can come by tomorrow and sign the contract. I'll do an inventory of what you have and what you need and we can start next week if we have enough to work with. Will that work?"

Stefanie seemed to relax her hostile glare a bit. "Yes. Come tomorrow at four o'clock and the contract will be ready. See you then."

Dismissed, Jock had the urge to turn down the job because Stumpy was being such a bitch. But it was good work and the building had a lot of potential. Her crew would finish the other job soon and they could take a long weekend. She needed to keep them busy because they were all good at what they did and other contractors would hire them away from her in a minute.

"See you tomorrow. Nice to meet you, Sika, and good to see you, Denny. You too, Stum…Stefanie."

She had to get out of there before she really said something bad. As she closed the door behind her and thought about it, she had to chuckle.

Women.

❖

Laurel placed a hot cup of tea on her desk, far enough away from her keyboard to prevent a disaster if she got clumsy. She had a break and had decided to come home so she could enter grades into her database before going back to the last class of the day. The doorbell ringing insistently was an unwelcome distraction.

"If this is a delivery person or a student, I'm really going to let them have it," she muttered as she stalked to the door and flung it open. There, in all of her tall, buxom, and fabulous beauty, was Kate, her younger and famous sister.

"Laurel. I'm devastated." Kate fell into her arms without preamble and started sobbing loudly but, Laurel suspected, never enough to smudge her perfectly applied makeup.

Hugging her warmly, Laurel said, "I'm fine, thanks. How are you?"

She was accustomed to Kate's self-absorbed greetings. She'd learned long ago that, for her sister, it really was "all about me." Kate was the beauty in the family, from the moment she was born. They had the same unusual green eyes and thick blond hair, but Kate was very outgoing, athletic in every way, and loaded with talent.

People told Laurel she was attractive, but she knew she couldn't compete. Where she was of average height and had a slight build—some called her fragile—Kate was taller and robustly healthy with a lot of sexy thrown in, and she had bigger breasts. Much bigger breasts. Perhaps growing up being the center of attention had something to do with her self-absorption; Laurel wouldn't know. But she loved her sister, and when the chips were down, Kate usually came through.

"That bastard Luis was fucking around on me," Kate continued. "Me! Can you imagine?"

Leading her to the worn leather sofa in the small living room, Laurel sat her down and settled beside her. "Kate, honey, it's only hard to imagine that he beat you to it. I'll bet that stung."

Sniffing, Kate shot her a sharp-eyed look and then relaxed her shoulders. After a few seconds, she chuckled. "Yes, well, I do always like to be the first to break up. The tabloids are going to say I was dumped." Her face scrunched up as she prepared to open the spigots again.

Hastily Laurel said, "No, not at all. You'll be seen with another gorgeous hunk before Luis has time to announce it. Get one of your closeted gay boys to club crawl with you tonight. It worked all the other times. You're more photogenic anyway. Add a bit of cleavage, and voilà. You'll scoop him." Laurel had been down this road before.

The back door slammed and Rochelle yelled, "Laurel? There's a cab out front. Who's…Kate!"

Rochelle's face transformed from irritation to delight within two seconds. She rushed over to Kate and hauled her to her feet, giving her a hug by smashing herself against the entire length of Kate's body and snuggling her too tightly, for too long.

Laurel's face grew warm with embarrassment as Kate finally pushed Rochelle none too gently away. Rochelle had always had the hots for Kate, but her flirting was getting out of hand.

Kate gave her a tepid greeting. "Hi, Rochelle. Laurel and I were just catching up."

"Why didn't you tell me your sis was going to visit? I might have missed her." Rochelle tore her eyes away from Kate long enough to glance accusingly at Laurel.

"Because she didn't know I was coming," Kate said before Laurel could speak. "I just flew up for a short visit and advice from my big sister."

"I've been so busy we haven't had a chance for our usual sister chats." Laurel tried to smother the defensive note in her voice. She could tell from Kate's tone that she was trying to get Rochelle to leave them alone.

Rochelle was oblivious to the hint. "How long can you stay? Why don't we all go out to lunch?"

"Don't you have a class to teach?" Kate asked politely.

Kate had a ton of lesbian and gay friends, and had never said a bad word about Rochelle, but Laurel knew she didn't like her. Although Kate flirted with just about everyone, she had always seemed uncomfortable with Rochelle. Perhaps because Rochelle didn't respect the boundaries most "in-laws" found appropriate.

Rochelle shrugged off her work commitments, insisting, "I know some of my colleagues would relish the opportunity to say hello. They're such fans of your work. I could have them meet us at Chez Panisse." She moved to put her arm around Kate's shoulders, but Kate expertly avoided the touch.

"No can do, Rochelle. There's a reason the cabbie is waiting, besides the promise of an autograph. My flight leaves in an hour. Some other time."

Undaunted, Rochelle said, "I'll tell him to go and I'll run you out to the airport myself. We can catch up that way. I'm sure Laurel has to get back to school anyway. Right, Laurel?"

With a knot growing in size in her gut, Laurel quietly said, "Rochelle, Kate came to visit me for a bit so we could talk. Just sister stuff. Is that okay?" She hated the "asking permission" tone in her voice, hated her sister to witness it. But she loathed Rochelle's temper even more. She sought the middle ground, knowing it rarely worked to be confrontational with her partner.

Rochelle whirled on her, but then seemed to catch herself in front of Kate. "Oh, sure. No problem. I have an important meeting anyway. Well, next time, Kate." She smiled thinly and disappeared down the hall.

Exhaling, Kate said, "Rochelle is rather intense, isn't she? I get that kind of insistence with guys all the time." Sitting, she took Laurel's hands in hers and asked, "Is everything all right? I mean with the two of you?"

Laurel stared at their hands. "Oh, sure. Rochelle is just starstruck. Like you said, you get that all the time."

Kate was quiet for a moment, staring out at the hallway Rochelle had taken. Then, uncharacteristically, she dropped the subject, much to Laurel's relief.

Laurel tried to lighten the mood. "So, are you making calls to reserve your gorgeous men?"

Kate finally met her eyes. With a warm smile, she said, "I guess so. I'll fix the little bastard. I'd better go." They stood and she slid her arm around Laurel's waist as they walked to the front door. "If you ever need anything…maybe even a place to get away for a few days, you know you're always welcome, sis."

Struggling to talk around the sudden lump in her throat, Laurel managed, "I have a really packed schedule up here. Besides, getting away to your place is like escaping to the circus. A little more stimulation than I'm used to."

Laughter lit Kate's face and her eyes deepened to an even richer shade of emerald. "Oh, come on. It would do you good to have some fun for a change."

The comment was tactless, but Laurel couldn't deny the truth that lay behind her sister's assumptions. She couldn't remember the last time she'd had a genuine belly laugh about anything. Pushing the depressing thought away, she opened the door and waved to the driver, who returned the wave enthusiastically, his eyes never leaving Kate's body.

"Go. And don't worry about me. Rochelle and I are fine." Laurel wished she could sound more convincing, but Kate could see through her, so why bother?

A sense of gloom came over her as she watched Kate drive away, and she retreated slowly back in and closed the door. Maybe if she gathered her things quickly, she could get out of the house before Rochelle realized she was gone.

"Have fun with your sister?" Rochelle's voice was so close Laurel jumped. Why did Rochelle always have to sneak up on her?

"Rochelle, you scared the crap out of me. And not really, if you must know. Kate just came up to complain about another boyfriend disaster. It didn't help to have you drooling all over her." The words popped out before prudence could shut her up. The knot that seemed to be making a home in her stomach these days got bigger.

"What are you talking about? She's my sister-in-law. I was just being friendly. Why do you have to make everything such a big deal? You have no idea what you're talking about." Rochelle stalked away, the subject closed.

Laurel had just started to breathe again when Rochelle halted, turned, and retraced her steps, eyes glittering with amger. Grabbing Laurel's arms, she squeezed so hard it brought tears to her eyes. "Don't ever talk back to me in front of your sister again."

She shoved Laurel hard against the door, then left the room and slammed into her office. Laurel rubbed the circulation back into her arms, swiped her face to get rid of the tears, and fled the house for the safety of her classroom. Her life was certainly not what she'd dreamt of, that was for sure. Instead of a wonderful long-term relationship with the ideal woman, she had become the live-in maid of a tyrant. She might have taken comfort in a stellar career, but instead of heading steadily toward tenure, intellectual exploration, and recognition, she was held in limbo by the whims of her partner and boss.

Laurel loved teaching. She sat on committees as she was expected to and usually ended up being the recording secretary because no one else wanted to do the boring stuff and she didn't seem to be able to refuse. Those meetings were full of bombastic blathering, with little actual work getting done. She used to think the men were the problem, posturing for each other. But most of the time-wasting involved the full professors, male or female, liking the sounds of their own voices and arguing minutiae. It had taken a while for Laurel to realize Rochelle was no different from the others, and the handsome academic she'd fallen for was nothing more than a petty, grasping woman who spent all of her time making sure everything in her life reflected her own illusion of herself. And Laurel was one of her mirrors.

Between teaching so much and the number of committees Laurel was on, she barely had time to publish one small journal article a year. And those weren't earth shattering, just the result of hard work and pulling together research. Rochelle almost patted her on the head, in a way that had become increasingly irritating.

❖

Laurel returned her concentration to the students filing out of her last class for the day. One of them met her eyes and smiled, a pretty young woman she was allowing to audit without formally registering and therefore paying. She'd done that before, reasoning that the desire to learn trumped the administration's desire for more money. So, once or twice a quarter, she let a student sit in. No one ever complained. A good thing, too, because Rochelle would have a fit if she knew.

The young woman reminded her of Kate, with a few big exceptions. She had the beauty but little awareness of that beauty, and she always tried to keep a low profile. She'd made a few friends but usually kept to herself. Today, however, she'd been excited about her new job, assisting a contractor renovate a building that would eventually become a women's hotel. Most of the renovation crew was female and the project sounded very ambitious. From what Laurel overheard, the women in charge were dynamic and honest. The job sounded like fun. Especially to Laurel.

CHAPTER FOUR

"Who is that?" Stef stared at the back of a gorgeous young woman clomping down the hall, covered in dust and lugging a bucket full of tools.

"I don't recall seeing her before," Denny said. "I would have remembered."

Behind them, Jock announced, "That, ladies, is Ember Jones. The old woman downstairs asked me to give her a job. I thought you knew about her."

"Knew what?" Stef asked.

"From what I can tell, she's living here now. Maybe she's a grandchild. Anyway, I need a gofer and she works hard, doesn't complain, and is certainly easy on the eyes. What's not to like?"

"You're saying Mrs. Castic has a roommate?" Stef was astonished. "I've never seen her with anyone. That's not allowed."

"Maybe she's just visiting, helping out," Denny said.

"Then Mrs. Castic should have informed me of the situation."

Denny shrugged. "She's not doing any harm."

"We have rules." Stef realized she was wasting her time trying to explain her position, but she persevered. "Making exceptions sets a bad precedent. What next? She invites all her friends to move in to the rooms around hers?"

"Mrs. C wouldn't do that. She isn't a drunk or a thief, either, and we gave our word that she could stay. We can't throw an old lady out on the streets just because she has a relative in her apartment." Denny was looking at her with confusion.

Jock folded her arms, a scowl on her face. "From what Ember says, she was on the streets when Mrs. C offered a place to her. A kid that looks like that wouldn't last long out there."

Whirling on her, Stef snapped, "I thought you said she could be a grandchild. Why did you lie?" She knew she sounded petty but that didn't stop her. "And she *is* just a *child*, so keep your distance."

Taking a step back, Jock retorted, "I guess I thought you'd use any excuse to evict the old woman. She's a nice lady, bakes cookies that Ember brings for the crew. It's kind of cheap that you make her live here during the remodel."

Stef snorted. Jock set her teeth on edge and always had. "Listen, we offered to pay for a room for Mrs. Castic during the construction, but she refused. And I didn't say anything about evicting her... Never mind. You have no idea who I am. Just leave the kid alone."

Jock colored. "What kind of a crack was that? She's eighteen, legal, and I'll do whatever I want. Without your permission."

Knowing Jock was right, and resenting her for precisely that reason, Stef sought a deflection. "I just don't want any more problems caused by another contractor."

"Whatever. Listen, I'm taking down that west wall in this unit, so there's going to be a lot of racket today. You might want to stay on a different floor for a while. Wouldn't want you to get mussed up or anything." She did nothing to hide the insolence in her voice.

"That's why I'm here. I want to make sure you don't screw something up while you demolish the wall. There could be old pipes in there that tap into another area."

Stef could feel Denny glaring at her, irritated that she kept trying to goad Jock, but, dammit, she had a right. The hotel was her responsibility, her risk, and she still thought they were making a mistake hiring Jock Reynolds. In college Jock had been nothing but a basketball player and a flirt, bedding any woman she could. Stef had made a few attempts at being nice, only for Denny's sake, but she was ignored. It was like she didn't exist because she didn't flaunt her tits. Now she'd reluctantly placed her future in Jock's hands. But she wasn't going to stand back like a cheerleader. Jock had better damn well get used to being supervised. This was no game.

She watched Jock's shoulders straighten as she marched into the room that contained the wall they were arguing about. She picked up a sledgehammer leaning against a cart and kept moving. Stef suddenly had a bad feeling and scurried after her. Once inside the door, Jock stopped and Stef narrowly avoided crashing into her.

"That the wall you're worried about?" Jock asked.

Stef nodded. "I don't even know why it's there, it's not on the blueprints. It will open up the room considerably, and we could…"

Her words were lost as Jock strode up to the wall and let the sledgehammer fly, placing a six-inch hole in the plaster and the old and rotting wood slats behind it.

"What do you think you're doing?" Stef yelled. "I said to be careful."

Jock struck again, widening the hole, then again, and again. She was about to swing the sledgehammer once more when Denny yelled, "Stop!"

The room was quiet. The new kid, who'd returned and picked up a broom, stared slack-jawed as Stef and Jock squared off. Two other crewmembers poked their heads in the doorway.

"How dare you." Stef's hands were on her hips and she could feel the blood rushing to her face. She was going to fire this woman. "I gave you an order, and you ignored it. You work for me, Jock Reynolds, and I will not tolerate your disrespectful attitude."

"If you think I'm going to let you tell me how to run a job, then you can take this hotel and shove it." Jock loomed over Stef and wasn't about to back down.

Denny stepped between them and pushed them away from each other. "That's enough. Both of you, take a breath. We're going to have a meeting and I'm going to be the mediator, *and* the one who decides. Now."

A higher-pitched voice intruded enough to get their attention. "Maybe you'd better decide about this, too."

They all turned to the kid, who was staring into the hole Jock had just put in the wall. She aimed a flashlight she must have pulled from the bucket of tools.

Automatically, Stef asked, "What is it?"

Ember never took her eyes from the hole. "Looks like a coffin to me."

❖

Jock muttered, "Well, I'll be damned."

The air was stagnant and thick. Stef, Jock, and Denny peered, as a unit, into the hole. Ember obligingly held the flashlight. The beam played weakly over an oblong wooden box, among a few possible wardrobe trunks and very old filing cabinets. There was also a desk of sorts, covered with detritus.

Stef thought her heart had stopped. Both she and Denny turned and slid down the wall to land heavily on the floor, trying to absorb what they were faced with. "I can't believe it. Just when we were back on track. This can't be happening." She felt tears threaten, and tried to will them away.

Denny placed a comforting arm over her shoulders. "Hey, it's okay. We don't know for sure that it's a coffin. We have to look. Let's not borrow trouble."

"Why are you upset?" Ember asked. "Isn't it exciting? I mean, what if it's a mystery? How cool is that?"

Ah, youth. Suddenly Stef felt much older than her years. Wearily, she said, "Because if there *is* a body in there, construction stops. Everything stops while an investigation occurs. No jobs, no money, no extensions on our loan, nothing. For however long the powers-that-be take to decide what to do with it."

That piece of information seemed to deflate the excitement the discovery had generated. No one wanted to be out of work.

Sighing, Stef got to her feet and pulled Denny up. "Okay, let's take a look. Jock? Why don't we finish what you started."

With that, Denny took the sledgehammer and Stef wielded a crowbar and they beat the crap out of the false wall, enough to work out some frustration and be able to crawl through to the space they'd uncovered. After about fifteen minutes of swearing and sweating, they dropped the tools.

Stef said, "Kid, would you give me the flashlight and see if you can find a few more? Thanks."

Ember handed the torch to her and left the room. Five minutes later Stef, Denny, and Sika, who had arrived to see what the commotion was about, picked their way into the confines of the interior.

"Stef, you should be the one to open the coffin, I mean box." Sika evidently couldn't edit her thoughts in time.

"Someone hand me a crowbar." Stef knew her voice sounded close to hysterical, but she was beyond caring.

As her fist closed around the crowbar Denny passed her, she said a prayer that this really wasn't a sarcophagus and shoved the pry between the lid and body of the box. It only took two or three pumps to pop the lid, the rusty nails breaking easily. Dust rose and filled their nostrils, sending them all into coughing fits.

"Let's get this off of here," Denny said.

They raised the lid, and Sika directed light into the box. "Clothes." Her deep voice was almost a whisper.

Stef cautiously put a hand inside, preparing to run into skeletal remains as she pressed down on the faded burgundy-colored material. The sensation of age and secrecy ran through her, the material felt fragile but somehow thick and sturdy. An involuntary shudder played over her shoulders.

Behind her she heard Jock say, "Are you okay?" Her voice held none of its usual bravado; she sounded sincere.

Stef could only nod once, not feeling okay at all. She pressed gently down and ran into hard edges but nothing like a skeleton. She exhaled at last.

"I think it's just more books." Her voice sounded weird to her, but it was the best she could do.

She heard Jock behind her yell, "Good news, no bodies," and a small cheer went up from the crew, who'd gathered nearby in concern.

"All right." Stef was so relived she almost staggered as she sought to lean against the false wall. "Let's get this stuff out of here and get on with it."

"Wait, Stef, what will we do with this discovery?" Sika asked. "We don't know anything about it. There could be some valuable items here. I think we should treat everything carefully and with respect."

Resisting the urge to stamp her feet and say what she was really thinking, that she wanted to shred the stuff for almost giving her a heart attack, Stef said, "Okay, Mamaka, we'll move all of this to the vacant apartment at the end of the hall on my floor. That way we can look through it later." She made her way out of the airless space and addressed the young woman who evidently lived with Mrs. Castic. "Kid? What's your name?"

"Ember." She offered nothing else. Her tone hinted at defiance, but her expression suggested nerves.

"Amber. Listen, take one or two others and get the stuff—"

"Ember." The kid straightened to her full height, a lot taller than Stef, and set her jaw.

Attitude, great. "*Ember*. Would you please take this stuff, carefully, to the apartment at the end of the hall on Mrs. Castic's side? You know where that is, right?" Stef had just about had it for the day. The adrenaline surge from the discovery was wearing off.

"I thought you were gonna be next to Mrs. C."

"No, the *other* side of Mrs. Castic, end of the hall. I'll come down and unlock the door." Stef loved working with mostly women, but it had its downside. All this being nice stuff. She was impressed, though, that word had already spread that she would be moving into the apartment next to Mrs. Castic's. She hadn't even started cleaning it out.

Denny and Jock were smiling at her when she turned back to say something.

"What?" Even Stef had a hard time keeping a grin off her face. They knew exactly how polite she enjoyed being.

Jock gave her a break and ordered, "Let's clear the room and then take a half-hour lunch break. Move it, folks, show's over."

Stef had never been so grateful to escape to her office. She felt like she'd narrowly avoided disaster.

❖

Jock strode quickly down Powell toward Market. She'd left work for the day and needed to get cleaned up, but finding a dark place for a beer sounded better. South of Market had more working-class bars where she would fit right in. Hell, it was where she belonged anyway. Being around rich kids like Stefanie Beresford gave her a headache. She'd gone through college on basketball scholarships. It was that or being stuck in Barstow, California, at her father's construction company.

"Hey, Jock, wait up." Denny came running toward her and halted six inches from her face. "Want some company?"

Jock had to grin. Denny always made her smile, no matter what the situation. In college Denny had tutored her and helped her pass her classes so she could keep her scholarship. She was a true friend.

"Are you sure you want to be around me? I'm looking for a beer and I'm not particular where I find it." From the look on Denny's beautiful face, Jock could tell her remark had come out rough and uninviting. Quickly, she said, "I'm sorry, Den. I'd like some company, if you don't mind a foul mood like the one I'm in. I was just heading to that dive we used to hit when we were in town for a game. Are you sure you want to risk your health?"

"La Cucaracha? Oh, hell yes. As long as we drink from the beer bottle and avoid anything raw, we should live. I could use some nachos after today."

They silently fell in step, two very tall women who always got curious looks from the much shorter general population. They were heroines in college, and everyone knew them. After school, well, for Jock at least, she became just another construction worker, most often assumed to be a man, or she was considered an oddity.

When she started her own company, the best of the female

tradeswomen were more than happy to come with her. Straight or gay, they liked to work with other women and get things done, minus the politics and the men who usually took or were given the credit for their hard work. The company's reputation was impeccable.

The bar hadn't changed. Small, crowded, but relatively quiet at this time of day. Most of the patrons there were just off work and tired, like Jock and Denny. They managed to snag the last tiny table and eventually order beer and nachos.

After a few sips of beer, Denny asked, "So, having fun?"

That was all Jock needed. "That damned Stump. She won't cut me any slack and never misses an opportunity to complain or try to order me around. God, what's her problem?"

Denny sighed. "I know Stef has been a real pain to work with. She feels personally responsible for the Kevin screwup, and her family is just waiting for her to fail. Thanks for not just stomping off the job."

"I understand where she's coming from, Den, I really do. But this seems personal. Jeez, we never dated, she should feel grateful. You were right to declare her off-limits when you two were roommates."

"I just didn't want to listen to another brokenhearted woman carrying on about how the star center on the team dumped her after only a few dates." Laughing, she added, "It could be a whole lot worse for us now if you had dated her, believe me. So yeah, I guess I was right."

Jock studied her. "She's your best friend, so she must have some redeeming qualities. And she's hot. I would have gone out with her in a second. You saw something about me that made you warn me off. Smart woman."

Denny cocked her head and Jock flinched inside, hoping she hadn't revealed too much. "Jock, what do you mean by that? I didn't put Stef off-limits because you were a bad person. Just...a rolling stone. You were having a great time and weren't ready to be all 'let's get serious' with anyone. We were kids."

Staring at her beer, Jock said, "Yeah, kids."

The waitress appeared and they ordered more beer and a

huge plate of appetizers they could share for dinner. Just like old times.

After a few more minutes of small talk, Denny said, "So, did you date yourself into oblivion? Because according to your crew you don't go out much these days, or at least you don't brag about it. That doesn't sound like the Jock I know." She placed her hand gently on Jock's forearm.

Meeting her eyes, Jock found only warm acceptance there. She'd never been able to lie to Denny. She was perhaps the one woman in the world Jock wouldn't try to manipulate. "I'll bet you're like your mom, aren't you? She gets the absolute truth out of anyone she talks to."

"I hope so. She's my hero. Now, are you going to answer my question?"

Sighing, Jock gave in. Maybe telling someone would help her deal with the guilt. The risk was that Denny would be so disappointed she would stop being her friend. After two beers and the day she'd had, that would be one blow too many. The words came out anyway. "Do you remember Melanie Rippitoe?"

Denny looked across the room, probably trying to pull out a face for the name. It didn't take long. Eyes widening, she said, "Do you mean that girl from the tiny town in Arkansas? The preacher's daughter. Okay ball player but always telling us about our sinful ways? Sure, I remember her. Don't tell me you bedded her."

Jock nodded, staring at her beer.

"My God. I'll bet that went over well with her daddy. When we were in school?"

"Summer after graduation. We were both on campus for classes. After our senior season I blew off an econ class and had to repeat it. She was doing something similar. We ran into each other."

"So you took her out?"

"It gets worse, Den. You know how I was then—fuck 'em and forget 'em. She kind of let me know she liked me and I turned on the charm. I thought what a cool thing if I could score with a preacher's daughter. I didn't give one thought to the ramifications of that, not one."

Denny only nodded, but it was enough.

"We went out, I was my usual charming self, and we ended up fucking our brains out for a few weeks, probably longer. She was insatiable. I thought it was great, even though afterward she usually was quiet before coming for me again. Usually with tears in her eyes. Everyone's different, so I just went with it. To tell the truth, I didn't care, I was getting laid constantly."

Their platter of food came, and a third round of beer. After a few moments to eat, Denny said, "Well, she was a consenting adult and you brought her out."

"One night, we didn't do much talking. We'd been going at it for hours and she told me that she was going to apply to a Bible school for graduate work and she'd probably be moving to Oklahoma. I said I thought that was cool for her. She got all happy and started going on about how I could probably find a job in Tulsa and although we'd have to be in the closet, we could still be together. Eventually she'd have to tell her family, but not at first. She had it all planned."

"So you would be her secret stud muffin?"

"I hadn't thought of it that way. But yeah, I guess that's just what I'd be."

Denny put her beer down and leaned closer. "What happened?"

"I told her that I was sorry if she misunderstood, but I had no intention of moving to Oklahoma to be in a closeted relationship with anyone. I was out and not about to apologize for that. So she could make whatever plans she wanted, but count me out."

"Did she accept that?"

Staring, without interest, at the plate of food, Jock said, "She started ranting about how could I expect her to stay with me but still be a good Christian? She had to go back home, and her solution was the only way we could be together. I...wasn't very gracious."

"Go on." Denny waited patiently, just like always.

"I said that we had never mentioned the L-word and I didn't need her to stay with me. I was happy to share what we did and she was dynamite between the sheets, but that was it. When school was over, so were we." Jock could barely get the last part out, trying not to feel the cruelty of her words.

After a few seconds, Denny said, "What happened next?"

Jock felt her eyes slam shut but forced the words out. "She got dressed, walked out to her car, and left. The next day it was all over the campus that she had driven her car off of a bridge and was dead. Terrible accident. But I knew better, I knew she'd committed suicide. Because of me."

The noise in the tiny bar was raucous but Jock heard nothing. The truth was out, and as horrible as it was, she was relieved to finally tell someone.

Denny's sweet deep voice intruded on her. "I agree she may have killed herself, Jock. But if that's true, you weren't the only reason."

For the first time since the confession began, Jock was sure she revealed her shock. "What are you talking about? I could have agreed with her, tried to take some time to make her see it wasn't right. I could have realized she might do something like that. I was such a self-centered ass. If only I'd—"

"You were a kid, Jock. Was this the first time you'd heard of her plans about moving?"

"Yes. All we did was fuck. I even offered to take her out on a real date, but she only wanted to get in bed. I was fine with that. As I look back on it, she was probably afraid someone might realize she was screwing a woman."

"Honey, Melanie's problems started a long time before you came along. She was a lesbian growing up the daughter of a Baptist preacher in a small Arkansas town. She'd probably liked girls for a long time and resisted it. She watched you bed every woman in town and maybe fantasized about it. Then, there you were, ready to make her erotic dreams come true, and she couldn't help herself."

"I should have known how she'd react."

"Bullshit. How could anyone anticipate that?"

"Because when I told her I wasn't going with her, she got weird. Her eyes sort of went flat and she got a little smile. She never said another word, just got her clothes on and left. I was relieved, to tell the truth."

"Sounds to me like you're assuming far too much. Even if she did take her own life, no one does that over one rejection. Your decision could have been the final straw for her, but that's just a possibility. And even if it's the truth, I repeat, you had no way to know. You weren't responsible for her messed-up thinking or the way she was raised."

Sighing, Jock said, "Well, I haven't really dated since it happened. Except for the occasional hook-up with an anonymous woman, that's it. I think I did enough damage, don't you?"

Denny stacked some of the plates to make room on the minuscule table and leaned on her elbows. "I think the real question is, how long are you going to let this dictate how you live your life?"

CHAPTER FIVE

Stef was busy juggling which bills she could pay when her direct line rang. She smiled when she saw her younger brother Jason's cell number. "Hey, bro, what's up?"

"I hear your contractor screwed you over." Jason must have been in his BMW roadster because the traffic noise made him hard to understand.

"My, my. News travels fast. Where and when did you hear about it?" Stef tried to keep her voice light. She didn't want Jason to know how serious the situation was. He had a hard time keeping his mouth shut around George and their father.

Snorting, Jason said, "Where do you think? Contracting is a small community. I'm sure someone told George, and he couldn't wait to tell Dad. I'm sorry, sis, but that bastard cokehead had a reputation. If you'd asked, I could have found out for you. Hey, got time to grab a bite?"

"You're in San Francisco?"

"You bet. Meet you at Sears in fifteen?"

"Deal. Get a place in line. I might be five minutes late."

Sears was a tiny diner that had one of the best breakfasts in town and had been in business since the late 1930s. Although recently sold, the place had kept up quality and the waiting lines were legendary. People moved in and out pretty quickly, prompted by the hungry faces of those in line, staring through the window. It was fun to go there and pig out on Swedish pancakes, the signature dish.

Jason was already waiting when Stef arrived. It was hard to do anything but love the man, he was so sweet and naïve and probably always would be. Those qualities, plus his looks and name, had women flocking to him.

Once settled into their seats, they ordered and endured the weak diner coffee slopped into their cups by a very busy waitress. No one dared to ask for tea, and it just tasted like more watered-down coffee anyway.

"So, why are you in town?" Stef asked.

"To see my favorite sister, of course. Why else would I come to this beautiful city with all the hot women?"

He tried to look sincere, but Stef could tell he was the messenger from her dad and brother. She'd seen the look before. Poor Jason. He was a lousy poker player, too.

"You are such a bad liar. What do they want—to tell me what a dumbass I am for being fooled by that jerk? Tell them thanks, I already know that."

"George says he isn't surprised you'd leave the company for some idiotic project like this." Jason never had the guile to soften the blow.

Stef choked. "By the way, Kevin told me he and George were friends. And I already have another team in place, working away. So fuck off." Seeing the hurt in Jason's eyes, she quickly amended, "Not you, bro, just them. They can't wait for me to fail."

"Maybe it's not that bad."

"Yeah? How bad is it?" It was all she could do to not shout at him.

Jason brightened. "Dad wants to give you a loan. He said same terms as a bank, but more lenient on payments. Keep everything in the family, right?"

They stopped talking so the waitress could plop down their delicious-looking food. Stef took the reprieve to try to think rationally. The urge to leap at the finance offer was strong, but she knew there would be ropelike strings attached.

"You know I can't do that," she said. "They want me to fail, and financing the hotel would give them control. I've seen them be 'lenient' before, then tear the property out from under the poor owner's feet. No."

"But how are you going to pay for it?" Jason drowned his pancakes in syrup and butter.

"I've got it handled." She'd be damned if she'd tell Jason, who would then blab to George and her dad.

He passed the almost empty syrup container to her. "I think Dad secretly admires you and wants you to succeed. He really seemed sincere."

"George must have loved that. I'll bet he told Dad he'd handle the loan papers."

Stef didn't know why, but George seemed to despise anything she did. He was the eldest and a son, her father's favorite. She couldn't figure out why he never cut her a break. She halfheartedly fixed her pancakes, her stomach sour from the conversation.

"Yeah, he did." The implications finally dawned on Jason. "That's not good, is it." Her silence confirmed the answer. "Damn."

"Look, tell them thanks but no thanks. I have additional financing arranged." She didn't, but she had a lead.

They ate in silence, then Jason's head jerked up. "You're going for hard money, aren't you?"

He was referring to money loaned privately at higher interest rates and from sketchy sources. Stef had a number to call that her loan officer at the bank had given her. Leaning closer, she said, "Doesn't matter, Jason. I'm going to get the hotel finished and open for business and it's going to be a success. Tell that to Dad and George."

"You've really bet everything on this, haven't you?" He sounded proud of her. "I heard you're living in the hotel now."

"Who have you been talking to? Yes, I'm living at the hotel, and yes, I have put all of my money into it."

He chased the last bite of pancake around the plate with his fork, careful to dredge it through a puddle of syrup. He'd done that all of his life. No matter how expensive the clothes or manicured and barbered the man, he would always be her little brother. "You think you can survive with only women as clientele?"

"Yes, I think it can do really well with *only* women. Anything else?" She didn't care if she hurt his feelings—he was pushing. He'd been listening to George's dreck for too long.

Jason studied his plate for a moment, then held up his hands in surrender. "Sorry. I just worry about you, that's all. I want you to be a huge success, sis. I'm rooting for you, I promise." He reached for his wallet. "Let me buy breakfast."

Feeling terrible for taking her anxiety and anger out on him, Stef prepared her apology as he settled the bill. When they were ready to leave, he gave her an envelope. Her eyes must have asked the question.

"It's not much, but it might tide you over until you can arrange the money. I'm guessing you're paying your crew by the week. If they're working for less, they want it in cash." He kissed her cheek. "It's all I could put together, but I hope it helps."

Her eyes stung and she fought to not break down in front of him. She couldn't even think about turning it down; she'd been desperately trying to figure out how to meet this week's payroll. They made their way out of the busy diner, and once on the street she hugged him close. She glanced at the check and was thrilled. This gave her at least time to get the financing lined up.

"Thanks, Jase, I'll pay you back, I swear. I'll write out a note for the money as soon as I get back."

Squeezing her to him, he said, "I'm not in a hurry, I know you're good for it. I couldn't invest in a better operation. Now, go be a success and screw George. I still think Dad is rooting for you."

❖

Ember was reading from a text that Professor Hoffman had assigned. She'd bought the book used from another student. She knew she didn't have to study, since she was basically sneaking into the class, but someday she'd be a real student, with a student ID and everything. She found women's studies fascinating.

She made good money in her new job and was finally saving. Although the thought of returning home crossed her mind daily, she couldn't do it. She knew Heather would have been pleased with the way she was taking responsibility for herself now. She owed it to her to follow this new life wherever it was going to lead, and she owed it to herself. One day she would have something worthwhile to show Heather. That thought made her happy.

Mrs. C was in the tiny kitchen, making something out of nothing for dinner for them. The woman was amazing. She was always busy, even though she couldn't get around so easily. She cooked simple but delicious and inexpensive meals, saying it was easier to cook for two than one. She kept Ember and the crew supplied with treats at least once a week, and that really upped Ember's numbers in the popularity department.

Ember insisted on paying her fifty dollars a week, and tried to pay more, but that was all Mrs. C would take. She said she wasn't paying rent during the renovation, so Ember didn't need to, either. But Ember ate most of the food. Mrs. C kept telling her that she didn't need much at her age, but Ember was still growing and worked hard. The fifty probably didn't cover groceries.

The tiny apartment was filling up with delicious odors when Mrs. C called her to collect their plates and bring them to the table. Mrs. C needed her cane and it was easy for Ember to help. She always set the table and did the dishes, after Mrs. C taught her how. Although Ember had worked as a busgirl and dishwasher for a bit, there was a big difference between moving around a small space with no dishwasher and scraping plates and loading an industrial-strength machine in a restaurant. Garbage detail was hers, too. She never forgot.

After they were settled at the small dining table, Ember attacked her spaghetti and meat sauce with relish. Mrs. C made the absolute best sauce, or *gravy*, as she called it. She told Ember that she learned the recipe from a friend of hers years before. They had it probably twice a week because it was cheap and Mrs. C could make a big batch and freeze it in smaller containers. Then all she had to do was boil the pasta and make a salad or vegetable.

Mrs. C finished before Ember, even though Ember was shoveling the food down. Mrs. C reminded her that she could eat that way when just the two of them were together, but nice manners were important when there were others present.

"Ember, you seem to be enjoying your studies. And you like your professor, too, eh?" Her accent seemed to get heavier in the evenings, maybe when she was tired.

Swallowing a bite that she knew was way too big for proper company, Ember wiped her mouth with the paper towel and grinned. "She's hot. And really smart. The other students love her. She makes the material seem important and answers all the questions. I wish every teacher was like her."

Ember just audited that one class because Dr. Hoffman was the only one who allowed it. But she talked to other students and overheard conversations.

Mrs. C's blue eyes were full of curiosity. "You mentioned her partner, Dr. Jacobs, I believe. What is she like?"

Ember glanced to the ceiling in thought. "Well, I haven't really met her. I actually avoid her because I'm not really even registered to audit, you know. She doesn't teach freshman, I guess maybe she just teaches grad students, those going for master's or Ph.D. degrees. I've heard she's a bitch. Oh, sorry, Mrs. C. Didn't mean to swear."

She always tried to watch her language as a sign of respect. Mrs. C never swore and seemed so refined. She reminded Ember of her grandmother and her friends, always genteel and a lady. It was tough sometimes, being around the construction crew and then classmates. *Fuck* was used as a noun, verb, adjective, adverb, and every other part of speech, she was sure.

Mrs. C graciously chose to ignore her lapse. "So, she's not liked. Do you know why?"

"Well, from what I hear, she ignores the students unless they are really pretty, then she flirts with them and has favorites. The rumor is that some get an A by, you know, um…sleeping with her."

She felt uncomfortable passing on that rumor, but Mrs. C had asked and Ember had heard it from more than one person. Like it was something everyone knew. Still, it felt disloyal to Dr. Hoffman.

"I see. That is unfortunate."

"No one can see why Dr. Hoffman stays with her. We're all hoping she dumps her." Ember blurted that out before she could edit herself. She was relieved when Mrs. C nodded thoughtfully. "Mrs. C? Could I ask you a question?"

Ember respected Mrs. C's privacy. She wasn't a talkative person.

Giving her a gentle smile, Mrs. C said, "Of course. What would you like to know?"

Her openness surprised Ember into a brief silence. She had a million questions but sensed she should start slowly, not wanting to offend this kind woman who had made her life so much easier with her friendship and support.

"When did you come to America?"

Sitting back in her chair, Mrs. C stared into space. "Oh my, that was a long time ago. I became a dual citizen in the 1950s, if that is what you are asking. Is it?"

Ember looked at her plate. "Well, no. I guess I was asking where you are from. What is your accent? Those things."

"Ah. I was born in Yugoslavia, Belgrade, to be exact. It is now Serbia. My family had some holdings there. We fled with our lives when the Nazis invaded. Only my mother and I made it out of the country. My father was sent to a concentration camp, when he refused to cooperate with the Nazis. We weren't Jewish but were Serbian Orthodox, and they wanted our land, so they treated us the same. He died there."

"God. I'm so sorry to have brought up such painful memories. I didn't mean to pry." Ember felt terrible to upset her friend.

Mrs. C reached over and touched her face, her hand trembling slightly. "It is quite all right, my dear. It was a long time ago."

"After the war, did you go back there?"

Smiling wistfully, Mrs. C said, "Oh my, no. After the war, the Communists took over and declared my father an enemy of the state. Then one dictator after another made up flimsy excuses to avoid recognizing our right to the land."

"I'm so sorry. Is it still that way?"

Mrs. C pulled her sweater tighter around her small frame. "Well, they say that it is changing. The Serbs want to be part of the European Union, and they have been told to clean up the titles to their land before that can happen. Serbia is very poor right now. Companies won't invest because it is still too much ruled by those you must bribe. I've been told that there are bad legal complications for outside corporations."

Fascinated, Ember asked, "So you might get your family land back?"

"Who knows? I did make the effort to go to Serbia and document all of the property before a deadline in two thousand five, but the country is poor and corrupt. I might not be alive if it even happens. I'm old, and I'm tired of the constant battle."

"But what about your kids? Maybe grandchildren? Those people stole it from you, it doesn't seem right."

For the first time since Ember had known Mrs. C, her eyes clouded over and she looked her age. Ember's heart broke for her. "My child, my daughter, died when she was a young woman. There is no one." Her voice faltered and she was silent.

Ember reached out and took her hand, cradling it with both of hers. "She must have been a special woman to have you as her mom."

Staring at their hands, Mrs. C said, "I'm not sure she thought so, but she was special. She didn't approve of her mother sometimes, though."

Ember was silent for a moment, the ghosts of Mrs. C's past evident in the room. Finally, she asked, "Mrs. C, why didn't she approve of you?"

Mrs. Castic focused on her and a small smile crept to her lips. "Why, the company I kept, of course."

CHAPTER SIX

Laurel entered the building and picked her way through the cluttered lobby to the blanket-draped service elevator Ember Jones had described. Pushing the button for the third floor, she stared at a stack of construction trash as the doors slowly closed.

When she'd heard the student excitedly telling her fellow classmates about finding a "walled-up" room and papers that were really old, Laurel's antennae were on full alert. She'd been wondering what dried-up, boring tome she was going to pull together to keep herself at least *on* the tenure track. The papers were probably insignificant, but she was curious anyway and a small flicker of hope had driven her to the hotel just in case the find of a lifetime awaited her.

She'd quizzed Ember for as much information as the young woman knew, which was very little. She said there were a "bunch of papers," and she'd helped move them to an empty room on the floor where she was living, the third floor of the hotel. Apparently they still had a few rooms they rented. Laurel thought that odd, since the hotel was under renovation, but the idea of undiscovered papers was much more interesting than building codes.

After getting the address, she did a bit of research. The hotel was built after the 1906 earthquake and fire that had devastated San Francisco. It had once enjoyed a prosperous clientele, but over the years, and as the bordering Tenderloin district grew more dangerous, the hotels west of Union Square had gradually turned residential and shabby. The odd part was that this hotel had led the way. It went from prosperity to ruin seemingly overnight. Now the area was enjoying a renaissance because of its proximity to the shopping and theatre districts of downtown San Francisco.

This hotel, reborn as Hotel Liaison, had been purchased the year before by a partnership, SDS-LLC, and had been in renovation since. According to the news article Laurel had found online, it was going to focus on women travelers. That was intriguing in and of itself. Between the name and the stated purpose, Laurel's imagination was filling in all sorts of blanks. She had to laugh. *Yes, Laurel, a hotbed of lesbians, all waiting to cater to your every whim.* Still, a girl could dream.

When the elevator finally made it up to the third floor, Laurel stepped out into a dingy hall that was carpeted with a wool runner complete with bare spots and a musty smell. She felt like an intruder and found herself almost tiptoeing down the hall.

Gambling on the element of surprise, she'd avoided the administration offices, thinking if she could get a peek, maybe she could determine the value of the papers. Depending on what she found, she would either write the visit off as a pleasant diversion in a tedious day or she would have unexpected ammunition for a confrontation. Three years with Rochelle had accustomed her to the idea that everything was a battle, so she anticipated having to argue her way into being allowed to examine the discovery. If it was meaningful, she was positive that Rochelle would want to take over, and then nothing would be easy.

But still, she had to take the chance. What if the papers were important? What if the discovery would put her on the fast track to being a tenured professor? Or better yet, have other universities vying for her services? She knew the chances were slim, but she mustered up the courage to try the first doorknob she reached, hoping it would be unlocked. This was trespassing at the very least. Maybe she could be hauled away. If the owners discovered her they might ban her from the property. Then they could give the right to examine the material to someone else. This was a terrible idea.

"May I help you?"

Laurel whirled to see a woman a bit shorter than her, with chestnut hair and intelligent brown eyes, holding what looked to be a large, heavy box. "Oh! Oh, dear. May I help you with that box? It looks heavy."

Laurel scrambled to find some excuse for her presence. This woman must work on the property. Her mind raced as she hurried over to help. The woman stared for a moment, then seemed to remember the box and almost lost hold of it. Laurel got there in time to take some of the load and steady her.

The stranger said, "Thanks. I'm just moving in here temporarily."

Laurel couldn't help but notice how nicely she filled out her jeans, but she shook her head to erase the thought. She held most of the weight while the woman fought to extricate a huge lump of keys from her pants. Finally, she was able to get the door open and plop the box on the floor in the empty room. It seemed spacious, not the tiny, cramped room her research had led her to expect. The wooden floor was scratched and almost black with age and it had a sour smell, but there were windows, too. She imagined that if the film of age and neglect were scraped off, there would be a lot of light.

Holding out her hand, the woman said, "Hi. I'm Stef. And you are?"

Laurel quickly shook her hand and couldn't seem to stop shaking it. She self-consciously pulled away when she realized the woman had a curious look on her face, studying her. "I'm Laurel Hoffman. I…was just trying to locate one of my students. I understand she lives here. I teach at Cal."

That really didn't explain much, but she hoped maybe this Stef person would let it go. Laurel cringed inwardly. She'd been discovered lurking around in a building she had no right to enter without the owner's permission. The woman in front of her folded her arms across her chest, and looked her up and down dubiously.

"She lives here? What's her name?"

She had no choice but to tell the truth. "Ember. She's a pretty young woman who audits a class I teach in women's studies. Blond hair, blue eyes, likes to wear baggy clothes. She's very nice."

With a slight scowl, Stef said, "I know her. She's at work upstairs. I'll tell her you stopped by."

Realizing something wasn't right, Laurel added, "Is she in trouble? You seem upset. It isn't her fault I'm here. She was really excited about some papers that were found, and…I got curious. I wondered if I could get a look at them. So here I am."

That wasn't what she meant at all. She hadn't meant to blurt out everything. This intriguing woman made her tongue-tied. Stef's deep brown eyes narrowed and Laurel was on alert. She must have said the wrong thing again. She ducked her head and quickly exited the room, mumbling, "I'd better go. Thank you for your help."

Halfway down the hall, she heard, "Wait, where are you going? Don't you want to look at the papers?"

Laurel almost tripped over her own feet doing an about face. "Do you know where they are?" She realized she must look like a fool and tried to stop fidgeting like a five-year-old.

"Stef" slid her hands in her back pockets and cocked her hip. The look revealed full breasts and a very sexy figure. Laurel had schooled herself to not react to her students, some of whom were breathtaking, but this woman was about her age and it was all she could do to not stare.

Probably reading her mind, Stef grinned. "They're at the end of the hall, corner room. I have the key. They're pretty dusty, though."

"I don't mind. I mean, it's not a problem, I've looked at old papers before."

Now she felt bad for maybe getting this woman in trouble with her employers. She couldn't be doing that well if she was forced to live in a hotel that was questionable before, but now was under renovation, for heaven's sake. Damn. Rochelle would have no problem with the small deception. Most researchers wouldn't think twice. Laurel was always having a problem with ethics. She had them.

Stef was still staring at her, waiting for something, and Laurel realized it was her turn. Sighing, she said, "Wait. You might get in trouble with your employer. I can't let you do that. Tell me where the offices are and I'll try to talk to them. They might prefer someone else to examine them."

The woman blinked, then straightened. Laurel swore her eyes turned a shade darker. Eighty-two percent cacao popped to mind. "I'm sure it would be fine if you looked. You're a professor, right?"

"Assistant professor," Laurel corrected.

"There were only ledgers and files and some clothes and things." Stef sounded genuinely regretful. "Boring stuff. Probably a waste of time for you."

Laurel grinned. "Remember, I'm an academic. I love boring stuff like that. So, if you're sure it's okay, I'd like to see them."

Stef's frank gaze made Laurel's temperature rise. "Oh, yeah. I didn't mean to insult you about the 'boring' crack. Okay, let's go."

❖

There was only a bare bulb hanging from the center of the room. The windows were as grimy as the other room. No furniture, no place to sit. Some of the boxes were wooden but might be rotten. There was a lot of material, enough to fill half the space. This was, indeed, going to be a project, and she had a class in two hours. *Shoot.*

Stef was still in the doorway. "Let me dig up a chair for you. Maybe a flashlight."

"No, no. I don't want to put you out any more than I have. Would it be okay if I came back later? I'll need to be wearing something to work in, obviously, and I can bring lights and things I need. I even have a folding chair."

She was thinking about disposable gloves, a dust mask, and maybe even klieg lights borrowed from another department. *Keep it simple. The more people you involve, the more the word will get out.* Much as she enjoyed the academic world, gossip was rampant and wanting to be in on a find was standard procedure. She reasoned that the worst that could happen was a small article to keep her on course for tenure. But there was something here, she could feel it up and down her spine. She was lost in thought when she heard Stef's voice.

"Fine. I'll be around."

"Wait, Stef?" Scrambling to the door, Laurel found her waiting, looking over her shoulder. The long red-brown hair flared around her face, making her look incredibly sexy. "How shall I get back in? It might be after five, if that's okay. May I have your phone number?"

Laurel was disconcerted at what sounded like a pick-up line. Maybe it was. Her cheeks were really heating up now.

Grinning, Stef said, "I'd like yours, too."

She said it in a way that seemed like flirting. Was that true? This good-looking woman was flirting with her? No, that didn't happen. They exchanged numbers, Laurel painfully aware that her blush had continued to cover her entire body. "What's your last name? I've been rude not to ask."

Stef didn't seem to hear the question. She reached for her key ring and searched, then removed a key. "Here, have a copy made and get this back to me later. Okay?"

Only able to nod in gratitude, but wondering why this woman would trust her since they just met, Laurel took the key and clutched it tightly in her hand.

Stef must have read her mind again, because she said, "I know you'll return it, and I probably won't be around every time you want to get in. You will need to make arrangements to get in the outside door if it's after six. Okay, see you later?"

"Yes, thanks. I'll get a copy made today. Could I, could I bring a pizza and some wine? To repay you for your kindness."

Silent for a moment, Stef nodded, then said, "Not necessary, but sure. What time? I'll meet you downstairs to let you in."

❖

Driving across the Bay Bridge to get to the campus, Laurel was astounded at her own temerity. She had not only barged into the old hotel and practically commandeered the mystery papers, she'd asked a woman for a date, kind of. *Well, you haven't really asked her out, you merely want to thank her.* She thought about the half-truth of that, and tested her guilt meter. It registered a six of ten.

Her thoughts immediately detoured to Rochelle. She wasn't going to be home tonight. She'd already said she would be out at another of her endless meetings with her cronies that resulted in coming home late and half smashed. She'd never know that Laurel was gone.

"I should tell her," Laurel mumbled beneath her breath. "I should tell her about the papers, too. After all, she's my partner, not to mention chair of the department."

As soon as she said the words aloud, the joy of the new discovery was lost. She imagined that most people would be excited to tell of their possible career-making discovery. Their partners would be happy and help them celebrate. But her reality was much less inviting. The first thing Rochelle would do was downplay the possibilities, talk disparagingly about the papers, the hotel, the area, anything to make Laurel feel stupid for even checking out her hunch. Then, if there really was something there, she'd want most, if not all, of the credit. She was supposed to be publishing a lot more often than Laurel, and she'd been coasting on tenure for some time.

No, Laurel decided, the thing to do was to keep quiet until she knew what she was dealing with, then she could decide what she would tell Rochelle and when. Meantime, she had a class to teach and, later, a room full of possibilities to explore. Not to mention dinner with a really attractive woman. Her spirits were suddenly soaring.

❖

Stef whistled as she loaded another box onto the cart. That professor had such intense green eyes, a real knockout, and she was so earnest, Stef had to chuckle. Shy, too. *Hmm, we now have a quasi date. Wonder how that happened?*

Denny came up and shoulder-bumped her. "What's up with

you? I haven't seen a smile on your face since before Kevin sniffed up our budget. Did you find a trunk full of money you'd forgotten about?"

Surprised to feel her ears tingle, Stef kept her attention on the boxes. "No, nothing that good. I wish."

A hand on her shoulder stopped her. "Are you blushing? You are! What happened? You get laid? Dawg, I am so jealous." Denny stood back and grinned.

Holding both hands up in surrender, Stef said, "Whoa. I wish for that, too, but no such luck. I did, however, meet a really hot professor." As Denny's eyes widened, she added, "Seems little Miss Ember was bragging to her *classmates* at Cal about the hidden room and its contents."

"She's in college? At Cal?" This was news to both of them and probably would be to Jock.

"Well, from what I understand from her professor, *Laurel,* I mean Dr. Hoffman—the one with the amazing green eyes and honey-blond hair down to about, oh, her breasts—she's auditing."

"Oh, *Laurel,* is it?" Denny leaned closer. "And you know her how?"

"Well, I offered to let her get a look at the papers we dug out of the hidden room. And, to repay my generosity, she's offering a hot, tasty"—Stef indulged in a heavy pause; she loved to tease Denny—"pizza and some wine. Tonight."

Denny started tapping her toe. "I thought you were going to quietly dispose of that stuff, since there was no dead body. That's what you told me. Suddenly a pretty face turns up and asks all nice and you turn over the goods. What if she finds something that would stop construction?"

Stef hadn't thought of that and could tell that Denny was only half joking. "Look, Den, there are no organic parts in that junk, other than maybe a few desiccated rat carcasses. And when the professor discovers those, she can come screaming to me, and I'll dispose of them. Brave person that I am."

"Uh-huh. You're a sucker for green eyes. You always have been."

Getting busy with the boxes again, Stef muttered, "Yeah, well, it's only pizza."

Still, she was looking forward to the meal with lovely green-eyed Laurel, and hurried to finish so she could shower and change. Denny got distracted with a phone call and didn't bring the subject up again, for which Stef was grateful. There was something about Laurel that she was drawn to. Perhaps her attraction hinted at the early promise of a friendship, but it didn't feel like that. Hell, she didn't even know if Laurel was gay, but she knew that Laurel had checked her out. She didn't want to jump to conclusions, she just wanted to see where it would go.

Laurel seemed honest, and genuinely nice. She hadn't wanted to get Stef in trouble for letting her in the room. Of course, Stef hadn't mentioned her last name, which would have been a dead giveaway as to who owned the hotel. She wasn't sure why she'd avoided that disclosure. Maybe she didn't trust Laurel after all. Or maybe she just didn't want to be a Beresford for a while. It had been her experience that once someone heard her last name, the relationship changed. She'd been used before and was sick of it. The truth would come out soon enough. Meanwhile, perhaps she could just enjoy herself with a woman she was attracted to.

CHAPTER SEVEN

Stef had to struggle not to laugh when she came down to open the locked exterior doors. Laurel was balancing the pizza on top of pads of paper and file folders, carrying bags containing all sorts of crap, and lugging a backpack that looked like it weighed more than she did. She looked cute, a word that rarely entered Stef's mind. She was dressed in jeans, a large denim shirt over a white tank top, and sneakers. Her hair was hastily piled on top of her head and she wore glasses.

They schlepped everything into the elevator and along the hallway to the corner room where the papers were housed, and settled in, only to realize that the electrical outlets were ancient, with no grounding port. Stef dug up an extension cord and power strip and ran it from her room. She'd had an electrician rig a temporary setup that would safely support newer electronics until the remodel reached the third floor. She'd also done that for Mrs. Castic, but her own tiny kitchen would have to struggle along with only a microwave. She didn't mind because Sika always made coffee and breakfast in the kitchen for the three of them and anyone else who wandered in hungry.

They couldn't plug in all the lights that Laurel had brought, but Stef suggested they use her place if they found anything interesting. She stopped short of offering Laurel a key to her room, puzzled by her impulse. She seemed determined to give the woman anything she wanted. This had never happened before, even with former lovers.

Stef had taken the time to sweep the room before Laurel arrived, so they sat on the floor and enjoyed a good bottle of wine with the pizza. Their chat focused on the papers, the logistics of examining them. Laurel had brought a box of disposable gloves to protect the papers and their hands. She also had a camera and wanted to photograph everything before they started. She took a few pictures with Stef in them, too. Then Stef took shots of her, the professor with her find. Through the viewfinder she saw grace and elegance, and those unusual green eyes tinged with what she thought might be sadness. She wondered about that.

Once work commenced, they fell silent. Stef wasn't sure what she was looking for, but Laurel assured her that anything interesting was fair game. They spent time just getting to know the material, randomly perusing. The earliest that they found dated from 1912. The guest registration was interesting in that it was easy to read, even though badly faded. Evidently, penmanship was stressed back then. The record began with a Mr. and Mrs. Thisandthat, but after 1915, after the Panama-Pacific Exposition, there were single names, usually Mrs. Somebodyelse, occasionally Miss Whatever, but always a woman.

Musing out loud, Stef said, "Well, I guess the hotel was primarily for women travelers almost from the beginning."

Carefully moving papers around, Laurel commented, "That makes sense. Single women were not supposed to travel alone and definitely not supposed to sleep in the same buildings as men. There were several San Francisco hotels for women only."

"Weird that they sign their names as Mrs. Mansfullname," Stef said. "What's that about? Why can't they just say Mrs. Jane Fullname? It's like they don't even exist except as property. Look at this, Mrs. Nelson Doubleday." She didn't mention that her stepmother relished saying she was Mrs. Wellington Beresford the Fourth. Like that meant something.

Without looking up Laurel replied, "That about sums it up. Women traveling alone sought a measure of safety by using their husband's name, as well as observing propriety. Emily Post would have swooned any other way."

"Swooned? Oh my." Stef thought the remark was utterly charming.

She got up and found the wine bottle to refill the glasses she had supplied. She didn't have much in her rooms, but wineglasses were a must. She observed Laurel, completely engrossed in a ledger, blond hair falling around her face in disarray. Her long, gloved fingers were tracing the lines, tapping to an internal rhythm. *Some kind of mental sorting system perhaps.* She was lovely.

"What?" Laurel was looking at her directly.

Stef felt her body stiffen and her face start to warm. What an odd reaction to a simple question. "Hmm? Oh, just wondering if you'd found anything interesting." She thought she saw a hint of disbelief, but, hey, it was the best she could do. She'd been caught nakedly ogling. Okay, she had to rein in this thought process.

"Actually, some of the names are familiar. Something about them...I can't put my finger on it." Laurel tapped a ledger page absently.

Not terribly interested, Stef took a sip of wine and scanned the room Laurel had quickly organized when she arrived. Registration was in one stack, bookkeeping in another, room diaries in a third. They still had a long way to go. She reluctantly checked her watch. "I can get some fresh boxes and bring them down tomorrow. A lot of these are falling apart."

"You're right, it's late. I'll get over tomorrow as soon as I can. We can put them in chronological order and go from there. Maybe by decade." Laurel stared at the registration ledger she'd been leafing through, then grabbed the one Stef had abandoned a few moments before. "Wow."

"What is it?" Stef asked.

"The name right under Mrs. Nelson Doubleday. Daphne, Lady Browning."

"So? Blue blood of some sort?"

Laurel had a small smile on her lips. "Yes, but that's not what is interesting." Her eyes were almost sparking. "Lady Browning was the married name of Daphne du Maurier. Ring a bell?"

After a moment, Stef offered, "She was a writer in the thirties and forties. Didn't she write *Rebecca*? I've seen her name a lot. Didn't know she was royalty."

The reference to royalty seemed to amuse Laurel. "Du Maurier was in love with Doubleday. As far as I know, it was unrequited, but it's been fairly well documented. In the least, they were dear friends. And, evidently, traveled together." She carefully closed the ledger and pointed to the one she had been going over. "This name. Miss Harriet Brown. This ledger is from nineteen thirty-one."

Peering over Laurel's shoulder, Stef forced herself to not react to the fragrance she was wearing and kept her distance from the curve of her neck. "What about it?" She was so preoccupied, she almost missed Laurel's reply.

"'Harriet Brown' was an alias Greta Garbo sometimes used."

Stef stared down at the spidery signature. "So what you're telling me is we could sell this on eBay?"

Laurel evidently didn't realize she was only kidding. She seemed stunned and replied seriously, "What I'm telling you is your hotel probably was a destination for some very famous women. It's never been reported before. This hotel could be an important part of women's history. Our history."

❖

Laurel couldn't sleep. She had driven home in a haze of anticipation. For once she was grateful that Rochelle had been drunk when she got home, because if she'd paid attention she would have realized that Laurel had only just arrived herself. But she'd stumbled to bed and passed out on her back, snoring loudly.

As had become her habit, Laurel went to the guest bedroom. It used to upset her that she had no real reason to sleep with her partner anymore. But over the past year, she'd begun to see the smaller room along the hallway as her refuge, and was always relieved to close the door and be alone with her thoughts. She rearranged her pillows, knowing her usual nighttime rituals would not transport her to sleep. She was still too excited to relax. After discovering the famous names, she and Stef had quickly scrambled through some of the other ledgers. They found several more references to the name Harriet Brown, and also some other aliases used by Hollywood women. Some, Laurel was sure, were anagrams for still others. She couldn't wait to return to the hotel and continue the search.

The thought troubled her almost as much as it excited her. Knowing that Rochelle would try to usurp the project, she couldn't share what she was doing, for practical reasons. Yet her emotions were also involved. Rochelle was her partner, but she didn't want to share her joy with her. That was just plain wrong, and Laurel refused to accept the entire blame for her reservations. She took her feelings for what they were, an indication that her relationship was in serious trouble.

She went through a litany of alternatives that might help bring her and Rochelle closer together. *More sex*. No. *Okay, get a dog*. She wouldn't bring a dog into this house. The poor thing would be terrified. And if she wouldn't do that to a dog, she sure as hell wouldn't do it to a child. Couples therapy was the obvious step, but Laurel was shocked to realize that she didn't want couples therapy. That was for people who really wanted to stay together. A normal couple would try to talk things through, and Laurel had made attempts in the past. That was the problem, she already knew what to expect. When Rochelle was sober, she was usually hungover and rarely had a kind word for anyone, especially Laurel. Finding time to just sit down and talk about their relationship issues would never happen. Rochelle would start yelling almost immediately, blaming all that was wrong on Laurel. The situation would then escalate, and Rochelle was becoming increasingly willing to use violence to win any argument.

Laurel broke out in a cold sweat and searched for something else to think about. Stef. She felt her heartbeat slow, even as her body warmed. She didn't know the woman's last name, and all they had done was share a pizza and some wine. They'd talked about the project, nothing else, yet there was an intimacy between them. How was that possible?

Laurel rationalized that she was looking forward to delving into the project and was excited by the possibilities, but the truth was not quite so simple. She couldn't stop thinking about the woman she'd spent less than five hours with, a woman she knew nothing about. *Well, puzzle solved. You can fantasize to your heart's content. As soon as you get to know her, disappointment will set in.* Laurel was pretty sure Stef was gay, but she hadn't asked. She also suspected she might be single but hadn't asked about that either. And the reason she'd avoided those obvious questions was that she didn't want to answer them herself. What a farce.

Her personal life was a mess and she refused to involve anyone else in it. The idea that Stef might want to know more about her was a delusion anyway. She had so much going for her; why would she be interested in a bookworm like Laurel?

❖

"How was your date last night?" Denny and Sika were seated at the breakfast table when Stef appeared.

Catching the interest in Sika's eyes, Stef busied herself with filling her plate with some toast and scrambled eggs. Mamaka could always read her with crystal clarity. Moving to the espresso machine, she tried for nonchalance. "It wasn't a date, just a thank-you for letting her look at that stuff from the secret room."

"How was that? Find any buried treasure?" Denny wasn't going to let this go.

"No. We just organized, really. Some of the guest registration ledgers were interesting, though. There were a couple of entries that could have been from celebrities back in the thirties. Like Garbo." From the looks on their faces, that got their attention.

Sika asked, "Who else?"

Satisfied that the conversation had been diverted from her, Stef said, "Writers, intellectuals, some very wealthy, all women. So I guess my idea of a hotel just for women travelers isn't that original. This place was on the map decades ago."

Denny seemed thrilled with the idea. "Wow. We should use that history for promoting the hotel. 'Destination for the stars.' That has a ring to it. Right?"

"Yeah, we could get some old photos and have them blown up, maybe have an exhibit of the article Laurel will write. It could be great for us." Stef loved the whole idea, especially because it would provide a legitimate excuse to hang around Laurel. She steadfastly refused to examine why that thought was so inviting. "What do you think, Mamaka?"

Sika looked pensive. "I think we should tread lightly. Let's wait and see what your friend discovers. Perhaps there were other reasons these women came here." With that, she stood and excused herself, saying something about needing to get to the flower mart before everything was picked over.

Staring at the swinging door, Denny said, "Well, that was strange. I would think Mama would be very excited about this. She loves women's history. And we're always talking about ways to promote the hotel."

Stef shrugged. "I have no idea."

Sika apparently changed her mind because she reappeared with a fresh cup of tea in her hand and sat down. "I would like to hear more about everything you've discovered, especially from the professor. Do you think she'd like to have dinner with us?"

"That's a wonderful idea," Denny enthused. "We could make something special and eat in the dining room. Tell her about the restoration plans. Show her around."

Denny had it all mapped out, a plan to impress one of the only women Stef had felt a flutter of interest in for years. She wasn't sure how she felt about her best friend immediately stepping in to charm the captivating academic. She was sure that Denny's motives were purely to help the hotel, but suddenly things felt like they were moving too quickly in an unknown direction. She didn't want complications at this point in her life. Her plan was to slowly explore a friendship with Laurel. She needed to stay focused on that.

There was only one problem. Her plan had already dissolved

into a process that had taken on a life of its own, one she had lost control of. The thought was extremely unsettling.

"I'll ask her later this week," she said with weakening resolve.

❖

Stef knocked on the frame of the open door to announce herself. She'd observed Laurel deep in thought, flipping back and forth between several ledgers and making notes on a pad of paper. She was in her customary uniform of baggy jeans and shirt, hair pulled back, glasses on, latex gloves in place. She was breathtaking.

Laurel gave her a luminous smile of recognition and welcome. She knew she must have matched it because her heart was pounding. She had avoided visiting for most of the week, reasoning that it would be pathetic if she found excuses to hang around all the time.

Now, seeing Laurel amidst the detritus of the hotel history, she had to admit that she'd missed the quiet professor. A lot. No matter how busy she got trying to arrange for financing, paying bills, making remodel decisions, there was a part of her mind that held the image of Laurel as a refuge, a secret place she would visit. The prospect calmed her amidst the storm. And that worried her.

This woman probably wasn't available and didn't know Stef existed other than as a nice person she had befriended and resource for her project. Besides, Stef had an unbreakable rule: Never mess with a married woman. And she was pretty certain that's what Laurel was. Not only did pining for unavailable women lead to heartache, it messed up any professional relationship going forward. She'd seen it before and had no intention of falling victim. No matter how much she was attracted to Laurel Hoffman, fantasy was going to have to suffice.

"Hey. How's the project going?" She ambled in and tried not to have a visceral reaction to the unusual color of Laurel's eyes. She'd been thinking about that color constantly and couldn't name it. Green, but not dark or turquoise, more like lime. But not dark lime. She'd eventually gone to the paint charts and decided on chartreuse. But green chartreuse. Jade with gold flecks. She longed to study

Laurel's eyes, but knew she couldn't be that close to Laurel without kissing her.

"What color are your eyes?" That one popped out before she could stop it. Nice self-control.

Laurel seemed startled by the question, then blushed and lowered her gaze. She was beautiful when bashful, which didn't help Stef's vow of detachment.

"Green, I suppose." She tilted her head as she answered the question, as though studying Stef.

"Uh, yeah, but what shade? It seems unusual to me." There, perfectly reasonable question.

"Well, my dad has blue eyes and my mother hazel. It must be a combination because my sister and I are the only ones with this color."

"Your partner must love it. I mean, because it's unusual, you know?" So very, *very* lame. Why not just come right out and ask what she really wanted to know: *Are you single and are you interested in me?*

The amused curiosity that had been present in Laurel seemed to disappear. With a noncommittal shrug she went back to her ledgers immediately. Subject closed.

Casting around for something, anything to change the topic, Stef asked, "Have you found out any more about movie star guests?"

Laurel smiled briefly, but her demeanor was neutral. "Not as yet, but I'm going to search the room diaries after I look through the rest of the ledgers quickly. I have a few more names that seem interesting."

"Like what?" This felt better, nothing personal. Keep it work related.

"Well, for one thing, I think some very famous women stayed here regularly. I've seen their maiden names, married names, what could be anagrams, that type of thing. At first, I thought it was a coincidence. This hotel must have been the 'in' place for the rich and famous for a time. But it was solely women, not their husbands or male lovers."

Stef was listening intently, drawn to the animation of this

normally quiet woman. Her eyes were now definitely a lime color; fresh, sparkling. Without realizing it she must have moved closer. "Do you think it was a women's club? Or some kind of sorority? I was in one in college, secret handshake and all."

Deep in thought, Laurel stared at the pile of ledgers. "I considered that. The secret part, yes, definitely. I even wondered if it was similar to Marlene Dietrich's infamous 'Sewing Circle' from the nineteen thirties and forties."

"What was that?"

Laurel finally met Stef's gaze. "A group of beautiful, rich women who were decidedly bisexual. They got together and ate and chatted and bedded each other." She was blushing by the end of the sentence.

"Oh." That was all Stef could utter.

She was absorbed in Laurel's response, the subtle color on her porcelain cheeks, her darkened eyes. She was closer than before. So close that her lips seemed within touching distance. Her lips. Stef couldn't tear her gaze away from them. They begged for attention, pleaded to be met with her own.

Laughter in the normally quiet hallway broke the spell that had them within inches of one another. They flew several feet apart as the current between them was severed.

Ember appeared in the doorway with Mrs. C on her arm, the two smiling broadly. She started to enter, probably oblivious to the interruption, but Mrs. C held her back for a moment fussing with something she was holding. When they came in, Ember quickly retrieved two card table chairs, as she had the first time they visited. Mrs. C continued to peruse the stacks of papers as Stef tried to reorient. She wasn't sure what had just happened but she'd never experienced anything like it before.

Laurel seemed flustered, standing and looking furtively around, as if she'd misplaced something. She was rubbing her thighs with her palms, like she was trying to dry them. It was all very confusing.

Once seated, Mrs. C presented some delicate tea cookies and they each had one and talked about the research project.

After a moment, Laurel, evidently fully recovered, asked,

"Mrs. Castic, do you have any knowledge about the women who used to stay here?"

The blue of Mrs. C's eyes seemed to pale as she focused on the ceiling. "There was a society, an organization of women who were concerned about the times we were living in. We met fairly regularly, always here. We discussed books, events, all sorts of things."

Laurel said, "So you were a member of this society."

"Yes, I was."

"Do you know when it was formed? Where I can find more information about it? I tried to look it up on the Internet and, as yet, nothing like you're describing shows up. Was it secret? Were there dues? Was it a ladies' book club type of thing?"

Chuckling, Mrs. C answered, "My, you are a researcher, aren't you? So many questions. I'm not sure when it was formed, but it predated the San Francisco earthquake and fire, I think. I don't believe it began in San Francisco, perhaps in New York or Paris. We discussed more than books, I can assure you. There were dues, but each woman paid according to her ability."

"Were the members lesbian or bisexual?" Laurel seemed surprised by her own straightforwardness and quickly looked away, blushing.

Stef was riveted to Mrs. C. Her gaze remained steady. She seemed amazingly unflustered.

"In those days, most women were married or saw men. It was necessary."

From nowhere, Ember asked, "What about you?"

After a moment, Mrs. C replied, "I did what was necessary."

"Don't we all," Laurel said quietly.

CHAPTER EIGHT

L aurel slipped on a pair of nice jeans and chose a light sweater that she was always complimented on rather than the huge denim shirt she normally wore. She'd been out for the past three nights, foraging through the material at the hotel. Sometimes the task was tedious, but it was always better than sitting in the library trying to coax a paper out of the archives.

She had to admit that much of her pleasure in the project was the chance of seeing Stef. Over the past month they'd developed a friendly relationship, but Laurel was aware that they were intentionally keeping their distance. Except for Stef's comment about her eyes and a partner, which Laurel had sidestepped as best she could, they still hadn't spoken about anything except the material they were examining and progress with the hotel renovations. Laurel was content to avoid treacherous personal conversations. Even though Stef's face occupied a great deal of her daydreaming, it was safer to see her in a purely professional capacity.

"Are you going out again tonight?" Rochelle stood in the doorway of the bathroom, a cocktail in her hand. It was one of the rare nights she was home, not having stopped at the bar with her buddies. She didn't look pleased.

"Yes. I told you, I'm researching my next paper and I have work to do." Well, it was true.

"You look like you're going on a date."

Laurel tried to sound casual. "I get sick of wearing my crappiest clothes to the library. I'm confused for a student so much of the time. Besides, they're dirty." Okay, that was a partial lie. She wasn't going to the library, but the rest was true, almost.

Rochelle studied her. "Well, you look good. Don't be too late, we haven't seen each other in a while. I thought we'd cuddle tonight." She grinned wolfishly and Laurel's heart sank.

"I might be a little late, but I'll try to get home soon. I left your dinner in the fridge."

"Fine." Rochelle checked her watch. "Oops, time for my show. See you later."

Letting out a sigh of relief, Laurel quickly finished and left the house before her partner changed her mind and insisted that she could do research some other night.

The woman at the door was beautiful. Her golden blond hair was loose around her shoulders, framing her oval face perfectly. The sweater she wore matched the green of her eyes and clung to the delicate curves of her slim body. Her jeans were not the baggy ones Stef had seen before, but fit like a glove, promising shapely legs and a perfect derrière.

Opening the door, Stef managed, "Hey, Laurel. You look great. Thanks for coming over."

The conversation was loud as they entered the small dining room, Denny had invited Jock and crew, and although Jock still irritated the hell out of her, Stef couldn't begrudge the invitation. They'd worked their asses off for weeks now, meeting deadlines, correcting the shoddy mistakes of the previous contractor as they went. When Denny had suggested making the dinner more of a team celebration, Stef couldn't see any reason to refuse.

Even Mrs. Castic, escorted by Ember Jones, was there. It was hard not to like the old woman because she was very sweet, made killer cookies for the crew, and Stef had noticed that Ember seemed devoted to her. No matter what the girl's background was, Stef was glad she had a place to stay, rules or not. She was a nice kid. As she glanced around the room, it dawned on her that these people had become a family of sorts to her. And for whatever reason, Laurel's presence seemed to complete that picture. That thought, after being labeled "ridiculous," was quickly stuffed to the back of her mind.

Sweeping her arm toward the festivities, she said, "Here's the whole motley crew. Let me…" But somehow words failed her as she was caught in the intensity of Laurel's gaze. She had no idea how long they stood together before someone clapped her on the shoulder and interrupted.

"Hey, Stump, aren't you going to introduce your friend?" Jock eyed Laurel with more than casual interest, from Stef's point of view. And there was that nickname.

"Jocelyn Reynolds, this is Dr. Laurel Hoffman. Professor Hoffman to you."

Jock grinned winningly. "Please call me Jock, Dr. Hoffman. Ms. Beresford likes to tease me. So nice to meet you."

Watching Jock turn on the charm grated on Stef's nerves. She was even more dismayed when Laurel said, "Beresford? As in the Beresford hoteliers?" She had a confused, then wary look on her face.

Stef shifted, not knowing what to say. "Yes, but they don't have anything to do with this hotel."

Her voice cooler, Laurel said, "But you do. You own this hotel, don't you. I thought you were employed by the owners."

Stef was silent, at a loss for words. She should have told Laurel sooner. After a month, her failure to mention her name looked like a deliberate deception.

Interrupting, Jock smoothly said, "Well, she works like she's employed by the owners. You know, Ember talks about how much she enjoys your class. If you ever want to come up to see what we're doing, feel free. We're on the top two floors now."

Laurel turned to Jock. "Well that was very nice of Ember." She looked around and spotted the young woman. "If you'll excuse me, I'll go over and say hello to her and Mrs. Castic. I want to thank her for the tea and cookies a few nights ago."

As they watched Laurel's lovely backside, Stef abruptly remembered herself and elbowed Jock. "Stop drooling on the professor. And, thanks for saying that. I meant to tell her, I just forgot."

"No thanks needed. You always hated to tell anyone your last name in college." Rubbing her side, Jock teased, "Hey, Stump, do I detect some territory that you want to keep to yourself?"

Stef snapped, "No. It's just that she's got a lot of class and deserves more than a one-night stand, so I suggest you stay away from her." She was surprised to see Jock flinch at that description, since she remembered her priding herself on doing just that in college.

Jock recovered quickly. "Are you dating her?"

"No, I'm just keeping an eye on her and the historical stuff. After all, I'm...*we* are the owners of the hotel." Stef sounded like an ass, even to herself.

"Uh-huh. You don't even know if she's available, do you?"

"Well, I..." Now her neck was starting to itch. Stef knew that meant she was blotching from embarrassment. Double dammit.

"Do you know if she's a lesbian? Bi? Het?" Jock rocked back on her heels, obviously enjoying the tease. Just like old times.

Stef hated it. "Back off, Jock. It's none of our business and you know it."

"Ladies? Do I sense tension here?"

They whirled to meet Denny's vigilant brown eyes. She'd always been the mediator between them, and Stef was glad to see her. She couldn't let her temper get the best of her. They needed Jock.

"Sorry, Denny. I know I promised to be good." Offering her hand to Stef, Jock said, "Truce? I didn't mean to step on your turf. I was just curious. The professor is hot, that's all."

Stef hesitated only long enough to catch a meaningful glance from Denny, the kind that threatened great bodily harm if she didn't cooperate. She shook Jock's hand, and at that moment Sika called dinner. She'd prepared hearty food, with several kinds of lasagnas, salads, crusty garlic bread, and good Chianti, sodas, beer, or water to choose from. Laurel seemed to be enjoying herself, pitching in with carrying bowls and such to the long table that they were going to use for the buffet.

Everyone found a place to sit and dug in. Stef quickly arranged herself next to Laurel, reasoning that she needed familiar people around her. They ended up near Ember and Mrs. C, Sika, Denny, and Jock. The conversation was lively, with Laurel exclaiming over the delicious food, Denny and Jock regaling people with stories of their college days on the basketball team, and Ember asking Laurel, whom she insisted on calling Dr. Hoffman, about other classes at Cal. The young woman obviously wanted to attend as more than an observer.

"Mrs. C, how long have you lived at the hotel?" Laurel asked after a while.

The banter paused as all turned their attention to the small, delicately boned woman with the lively blue eyes. Her reserve and Eastern European accent served to make her more interesting.

"Let me see. I visited the hotel in the nineteen forties with a friend of mine, actually many times. That went on through the fifties, and I lived here, finally, in the sixties, I believe."

"Your name must be in some of the guest ledgers I've been looking through. I haven't gotten to the forties yet."

Mrs. Castic offered a slight smile. "Perhaps."

Well, that was vague. Laurel must have thought so, too, because she followed up the comment. "I was thinking about what we discussed the other day. That club you mentioned. Was it the Elysium Society?"

A noise from Sika's direction along with some coughing drew everyone's attention to a spilled glass of red wine. "Sorry." She stood and started mopping the mess.

Denny quickly disappeared into the kitchen and reappeared with several dish towels as they all tried to help and not get dripped on.

Sika recovered quickly and said, "Well, I think it's time for dessert. Laurel, will you help me?"

Laurel trooped after her to bring out the ice cream and

chocolate cake that everyone busied themselves with. There were exclamations of being overfed and happy, and a lot of the group thanked their hostesses and excused themselves. Their table was the exception.

Jock asked Laurel, "What is the Elysium Society? Sounds intriguing."

Shrugging, Laurel said, "I'm not sure. They seemed to hold regular meetings at the hotel, starting in the nineteen twenties. Mrs. C was telling me about being in a book club of sorts. I'll have to do some more research."

Ember, listening intently, piped up. "Why don't you ask Dr. Jacobs? She might know about it."

Laurel appeared to lose some of the color her glass of wine had placed in her cheeks. She'd also lost the smile Stef found mesmerizing. "Maybe so. I'll have to ask." Her voice was so soft Stef could barely hear her.

Ember must not have noticed, because she followed with, "Well, she's your partner and the department chair and all, so I thought, you know, she might help."

Stef lost all of the air from her lungs. She stared at Laurel, who seemed engrossed in her napkin, refusing to look up.

"Okay, well, it's getting late," Denny said, clearly picking up on the tension. "We all have early days tomorrow, so how about we wrap up for tonight?"

She must have elbowed Jock because suddenly Jock was standing. "Yeah, come on, kid, I want you on the job by seven tomorrow. Mrs. Castic, may I escort you back to your rooms?"

Mrs. C was quick to accept.

Ember seemed about to protest when Jock said, "I'll give you your list of chores for tomorrow as we walk back."

Before Stef could register more, she was watching the three of them exit the dining room, Mrs. C framed by the two tall women, one on each arm. Denny and Sika were clearing dishes. Stef offered to help but Sika told her to sit, she and Denny had it handled.

Laurel still refused to look at Stef, instead busying herself gathering her small backpack to leave. "Thank you for a great evening. It was such fun. Is it okay if I come back tomorrow to resume work?" She seemed to be asking permission, all over again.

Numbly, Stef said, "Of course. I might not be around, so if you could get here before we lock the outer doors, that would help."

It seemed they had both had held back critical information from each other. Stef knew she shouldn't be surprised to hear about the existence of a partner, especially after Laurel had dodged her only attempt to get personal information. But that didn't matter now, because her fantasy was shattered and the reality of the truth made her sad in a way she had never before experienced.

❖

Driving across the Bay Bridge toward Berkeley, Laurel was almost ill from the turn of events of the evening. Things had been going so well. The women were interesting, humorous, immensely likeable. Stef and Jock had almost argued over her, and she was so flattered she'd felt giggly. Although she was startled to learn that Stefanie was from one of the largest hotel families in the world, when she thought about it, how could she be angry when she'd withheld a much more critical piece of information?

Mrs. Castic was fascinating and obviously knew much more than she was saying about the history of the hotel. She'd been cagey in their few previous conversations, and Laurel had the feeling her measure was being taken. More questions bubbled up in her mind. She wished Sika hadn't spilled the wine the moment she mentioned the Elysium Society. Everything seemed to come to a crashing halt after that. Laurel could still see the look on Stef's face when Ember innocently dropped the bomb about Rochelle being her partner.

Even though the topic had never come up before, even though she hadn't lied except by omission, she felt guilty. She could argue she was being silly. After all, neither she nor Stef had ever been anything other than friendly and businesslike. Yes, very friendly, but why should that matter? Just because she had a partner, nothing would change. And that, she realized sadly, was the problem.

Aside from the fact that she didn't want to share the project for professional reasons, she didn't want to tell Rochelle for personal reasons, too. The hotel, the project, was *her* territory, the women *her* new friends. They liked her for who she was, not as Mrs. Dr. Rochelle Department Chair. Without Laurel realizing it, Rochelle had narrowed her world to just the friends and colleagues Rochelle knew. She controlled everything, and Laurel had allowed it.

The driveway gravel crunched as she rolled to a halt behind Rochelle's car. She could see the flickering of the TV in the living room. Rochelle had probably fallen asleep in front of it. With an audible sigh, Laurel locked the car and trudged up the walkway. Now she would have to rouse her out of her drowse and help her get to bed. Rochelle was larger than Laurel and often nasty when awakened. Laurel never knew what was waiting behind the door. She steeled herself and went in.

"You're late." Rochelle was standing just inside the door. The tone in her voice made Laurel's stomach tighten. It signaled displeasure and anger. She knew it well.

"I got home as soon as I could." Laurel tried to sound matter-of-fact but felt the tension in her throat. She knew Rochelle wouldn't miss the quaver in her voice and that this sign of weakness would only encourage her.

"Doing research, were you?"

The detachment served to elevate Laurel's anxiety. Rochelle knew something. She was setting a trap. "Yes. Why do you ask?"

"At the library?"

Laurel fought down panic, tried to think. Rochelle knew she hadn't been at the library. "No. I was in San Francisco, interviewing an elderly woman for my project."

"Oh, yes. Your *boring* research project. The one you are doing just to meet your minimum requirement to stay on tenure track. That one?"

Rochelle swayed just a bit, and Laurel fought the urge to run. Maybe it was all a ruse, maybe she was just upset that Laurel hadn't been home as much as usual recently. That alone was grounds for punishment.

"Yes. What's the matter, Rochelle? You sound upset."

Rochelle stopped a foot from her, now in the light. Her eyes were mean and Laurel could smell her breath. The alcohol scent was overwhelming. She tensed, hoping to talk Rochelle out of her anger and get her to bed.

"I talked to Harry De Silva."

Harry was Rochelle's best drinking buddy, a professor in the history department, and Laurel had never liked him. He hit on her, making slimy innuendos and trying to touch her inappropriately, always behind Rochelle's back. When Laurel complained Rochelle took his side and said it was all in her imagination. She'd never once protected her from him.

Feigning uninterest, Laurel said, "And?"

"He told me that the buzz in his classes was all about you and the great 'find' you've made in some hotel in San Francisco. Like you've unearthed the mother lode of historical feminist information." Rochelle suddenly grabbed Laurel by both arms, her fingers digging deeply and shook her. "Tell me about that, Laurel. Tell me all about it."

Trying unsuccessfully to pull away, Laurel said, "Stop it, Rochelle. You're hurting me." Lately Rochelle had been acting this way more often. She would shove Laurel, and even slapped her occasionally, but she always regained control of herself quickly. Something about her belligerence seemed different tonight.

"Who do you think you are, lying to me? You think you can pursue a find like that without me as your primary author? Do you?" She was spitting the words, twisting her hands to pinch Laurel.

Suddenly she let go and Laurel stumbled back, cracking her head on a nearby wall sconce. She tried to keep her feet under her and escape, thinking of the lock on the spare bedroom door. She'd used it before when Rochelle was drunk and would try to come in. Rochelle never mentioned those instances, either not remembering or pretending nothing happened. She lurched in the direction of the bedroom but Rochelle was on her again, this time grabbing her wrist and slapping her hard enough to send her to the floor.

Stunned, she lay still, trying to orient herself. Her mouth was open; she didn't know if her jaw was broken because she couldn't seem to move it. Before she could gather her thoughts, she felt a searing pain in her side as Rochelle kicked her hard enough to knock the wind out of her. After a moment, she sensed Rochelle still standing over her, panting.

"We're not through with this subject. I have an early meeting. I'm going to bed." Rochelle staggered and needed a wall for support but managed to make it to their bedroom, where she slammed the door.

Relief flooded through Laurel, then she hastened into the spare room, locking the door behind her. She wasn't going to risk Rochelle having second thoughts about her reprieve. Leaning on the door, she slid to the floor, the coppery taste of blood in her mouth. Her lips felt puffy, and she gingerly touched her face. She crawled to the only mirror in the room, an inexpensive full-length one she used to make sure everything was zipped and in order before she left for work each day. Even in the poor lighting, the results of her inspection weren't good.

Her lip was not split, but she must have bitten the inside of her mouth, because it was swelling. The side of her face showed Rochelle's handprint clearly, and now that the numbness had worn off, her jaw was aching. When she tried to open and close her mouth, she heard clicking and her jaw seemed to stutter. Tears fell as she sagged to the edge of the bed.

Rochelle knew about the project and would now demand to share the credit. She'd done so before, what was new? But what about the friends Laurel had made? What about Stef? She wouldn't be able to go into the hotel for a few days, not until she could cover the external marks with makeup. The thought was like another physical blow. The project, and the women involved in it, were her lifeline, all she looked forward to.

Hugging herself and rocking to help ease the pain from her bruised ribs, she decided that she would offer to share the project without complaint. That way, Rochelle would leave her alone and she might still be able to see Stef. With stunning clarity, she realized that seeing Stefanie Beresford was the most important part of the whole equation. Nothing mattered as much.

Laurel sank into the bed and carefully pulled her legs up to curl into a ball. Whatever she did, she wasn't willing to let go of the new, separate existence she led researching in the hotel. She had never been so happy or felt so relaxed.

Imagining Stef's beautiful face and smile gave her solace as she drifted to sleep.

CHAPTER NINE

Three days later, after class, Ember Jones lingered after the others left, which seemed to take forever. Although no one asked, the class had been subdued today, the students pensive. Once or twice one of them approached after they were dismissed, but seemed to reconsider and exited the room. All except Ember.

With concern written on her lovely young face, she inquired, "Dr. H?"

"Yes, Ember. May I help you?" Laurel tried to look neutral, professorial. She hoped it was working.

"Are you okay?" Ember looked embarrassed, staring at her boots and shifting her weight.

"What? Oh, you mean my face. Well, I am an absentminded professor, I guess. I was so absorbed in a book I was reading I walked into a door a few days ago. Almost knocked myself silly. That must have been why the class was so quiet today. Tell them I'm fine, will you?"

Looking unconvinced, Ember noted, "Haven't seen you at the hotel either."

Desperate to have the conversation over, Laurel said, "Well, other responsibilities took precedence, but I'll be back in a few days. Now, if you'll excuse me, I must be going. See you soon, Ember."

Ember gathered her backpack and slung it over her shoulder. "Sure. Next class." She started for the door and turned just before exiting. "If you ever need anything, you just let me know, Dr. H. I can come over really fast."

Touched beyond words, Laurel could only nod, fighting back the tears that threatened to form as she smiled at the young student, so noble and full of idealism. She was the second person, her sister Kate being the first, to offer help. Was the situation with Rochelle so transparent that others could see it despite her efforts to conceal?

Rochelle hadn't said much beyond a halfhearted and defensive apology. Laurel kept her silence, staying in for the past two days to nurse her face and side. Rochelle had brought home dinner for them each evening and kept her drinking to a minimum. She was nice to Laurel, but definitely wanted to know about the project. She explained that, as her partner, and most importantly the department chair, her help was essential if Laurel planned to publish in any prestigious journal. She also managed to use this logic to make the incident Laurel's fault for not telling the truth about the project.

Silent while Rochelle lectured her, Laurel was surprised to realize she didn't feel guilty for lying to her partner. She told her as little as possible, not mentioning what intrigued her the most: the Elysium Society. She had the feeling that there was more to the social group than Mrs. Castic had let on. A discovery of anything that wasn't commonly established before would guarantee a well-received paper in a good journal, perhaps even a book. As much as Rochelle talked, she hadn't had that many papers in those journals herself and would think nothing of coopting Laurel's work so she could take the credit.

Laurel collected her notes and left the classroom, her head down. She wasn't going to be bullied into handing all her research over to Rochelle. The very idea inflamed her and she almost knocked down the restroom door as she entered. Angrily, she splashed her face with cold water. All the feelings she managed to keep in check seemed to burst in her head, making her almost dizzy. She held the edge of the basin and took a deep breath to calm herself.

"Get a grip. Why the hell are you so angry? Rochelle is the chair of the department, her name would have to be on the paper. It's done all the time. And let's not leave out the fact that she's your partner. Your lover." The last words sounded so foreign to her that she stopped and just stared.

Would someone who loved her wreak such havoc on her face? She could barely walk upright, her side ached so badly. What kind of love was that? Never in her life had she ever thought she would be in an abusive relationship. She knew she should leave immediately. But what if all the nasty things Rochelle constantly told her were true? Could Rochelle make sure she was blacklisted from other universities? Was the only reason she was still at Cal her personal relationship to Rochelle?

What if Rochelle was right and, as a partner, she was as good as it would get? Maybe Stef would be just as abusive once she got to know her. But Stef had never been anything but kind and considerate, not just to her but to Mrs. Castic and Ember. It was obvious that Denny and her mother adored her.

Focusing on the wounded eyes in the mirror, Laurel said, "No. Stef is nothing like Rochelle. Nothing. But it doesn't matter, this is something you have to deal with by yourself."

She needed a plan. While the project wasn't the reason for her to leave, it was a catalyst. Rochelle's escalating drinking and violence had Laurel frightened, and she knew she needed to get out of her situation before something worse happened, and before Rochelle figured out that Stefanie Beresford was a factor in her decision to walk away.

Laurel allowed herself a shaky smile. She finally had the courage to do what she should have done a long time ago, and her attraction to Stef had everything to do with that. But she needed to keep her intentions hidden. If Rochelle guessed, it could push her over an edge she was already teetering on.

Stef was so full of conflicting emotions she was having difficulty breathing. Ember had come to her and told her about Laurel's obvious injury, and her concern. She said the rumor was that Dr. Jacobs had hit her. According to Ember, Dr. Jacobs didn't treat Laurel nicely, but no one knew of a history of physical violence, so perhaps Laurel's bruises were caused by an accident.

Jock had dropped by to mention that she'd seen Laurel enter the building. It was all Stef could do to sit on her hands for an hour or so before going down to see her. As she approached the work room Laurel had taken over, she rehearsed in her mind what she would say, how she would tactfully ask how Laurel was doing, suggest that maybe she should take some action, offer to help. But when she reached the door and saw the bruise on her jaw, the swelling on one side of her beautiful face, she wanted to destroy something. The thought of someone laying a hand on Laurel in anger made her crazy.

Watching covertly, from just behind the door, Stef tried to calm down but she couldn't. Laurel was deeply engrossed in a ledger, surrounded by the diaries and notepads of her research. She looked completely absorbed and terribly vulnerable.

"Laurel?" Stef did her best to strike a pleasant, innocent tone, as though she hadn't noticed the remnants of the huge purple imprint of a hand.

Laurel gave her a cautious smile. "I didn't hear you."

Stef came in and sat on a box close to Laurel. She studied her and reached to gently touch the bruise on her jaw.

"Don't." Laurel turned away. But when Stef didn't withdraw, she accepted her tentative touch.

"Who did this to you?" Stef's voice was rough with emotion. No matter how hard she tried, she couldn't hide her anger or pretend the evidence of an assault wasn't there.

Not meeting her eyes, Laurel said, "It isn't important. It's over."

"Yes, it is important. It's you." Stef pulled Laurel to her and in that moment, Laurel collapsed, clinging to her, breaking down completely.

Overwhelmed with tenderness, Stef held her and let her cry. When she tightened her embrace Laurel flinched and their eyes met. For a fleeting moment Laurel seemed afraid, then she focused on Stef, and Stef saw shame. Gently she eased back and, seeking her permission and receiving a slight nod, she lifted the tank top. Purple and yellow bruises covered Laurel's abdomen and ribs. Tears fell and Stef did nothing to hide them.

"You can't go back there." That was the one thing she knew in her heart.

Laurel looked away. "It's…complicated. I've decided I'm leaving, but I don't have a place yet, and there are my classes, my job. I just need a little time."

Stef tried to lighten the mood, reasoning with her, not making her wrong. "Laurel, why don't you try hotel living? This floor still has a few rooms left. You'd be closer to the project. Then you wouldn't have to commute so late at night. You could just go over to teach. You could eat here, too. Sika always complains she doesn't have enough mouths to feed."

Her eyes welling again, Laurel said, "That would be such an imposition. Besides, this is my problem, and I must deal with it. Rochelle is also my supervisor at the university. She could claim the project as partly hers."

Not able to keep the steel from her voice, Stef said, "You were the one we agreed to let examine the papers, and you are the one who will write about what we've found. The only one. Tell her that if you want."

Pulling away, Laurel sat up in the camp chair she used and straightened her clothes. She seemed embarrassed to have let down in front of Stef. "Thank you, but I'll have to handle this situation myself. There are so many things to consider."

"Listen, I'll let you get back to work. But the offer still stands. You can move into one of the rooms on this floor at least until we need to renovate, no charge." When Laurel emphatically shook her head, Stef amended, "Or a minimal rent. After all, these are not ideal conditions, right?"

"You've been more than generous, Stef, from the very beginning. I didn't mean to dump my troubles in your lap. It's just that this place feels welcoming to me. I… Don't worry about me, I'll be fine."

Stef was stung by her words, cut off from what had been such a strong connection only moments before. Standing abruptly, she started for the door. As she reached it, she felt a hand on her back and turned to see the woman she constantly dreamt about, just inches from her.

Laurel leaned and kissed her on the cheek. "Thank you for… everything."

It would be so easy to change direction, to take Laurel in her arms and kiss her passionately. Stef had to escape, needed to think. Now was not the time to complicate Laurel's life further. She nodded and left the room, numbly taking the service elevator to the top floor and then the stairs to the roof. There, she stared into the growing dusk, the tall buildings of San Francisco all around her. She wished she had a drink, then thought she should take up smoking. Her mood seemed noir; all she needed to complete the picture was a trench coat and fedora.

On cue, Jock was behind her. "Got woman problems?"

Stef started. "Where did you come from?"

"I come up here a lot at the end of the day. It's nice. Fresh salt air from the ocean this time of day, bustle of the city, I like it." Studying Stef for a moment, she asked, "How's Laurel?"

Stef felt her shoulders sag. "Bruised. Who told you?"

"Ember's been worried. We all like the professor. Want me to go beat someone up?"

Jock was serious. Her tough talk made Stef smile. "Stand in line. I offered to have her move into the hotel, but she said she couldn't."

Jock was quiet for a moment. "Want a glass of wine? I have a good Zin over there." She seemed a bit shy in the asking.

Surprised at the considerate offer, and who was offering, Stef nodded and followed her across the rooftop to a little sheltered area that was set up with a makeshift table of concrete blocks and a few metal patio chairs. Jock handed her a wineglass and poured the wine expertly. They swirled the wine and sniffed appropriately, then took a sip.

"It's good. Are you a wine devotee?" Stef couldn't see very well in the light but guessed that Jock was blushing.

"I've done work in some of the wineries in Sonoma and Napa and learned some things from their winemakers. One thing led to another, and now I just appreciate a good bottle of wine. Nice to share it with someone." They sat enjoying the silence for a while before Jock ventured, "Do you care for Laurel?"

Immediately shaking her head, Stef said, "I can't. She's in a relationship. Good or bad, she's with someone else."

Jock put a comforting hand on her shoulder just as Denny rounded the corner and pulled up short. "Oh, sorry, I didn't know you were entertaining." She did an about face and abruptly stopped. Whirling back she said, "Stef? What are you doing here?"

The tone in her voice fell somewhere between accusation and shock. For some reason Stef felt guilty and stood abruptly. "I came up for some air and found Jock and we were...what are *you* doing here?"

"Well, I came up to see what Mademoiselle was pouring this evening. Do I need an excuse?"

"Do I?" Stef knew she sounded defensive. Was she taking her frustration about Laurel out on Denny?

Jock interrupted them. "Hey, I have another glass. If you two *best friends* can calm down a minute, we can continue to enjoy the evening. Deal?"

Denny nodded and then seemed to reconsider her attitude. "I heard about Laurel. Have you talked to her?"

Stef deflated, taking a large gulp of wine as Jock poured a glass for Denny. "She looks like hell and there are bruises on her stomach. Looks like her bitch partner kicked her."

Jock asked, "How did you find out about her stomach?"

Stef heard only concern in her voice, so she answered and then explained how Laurel had just shut her out.

"She's ashamed, Stef. You need to give her some space to work it out." Denny stopped talking and they all sipped silently.

Stef finally added, "Maybe so, but if that woman so much as touches her again, I'm going to beat the shit out of her."

Jock raised her glass. "I call second."

Followed by Denny. "I call third."

Toasting required opening a second bottle. By the end of the evening they had shared a pizza, too, and Stef had begun to change her mind about Jock Reynolds.

CHAPTER TEN

Denny slipped into Stef's office and closed the door, leaning on it. "The suits are here. Think I should get my gun?"

Smiling at Denny's joke, Stef took a deep breath to calm herself. She had only needed to make one call before she came up with the money to continue the renovation. The loan officer who'd arranged the first mortgage had vouched for her. The representatives of the private investment firm were here to get her signature and hand over the check. The interest rate was excessive, so the monthly payment was going to be high, and there was a balloon payment after five years. She had to have the money to finish the hotel and get it producing revenue, then she could worry about the rest. Private investor groups usually made a ton of money off second mortgages.

"Are their names Bruno and Vinnie?" she asked.

Glancing at the closed door, Denny said, "No. One looks like a successful businessman. The other is a woman, more like an assistant, I think. The man reminds me of your brother George. Very expensive and well tailored. He was pleasant enough, but sees me as the secretary. I'm sure he's happy to be charging rates that border on usury."

Stef shrugged. "It's just business to them, Denny. Money. They've got it and we need it. Let's get this over with."

The suit was named Trip Boynton, a short, round man with perfectly manicured hands and a four-hundred-dollar haircut, if you counted the cost of the highlights to his mouse brown and thinning hair. His clothes were designed to obscure a soft physique, and he had a perfect tan. Unfortunately for him, his large nose and small hazel eyes made him look like a rat. A rich rat, and she was the cheese.

"Ms. Beresford, what a pleasure. My partners and I were happy to be of assistance in bringing this grand old hotel back to its former glory."

All this was said while he politely shook her hand, but lingered a bit too long before releasing it. Stef wanted to wipe her hand on the pant leg of her suit. Boynton's entire focus was on charming her, and it was making Stef want to grind her teeth. He introduced his assistant almost as an afterthought. Miss Agnes Brady was a plain, thickset woman who looked decidedly uncomfortable. She clutched her briefcase as though it contained diamonds.

"Why don't we get down to business." Stef wanted him gone, and soon. "I have other appointments and I'm sure you do, too."

"Of course. Miss Brady, papers please."

Stef suspected he narrowly avoided snapping his fingers at the woman.

Agnes Brady fumbled with the lock on her case and hastened to produce a thick sheaf of documents that made Stef's heart constrict. She was taking a huge risk, but there was no other choice. Gulping down her anxiety, she looked the contract over. The terms were as agreed upon with the usual inclusions. It seemed boilerplate. Boynton kept checking his microthin watch, as if he was late for something. Either that or he wanted her to notice how very expensive it must be. He had to have known she grew up in a house full of such watches. Maybe he just had a thing about it.

As soon as she'd signed the last form and Miss Brady pulled out her stamp and booklet to notarize it, Stef gave her fingerprint for the book and they were gone. Boynton breezed out first, leaving poor Miss Brady to struggle after him.

She hesitated at the door and looked over her shoulder uncertainly. With heartfelt emotion, she said, "Excuse me." Then she left.

Staring at the closed door, Stef said, "What was that all about?"

Denny and Sika sat in the chairs Boynton and Brady had just vacated.

Sika said, "Well, we have the money to continue. We are grateful."

Denny and Stef sighed at the same moment, Stef saying, "Funny, I don't feel grateful. I feel in debt. Enormous debt."

"It's our dream to bring this hotel back to life for women travelers, for women. Every man we've encountered has told us we cannot do it. It will never make money if we rely solely on women as clientele. Now how do you feel?" Sika was studying them. She always seemed to say the right thing at the right moment.

Stef felt her eyes narrow and her body straighten. She saw the same thing happen to Denny. "I feel like fuck…uh, screw…um…to hell…damn, Mamaka. It's hard not to swear when you're telling someone off."

Bursting into laughter, Sika hugged her and Denny. "Well, thank you for thinking of me, but I agree, to *hell* with them. They don't know women very well. We just have to get the word out. I'll work on that, you two get this hotel finished."

❖

Stef felt restless. Laurel was finally in the hotel again, after skipping almost a week, but hadn't been up to greet her. They'd been avoiding each other, so Stef wasn't entirely surprised to be ignored again, but she wasn't in the mood tonight. It was time they had an adult conversation, she decided, and stalked downstairs composing what she planned to say.

Laurel's door was usually open, but tonight it was closed and Stef could hear voices in the room. One was Laurel's, but she sounded different somehow. Stef waited a moment, thought about leaving, then knocked. When the door was jerked open, she was looking at a very angry stranger.

"What do you want?"

Momentarily stunned by the rudeness, Stef was speechless.

Laurel appeared at the woman's side, looking small and anxious. "Rochelle, this is Stefanie Beresford, the owner of the hotel."

She had stressed Stef's last name, as if trying to impress the rude woman. It must have worked because "Rochelle" was suddenly all smiles and extended her hand.

"Oh, Ms. Beresford. I'm Dr. Rochelle Jacobs, Department Chair of Women's Studies at Cal. Sorry, I was in the middle of examining the documents and was so absorbed that I forgot my manners. Thank you for letting me have access to these precious pieces of women's history." She pumped Stef's hand gratuitously, then dropped it to stand back and study her from head to toe. "Very nice to meet you indeed."

The tone of her voice made Stef decidedly uncomfortable. She was flirting. She probably expected Stef to be flattered. Coughing into her hand gave her the opportunity to think of a response. She glanced quickly at Laurel, who was studying the floor, blushing. She was probably thoroughly embarrassed. The urge to throw Rochelle Jacobs out made Stef's hands itch. She wondered what the woman was even doing here.

"I'm surprised to see anyone but Dr. Hoffman here. It's her project." Stef kept her tone neutral, her face schooled to match it.

Jacobs sought to clarify. "Oh, my, no. Laurel is an assistant professor, she doesn't have full tenure. With a find like this, she'll need my guidance to introduce it to the right people."

That explanation was supposed to impress, Stef was sure. "Really? Because she's the only one who has permission to be examining the contents of this room."

Jacobs's eyes hardened and her jaw muscles worked overtime. "Laurel is my employee. I need to show her how to handle the journals, how to introduce the material to the media. She's also my partner. She'll share."

"*She's* right here in the room. Maybe we should ask her." Stef had had about enough of this officious bitch.

They both turned to Laurel, and for the first time since Stef had known her, she looked afraid. Her hands were clasped tightly together, and she was slightly hunched as if protecting herself. If Stef needed any proof that Jacobs was the one who had abused her previously, this was it. The urge to go to her, stand between her and the tall, imposing, and pissed-off woman was so strong she had to fight for control. But Laurel gave no indication she needed her help. Except one. A pleading look that lasted no more than a second.

With that look, Stef understood that if she threw Jacobs out, or embarrassed her in any way, Laurel would pay the price for it. She couldn't allow that.

Jacobs said, "Laurel, explain to Ms. Beresford how the university system is organized." Her tone was light, patronizing, but Stef heard a threat in it and tried for damage control.

"You're right. I really don't want to put anyone on the spot. I just don't understand how all this works." Her false naïveté seemed to help.

Laurel went into a long explanation, probably memorized word for word, of the pecking order in the university. Only half listening, Stef was paying more attention to the body language between the two women. As the monologue went on, Jacobs seemed to get taller and Laurel to shrink, right before Stef's eyes. After she'd finished making her partner feel big and important, she cast another brief, pleading glance in Stef's direction.

Stef understood exactly what she needed to do. With a careless shrug, she said, "Whatever Laurel decides is fine by me. I guess I was just saying that I'd prefer if she were the only one who did the work at the hotel. She *must* be the only one with a key. This place is under renovation, as you can tell. We already have security issues and our insurance is sky high. She's signed a waiver releasing us from liability if she becomes ill from the dust."

Laurel tilted her head for a second before nodding vigorously. Playing her role, she added timidly, "Stefanie has kept me supplied with industrial masks." As if Jacobs would care about lung damage to her partner when there was prestige up for grabs.

"We should move all this material to the university." Jacobs was obviously salivating for compete control. "It will be safe there."

Shaking her head slowly, as if considering the idea, Stef said, "Can't allow that, sorry. It stays here. We need the material for promotion and stuff like that. We don't even know if this is all of it, and it isn't catalogued. We wouldn't know if anything went missing."

Frustrated, Jacobs offered, "Well, we'll catalogue the collection for you, naturally."

Smiling her best, Stef said, "That's what Laurel's agreed to do. You see, she's already tried to get the papers out of here and back to the university. But I wouldn't cooperate. I've been stung before, no offense to you."

Stef was damned proud of that lie. It would put Laurel on Jacobs's side and Jacobs could be upset with Stef instead. Maybe, if she was lucky, Jacobs would try to take a swing, physically threaten her. Stef would absolutely love to have a crack at her.

Staring hard at her, Jacobs seemed to force a casual tone. "Well, in my opinion, everything would be much safer at school. As you said, this place is a rat trap right now. Until it's remodeled, of course."

Why, you fucker. Stef was about to lay into her when Laurel said, "Rochelle, that's not fair. I've seen some of the top floors and they will be stunning, I'm sure. Stefanie is sparing no expense on the renovations."

Seeming to notice Laurel was still there, Jacobs insincerely said, "You've seen the rest of the hotel? Oh, my mistake. Please accept my apologies. Laurel, I think it's time we went to dinner. Some of our colleagues are meeting at a new place in Berkeley and we can get there only a little late. Ms. Beresford, a pleasure." She offered her hand in dismissal.

Stef took her leave, but not without trying to give Laurel a smile of encouragement. Laurel never took her eyes away from Jacobs, but her attention was not adoring. Stef read the body language with a sick feeling. Laurel was on guard and looking for the next blow.

❖

Laurel returned to her notes, searching for some juicy tidbit to distract Rochelle from her constant griping about Stef and perhaps act as a peace offering. Days had passed since the showdown at the hotel, and Rochelle was still brooding. The silence lasted maybe a minute, with Laurel acutely aware of Rochelle standing in the middle of her office, arms folded, staring at her.

"You're fucking her." The words were spat with such venom Laurel involuntarily flinched.

This accusation was a new low, even for Rochelle. And she was sober, too. Laurel's alarms were going off, big time. "What did you say? That's nonsense. I am with you, Rochelle, and I am working on a significant find. Why would I do such a thing?"

"That's how you got her to say that you had exclusive access to that shit. You're fucking her. Why else would she do it?"

Laurel was momentarily speechless. It was one thing to constantly degrade her, but why pick on Stef? "Because everything she said is true? Because she's honorable and is a nice person? Those thoughts never entered your mind, did they, Rochelle?"

Weary from the constant battle that was Rochelle Jacobs, Laurel had allowed the words to slip out, unedited. Rochelle's eyes narrowed dangerously.

"You have a crush on her. Maybe she hasn't fucked you, but you want her to, don't you?" She was leaning closer now and Laurel reflexively tried for some distance, feeling her face heat as she quickly searched for space. Unexpectedly, Rochelle started laughing. Her face contorted into a sneer and she spat, "Why on earth would you think a rich bitch like that would be attracted to you? Maybe Kate, but you? She could have anyone she wanted, and you're nothing but a junior instructor who takes all the pitiful leftovers anyone trying to dump a job heaps on you. And you just nod and do their bidding, Little Mary Bookworm. You're a joke."

If Rochelle had slapped her as hard as she could it wouldn't have hurt as much as those words. It was as though Rochelle knew how to cut her heart out and did it with surgical precision. Laurel's secret fear had always been that she would yet again be second to Kate. Rochelle had made it abundantly clear that that would have been her preference, too. Once Stef met Kate, any foolish dreams Laurel had would finally be put to rest.

"Why are you with me if I'm so unworthy?"

After a brief silence, Rochelle said, "I often wonder myself. Perhaps because I like being waited on, perhaps because I took pity on you. But don't push it, Laurel. And don't even think about trying to make it with Stefanie Beresford. You're not in her league." Straightening up, she dusted some imaginary lint off of her jacket. "If you try to screw me over on my new find, I'll bury you and I'll bury the information as well. I'll claim that they're all forgeries and I'll make it stick. I'll also find a way to discredit Beresford and her new *women's* hotel. Now get up and let's go. I want a drink."

As Laurel stood and gathered her purse and the papers she wanted to take home, she was amazed at how calm she felt. Maybe it was because Rochelle hadn't gotten violent, and she was relieved to have escaped the worst. Perhaps that was part of it. But something else had happened, too. As the cruel words spilled out of Rochelle's very sober mouth, Laurel knew that she would not put up with this poor excuse for a human being any longer. It might cost her tenure, she might have to give up the idea of being a professor, but she would be gone from this woman, and the sooner, the better. As for Stef, what did it matter? Rochelle was right about that, if nothing else. Stef was out of her league.

CHAPTER ELEVEN

On her way across campus toward the BART station, Ember stopped at one of the many coffee kiosks for a triple-shot latte. Working full time and researching stuff for Mrs. Castic in addition to the assigned readings in Dr. Hoffman's class was taking a toll. On top of all that, she'd overheard Jock and Denny talking about an incident last week between Stefanie, Dr. Hoffman, and that jerk partner of hers, Dr. Jacobs. Threats about the research project being coopted. Ember wished she'd never opened her mouth to the other students. It was her fault that Dr. Jacobs had heard about the discovery.

Morosely, she ordered the latte and leaned against the counter. Maybe she should go apologize to Dr. Hoffman since she'd obviously caused a problem. How was she supposed to know the papers were a big secret? She'd just assumed Dr. Hoffman would tell her partner, even if Dr. Jacobs was a skank.

As the waiter put her drink on the counter, someone slapped a twenty down to pay for it and a male voice behind her said, "I guess I owe you that."

Ember turned sharply, expecting to have to deal with an aggressive flirt. Instead, she was face-to-face with a very clean and shaven Joey G. She might not have recognized her heroin addict street friend if not for his bright smile. To say he looked different was an understatement.

"Joey G? Is that really you?" She couldn't believe it.

"Yup. 'Tis I. And I have you to thank for it." He bowed, gave her the change and her latte, and offered his arm. "Can I walk you?"

They found seats on the train to San Francisco and she studied him. "Joey, what happened? The last time I saw you, you were strung out and mugging old ladies."

"Yes, I was. Remember you gave me that twenty and told me get to rehab?"

"I remember. I didn't think you'd do it, though."

"You were right. I went straight to my dealer and tried to pay him with the twenty even though he told me he wanted fifty. He beat the shit out of me."

"Oh, Joey, I'm sorry I didn't have more. I didn't want you to get hurt." Ember felt terrible. The poor guy was a junkie, not a thug.

"I know, I know. Turns out it was the best thing you could have done for me. When I woke up in a pool of my own puke, and a few other things, I'd already started to withdraw. I barely made it to the ER. The doctor called my folks and they stuck me in rehab."

"Wow, what a story. Are you living at home now?"

"Nope. I'm taking classes and have a job. I'm too damned busy to use, and I'm paying my parents back for the cost of rehab. They don't have any money. They used all their savings."

Curious, Ember asked, "What job are you working? Where do you live?"

"I take care of a warehouse south of Market. Gotta start somewhere. Turns out there's not much call for a professional purse snatcher. I'm sharing a loft with a guy I met in rehab, Ben. He had a cocaine problem but we're both clean and sober now." He looked slightly bashful.

Ember picked up on his funny little smile. "Joey, is Ben your boyfriend?" They'd never really talked about much in those days, but Ember knew he'd turned a few tricks to support himself. Selling sex was part of life on the streets, a last resort she was always grateful she'd been able to avoid.

Joey's ears were pinking up nicely. "Yup. He's a few years older and much wiser. He's, like, a computer genius. Now he's developing software and beta testing and stuff like that. His employer owns the warehouse and he got me the job. It's very cool."

"I am so happy for you, Joey, really."

"You look great, too. Not on the street anymore either?" His gray eyes shone as he took in her clean clothes and scrubbed look. Not Abercrombie and Fitch, but not free at the church, either. She'd paid for them herself.

"I'm living in a hotel and working for the contractor that's remodeling it. Remember that old lady whose purse you tried to steal?"

"You mean do I remember getting that black eye you gave me? It was nothing compared to what happened later." He grinned, so Ember knew he was okay with it.

"Well, we became friends. She's really cool and I'm living with her. I help her out. She's, like, one of the most awesome people I know. You'd like her."

The train stopped at Market and Embarcadero and they both disembarked.

"I live about five blocks from here," Joey said. "You want to see it? We get to use some of the vehicles housed there, the ones our boss owns. A lot of it is mostly personal things owned by employees who've transferred, or they're on assignment or something."

"I'd love to, but I have to go now, I'm expected. Give me your cell number and I'll call you. I'm going to get a cell phone soon."

She'd enjoyed not being on call the way people were when they carried their phone twenty-four/seven. But Jock and Stef had been after her to have one for the job. Since they would pay for it, she could avoid having to show a phone company her false ID, just in case those papers she purchased making her Ember "Jones" weren't as good as she thought they were.

Joey scrawled his cell number and e-mail address onto a piece of paper for her, and they hugged good-bye. As she walked to the hotel, Ember was amazed and happy. She'd looked for him a few times and had been sad when she couldn't find him in his usual haunts around Union Square. She'd started to think she would never see him again, but now he was a friend. Thinking about the change in him sent her mind drifting to her family. She was also thinking of getting her own computer, rather than using the ones at the library or the job site. Wow, she was growing up.

❖

Stef unlocked the project room and entered, seeking the guilty pleasure of Laurel's ordered chaos. She'd come to think of this room as *their* room. She knew it was ridiculous, but she hadn't heard from Laurel since meeting Rochelle and she was worried. Being here made her feel closer and she hoped that maybe she'd find that Laurel had been here. She sat in Laurel's camp chair and looked around, listening to the silence.

A small cry from behind the closed bathroom door made Stef turn. She thought she was imagining things until she heard some rustling. The hairs on the back of her neck stood straight up and she crept to the door.

"Laurel? Are you in there?"

Silence.

"Laurel, it's me Stef. Open the door, please?"

Taking a breath, she tried the handle and found it locked. She listened with her ear resting against the smooth oak surface and heard a muffled sound, a gasp perhaps. A sound of distress. Fumbling to locate the bathroom master key, one of a set she'd never used before, she tried several before finding one that turned smoothly.

"Laurel, I'm opening the door now, don't be afraid."

She felt foolish for a moment, wondering if she was mistaken and there was a stray cat trapped in the room making that noise. They'd caught a few since the renovations began and had managed to find homes for them. Another thought filled her with dread. Maybe Laurel was in there and her partner was holding her at gunpoint. What should she do?

Terror started in her heart and radiated through her body. She opened her cell phone, keyed it to Sika's number, set it to intercom, and put it down on the floor. "Laurel, I'm coming in. It's me, Stef. Don't be afraid, I won't hurt you."

Cautiously, she opened the door and flipped the light switch. At first glance the room seemed empty, then she heard the sound again, coming from the bathtub. The old shower curtain was moldy and half torn, but pulling it back revealed Laurel, on her knees and curled in a ball, rocking. Dropping beside the tub, Stef gently put a hand on Laurel's shoulder and felt her shrink back.

"Don't." Laurel's voice shook. "Please. Go away."

Stef sat back on her heels, trying to catch her breath. There was no choice here. Trying again, she placed her hand on the trembling shoulder and said, "I won't leave you. I'll never leave you. I'm calling the paramedics."

"No. I'm fine. Just help me up."

"You shouldn't move."

But Laurel was trying to stand. Stef helped ease her over to sit on the toilet seat lid. Her face was swollen and she was going to have at least one black eye. Her lip was split. From the huddled position she was in, Stef would bet she'd been kicked in the ribs again.

"Who did this?" She'd instantly assumed the assailant was Rochelle Jacobs, but it was possible that Laurel was the victim of a random act of violence.

Laurel whispered something in reply, but Stef couldn't make out her words. The only thing she heard was, "I should have known better."

"So, it was Rochelle?"

"I can't talk right now," Laurel said.

Her voice was so thin, Stef could tell she was only just able to hold herself together. Treading carefully, she asked, "Can you walk?" When she nodded, Stef said, "We're going to my room. There's no place to lie down in here."

Just then Sika appeared at the door, out of breath. She took one look at Laurel and claimed the other side of her. They slowly made their way to Stef's room and got Laurel seated on the couch.

Sika asked, "When did this happen, Laurel?" There was no judgment in her voice, only compassion.

"A few hours ago." Laurel's speech was somewhat distorted

because of her lip. "She's been angry about what happened when she came here last week. We had a fight about it after work yesterday."

"I'm sorry." Stef felt terrible. Maybe she should have given in and just let the woman take all the documents. The project was nothing compared with Laurel's safety.

"Not your fault," Laurel said. "She came home early and found me packing my bags. She was drunk. It was the worst I've ever seen. I told her I was leaving her. I should have kept my mouth shut."

The effort it took to speak those words seemed to sap what strength Laurel had. She fell silent. Watching her, Stef felt so helpless. And so full of rage. She got a blanket and covered Laurel, then gingerly sat next to her.

Sika had her phone open. "You need a doctor, child."

"No, no. Please. No." Laurel reached for Stef's hand.

She felt so fragile, Stef had to school herself to not envelop her in a hug. Then she fought not to cry. This was no time to be blubbering like a wimp. She listened to Sika talking on the phone and deduced that she was discussing the situation with Denny.

When she ended the call, she said, "Jock's coming down to see if she can help. She was a paramedic for a few years."

That was news to Stef.

When Jock and Denny arrived, Jock's face was set in a professional mask. She quickly checked for anything broken or bleeding, asking questions as she worked. She listened to Laurel's breathing and heart, using a stethoscope that materialized out of— where? Her tool belt? Then she gently palpated her abdomen. Laurel sucked in air against the pain but was silent. Stef wondered if she'd been silent during the beating, too.

"I think you're battered but not broken," Jock concluded. "But we should get you to an emergency room to make sure, and to document this." After a long hesitation, she said, "You should file charges, Laurel."

Shaking her head, Laurel replied, "I won't file charges. It could mean her career."

Stef had had enough. "Laurel, you need to be checked out. Jock thinks you're okay but they'll take films to make sure. If anything were to happen, we'd all feel terrible, especially Jock. So while you're taking care of your abuser's career, why don't you take care of your friends, too." Shocked at the harshness of her tone, she quietly added, "You don't have to file charges if you don't want to."

All eyes were on Laurel, who was staring at Stef, one eye puffing closed. "You're right. Let's go." She struggled to stand and Denny and Jock had her upright in seconds.

"We'll all go." Denny was checking for her keys.

"No. I'll take her," Stef said. "You all have been great. Den, can you bring my car around? Jock, would you go with her, it's getting late."

The hotel had a garage, but it was still closed, housing only construction equipment and vehicles. They had to park in a nearby public lot until the hotel was completed. Denny could take care of herself, but Stef didn't feel like tempting fate at this time of the night.

Jock said, "Just what I was planning to do."

Sika was silent until Jock and Denny left, then she touched Laurel's arm. "You'll not go back there, Laurel. Not without an escort. I'll find some clothes for you to wear tomorrow. Call and cancel your classes for the week. You'll stay with me or with Stefanie."

Laurel mumbled, "Thank you for your kindness."

Stef squeezed the small hand in her own. "Laurel, that's what friends are for. We can count on each other in the bad times."

With a sob of despair, Laurel said, "I'm so sorry I dragged you into this. She'll know I'm here. I don't want to cause a problem."

"Let me tell you something." Stef kept her voice soft and even despite the temper flaring deep inside. "If Rochelle Jacobs shows her face in this building, there won't be a *problem*. There'll be blood. Hers."

Laurel looked startled and Sika concerned.

"Okay," Stef conceded, "I'm getting carried away. Let's just say she wouldn't dare."

❖

The emergency room was predictably busy, but Laurel was treated and discharged within three hours. They hadn't spoken much, but she'd held Stef's hand almost the entire time. Initially, Laurel went with the nurse by herself but hesitated after a few steps. Stef was instantly at her side and stayed with her during the exam. Their only separation was when films were taken of her ribs.

She left with prescriptions for mild painkillers and her abdomen wrapped. Nothing was broken but she was badly bruised and had some muscle strains and tears. Her lip would heal with a few butterfly sutures. Laurel surrendered Stef's hand to let her drive. Huddled in the passenger seat, she was gazing out the window at the quiet streets, seeming to doze.

"I'm going to park in front of the hotel and get you inside, then take the car to the garage. I'll call Sika." Stef reached for her cell when she felt Laurel's hand on her thigh.

"No, I'll come with you to the garage. It's too late and might not be safe. Two are better than one."

Stef wasn't sure that two women, one of whom was walking like a ninety-year-old and the other trying to help her, didn't present a better target, but the look on Laurel's battered face kept her from saying so. "Okay, thanks."

They parked in one of the spots reserved for those who paid monthly. It was well lit and patrolled. The elevator to street level smelled of urine and disinfectant. The street was a bit steep, but it was only a block until they reached the hotel. Stef knew Laurel was laboring but she didn't complain, only hesitating once in a while to catch her breath.

Once inside the lobby, they stopped. Stef wasn't sure what to do next. She wanted Laurel to stay with her, but Sika had offered, too, and Laurel might feel more comfortable there. "Laurel, let's go to my rooms and I'll call Sika. She lives close by and I can run you over there later."

She felt guilty that she hadn't done that before she parked. Laurel was the one who was out of it, not her. She should have insisted on taking her to Sika's, but she couldn't bear to be parted from her. That was why she hadn't argued when Laurel wanted to escort her from the garage.

Hastily, she said, "Or if you wish, I could take you there right now. I can go back and get the car."

"No." Laurel's voice fractured. Every breath was obviously a strain. "I'll stay here with you, if that's okay." Still no eye contact.

Stef knew this was not the time to be hopping around celebrating, so she concentrated on not grinning like an idiot. "Yes. I mean, of course, if that's what you want." Laurel swayed and Stef quickly forgot her victory. She took Laurel's arm. "Let's get the elevator."

"I hope it smells better than the last one." The attempt at humor made Stef feel better immediately.

"I'm having a talk with Jock about her subcontractors if it doesn't."

Laurel seemed to not be able to move forward, so Stef eased her arm around her waist, and together they made the final trek to the third floor. Settling Laurel into the bathroom, just along the hallway from the bedroom, Stef gave her a sleep shirt and closed the door. She was exhausted and had to be up early the next day.

After a few minutes of quickly changing her sheets and straightening her place in honor of her guest, she heard the bathroom door open. Walking down the short hall, she found Laurel standing in the doorway, holding the shirt, probably uncertain as to what to do next.

Stef led her to the bedroom, helped her into the sleep shirt, pulled back the covers, and tucked her in. Laurel seemed deeply asleep almost as soon as her body hit the bed. Smiling, Stef kissed her forehead and then both eyes. She shed her clothes and visited the bathroom herself, then slipped on some flannel sweats and grabbed a pillow and blanket from the closet, aiming for the couch. Fatigue robbed her of even the momentary pleasure of thinking of Laurel in her bed. She was asleep in minutes.

CHAPTER TWELVE

L aurel stirred, awakened from her drug and exhaustion-induced sleep by a noise in the other room. Pain forced her to move gingerly as she rolled to her back to listen.

Where am I? She felt like she was swimming against a strong current to make sense of her surroundings. Slowly the events of the past few days became crystal clear. The giddy feeling of freedom the day she'd decided to pack up and leave, breezing through her classes, laughing with the students, all the while making plans to go apartment hunting, maybe even move from Berkeley to San Francisco. The intense relief after she told Rochelle she was leaving.

She remembered humming to herself as she was packing her bags, her heart soaring with hope. She couldn't wait to see Stef so she could share the good news. The familiar tread in the hallway had made her freeze in shock. Terror constricted her chest when Rochelle lurched into view. She had leaned on the door frame and regarded Laurel with raw hatred.

Closing the door quietly, she accused Laurel of unfaithfulness, of screwing Stef. She told her what an ungrateful, lying, cheating partner she was. That it was no wonder she drank, with such a worthless piece of shit to come home to. Laurel knew better than to argue. She'd learned to stay still and quiet, and hope Rochelle would run out of steam or go searching for another drink. But Rochelle had only gathered momentum, and the list of transgressions grew until Laurel was responsible for everything wrong with Rochelle's life.

She was alarmed at first, then afraid. She'd tried to think of an escape plan. Maybe she could tip Rochelle over and skirt past her to the door. Run from the house without her packed bags. It didn't matter if she had to leave everything behind.

Rochelle must have seen her eyes darting or something, because she was on her in the next instant, plowing through the piles of folded clothing and sending garments flying. Absurdly, Laurel tried to reach for them. The next thing she remembered she was face down on the floor and Rochelle was standing over her.

"Cunt. This is all your fault."

Laurel had stayed down, trying to disappear, but she couldn't avoid the blows. When Rochelle finally stepped back, her chest was heaving from the effort of the beating. Laurel couldn't move at that moment; she was lucky she was breathing. She kept her eyes closed and it wasn't until she heard the room door click shut that the adrenaline kicked in and she crawled down to the guest room and locked herself in. She'd waited there until the house was silent. Rochelle would expect her to hide, as she always did, too ashamed to face the world. Instead, Laurel had crept out of the house to her car, and driven away knowing she would never go back.

She winced over a smile. Her lip reminded her there was not much to smile about. She'd driven to the hotel in a daze and made it to the project room without being seen. She recalled leaning against the bathroom door and then being overwhelmed with the need to get into the bathtub. Literally inching her way there around the blinding pain in her ribs, she knew it would be safe because when she was a child her parents always said if there was a tornado, get in the bathtub. That's how to protect yourself.

Laurel shifted position, trying to get comfortable. Glancing around, she realized she was in Stef's bedroom. The other side of the bed looked undisturbed. She wondered where Stef had slept. Sounds from the next room came into focus. Someone was crying, she was sure of it. Stef?

Moving to get out of the bed, she realized she was wearing a big T-shirt over an Ace bandage and nothing else. Her cheeks warmed as she thought about Stef undressing her when they got back from the hospital last night. She cast around for something to put on and spotted some flannel pajama bottoms neatly folded on a chair a few feet away. Slowly making it to the chair, she was grateful beyond measure for the snug wrap around her ribs, and had to sit to get the pants on. It took another few minutes of agony to stand, clutching the waistband to make sure the pants came with her.

She peered into the living area to see Stef, in the corner of the sofa, hands covering her face, crying. She hesitated, not wanting to embarrass her rescuer. After a few tentative steps into the room the floorboard creaked and Stef looked up. Their eyes met briefly before Stef scrubbed her face with her hands and stood.

"Are you okay? Do you need anything?"

Laurel was taken aback. Were the tears for her? Stef had so many responsibilities yet here she was, offering comfort to Laurel. She reached for Stef but pain stopped her from arriving at her destination. Gasping, she could only manage, "Could I sit on the couch with you?"

"Yes, of course." Stef shuffled over to make room.

Once settled, Laurel gazed deeply into the soft brown eyes of her hero. "What's happened? Why are you crying?"

Instantly averting her head, Stef began, "Oh, it's nothing to worry about. Just stress."

Laurel gently pressed her hand on Stef's arm. "Stefanie, I know how difficult it is to accept help and comfort from someone, anyone. I had that experience last night. I thought, perhaps, you might not mind my offer of friendship. Think of it as my way of repaying your kindness in some small way. How's that?"

Giving her a rueful grin, Stef took a big breath and shuddered as she let it go. "You may have gathered that I come from a wealthy family of hoteliers. What you might not know is that I split from my family several years ago. Well, that's not exactly true. I've been at odds with them since I came out, in college. Daddy doesn't approve."

Laurel nodded, not wanting to interfere with the most personal information she'd heard about Stef since they met. She longed to sit back and be supported by the couch, but that would have to wait.

"Long, boring story. Anyway, I worked in the family business, but when it was made clear that I wouldn't be able to advance much further than some fluff vice president in charge of doilies, I quit. Denny, Sika, and I searched and saved for years to find this place and sank every dime into it."

Laurel said, "Then that contractor betrayed you."

The pain was getting more difficult to ignore. Her back muscles were starting to spasm with the effort to compensate for the injured abdominal muscles.

"Here, let me help you lie down." Stef must have noticed.

"Thank you. May I use your lap for a pillow?" Laurel had no idea if this was flirting, but she couldn't think of a more comfortable place in the world to rest her head.

Hesitating only a moment, Stef grinned and murmured, "Of course."

She continued to spill the whole story about how she came to buy the hotel and how important the project was to her. Laurel reveled in the comfort of her voice and her soft touch. She must have dozed off because when she next opened her eyes, the room felt cool and neither of them had moved.

"You awake?" She whispered, not really wanting to break the connection.

"Yes. Just…enjoying."

"I know. I don't remember the last time I've been so peaceful. Stef?"

"Uh-huh." The low rumble of her voice in the fading light of late afternoon was sensual, that was the only word that came to mind.

"I'm afraid I have to break the spell. I can't get up by myself and I really need to use the facilities. I'm so sorry."

Chuckling, Stef said, "You've read my mind. Let me help you, then we'll figure out something to eat."

"Oh, I'm so hungry. Thank you." Despite her physical discomfort, she was having fun. Odd.

Helping her hobble to the bathroom, Stef said, "The others are worried. Would you be okay with having pizza with an abbreviated version of the crew? I'm supposed to be in a meeting with Sika right now."

Laurel stopped. "I'm not sure I'm ready to face anyone. Ember is a student. I don't want to see pity on their faces. I'm a professor of women's studies, for God's sake. And in this situation. Not much of a role model for my students."

"Laurel, it isn't a 'situation,' it's a mess. You were placed in that mess by the head of your department. That's the hypocrisy of the whole thing. You have nothing to be ashamed of." Laurel involuntarily flinched at her tone.

"Oh God, I'm not mad at you," Stef said instantly. "I'm so sorry, I didn't mean to frighten you."

Seeking shelter from the storm of her life, Laurel leaned into her and felt herself encircled and gently pulled against Stef's body. She gazed into the depths of Stef's eyes and saw compassion and understanding and something else. Something she'd never seen before, and it drew her closer. She studied the soft lips that waited for her to choose. One part of her mind screamed that she shouldn't, it was too soon. The other part, the one connected to her body and her heart, told her that the choice had been made for some time. This was only the expression of that choice.

The pain of her sutures didn't matter. Their lips touched, then touched again, then joined. Stef asked permission with her tongue, and Laurel granted entrance. Then she was in another place, a better place than she ever dreamt existed. She was breathless. At last, her caution kicked in, and she wasn't sure how she felt about letting the kisses go on, or what she could do to stop them.

She was sure that if she stayed here, alone with Stefanie Beresford, her life would get much more complicated than it already was.

❖

Sika put a sheaf of papers and magazines on Stef's desk and sat down, folding her hands in her lap. "Two things. We need an interior designer for the hotel rooms, especially the executive suites, and we need a designer for the restaurant. The kitchen itself I have ideas about, but I am calling a friend who I met in Paris when I was there. She and her partner live out here now, in West Marin County. She doesn't cook professionally any longer, but she and I could design a beautiful kitchen together."

Stef had known this day was coming but had been so immersed in putting the bones of the place back together and thinking about Laurel, she'd put it on the back burner. She'd made sure that the whole hotel would have the infrastructure to support any technology someone might need, now and in the future, and doing so had cost three times what she had estimated, mostly because of the security features she was hoping to put in place. She might not have the money to do everything immediately, but the technology was changing so quickly, they were constructing so that even the wiring could be changed out rather easily, without ripping walls apart.

Now, here was Sika with a real situation. Someone had to design what the public would see. The rooms, the lobby, the common areas, and the aesthetics of the hotel had to be unique. Stef was a meat-and-potatoes kind of girl, very good at making sure the building could survive an earthquake and the visitors would have all of their technology needs met and feel safe, zero in the design-for-the-eye department.

"We have a problem," she said. "The infrastructure renovations have eaten up a lot of money. I'm not sure how much we're going to have for the designer. I know how important it is, too. I'm looking for a loan add-on to pay for it."

Nodding, Sika seemed not at all concerned. "That's what I thought was happening. The hotel designer I've chosen is famous in Europe and is sought after in the United States, when she chooses to work. She has agreed to forgo her fee until after the hotel is up and running."

"You've chosen someone? How good is she if she doesn't want her fee?"

Sika gave her the look, and Stef squirmed. Privately, Denny and Stef laughed about that expression, but it was no fun to be on the receiving end.

"Stefanie, who is in charge of this part of the project? Who did we decide, because of your and Denny's lack of interest and my eye for color and texture, would pick those people? We have to get them going on their plans, and we have to do it now. She doesn't need the money. She's willing to trade."

"Who is this woman?" Stef couldn't keep the skepticism out of her voice.

She wished Denny were here because sometimes they could gang up on Sika. Denny was spending all of her time working with Jock and keeping an eye on the subcontractors. But what Sika said was true. She was in charge of the look and feel of the hotel. Trade?

Her eyes full of satisfaction, Sika said, "Carolyn Flemons. It was a real coup to get her."

"The name is familiar, would I know her?" Stef thought that the chances of her knowing an A-list interior designer were slim and none. But the name...

"She was married to the owner of the football team. She's a widow and her daughter runs it now. That's probably where you've heard the name."

"Oh, yeah. That was cool when the daughter took over. Do we at least get to see some sketches before we agree?"

"Yes and no. She's working on the designs and we will all see them and decide which we like." With that, Sika stood and put her hand on the stack of papers. "These are her resume, samples, and magazine layouts her work has been featured in. You and Denny read them. I have work to do."

She was almost out the door before Stef called to her. "Wait. You said 'trade.' What does that mean? Does she want free nights at the hotel?"

Sika smiled enigmatically, which always made Stef twitch. "Perhaps." And she was gone.

Swiveling in her chair, Stef stared out the window and said to the city of San Francisco, "And don't forget that I'm in charge."

❖

Two hours later a courier delivered two slim envelopes that needed Stef's signature. One was from the bank holding the first mortgage on the hotel. The other had the return address of the private investment firm from which she had gotten the second mortgage. She knew the address well as the building was owned by her family. Beresford Hoteliers' corporate offices were in the upper floors.

The courier collected the return receipts and then asked where he could find Irina Castic. He was holding several sturdy manila envelopes that looked like they had traveled a long distance. Stef offered to deliver them for him, but he told her he had to have her personal signature and needed to check her identification, too. He seemed pretty impressed himself. She gave him directions and sat down to stare at the envelopes.

She had requested additional money, and this must be their decision. She used the walkie-talkie feature on her cell and summoned Denny because she wanted some moral support. Sika had gone to an appointment with the interior designer. Laurel flashed in her mind, but she couldn't bother a woman still in a state of shock over her injuries and her disintegrating life.

Stef passed the envelope to Denny as soon as she walked in the door. She handled it like it had anthrax spores inside. Stef was starting to fidget by the time she read the contents and finally looked up.

"Well? What is it, Den?"

"They want a meeting. With you."

This didn't sound good. "Who? Which letter did you open?"

"Rat man's company."

That would be the private investors. Stef didn't know how to interpret that. "Perhaps to negotiate how much additional money we need."

Shaking her head, Denny said, "It says to contact their offices and make an appointment as soon as possible."

Stef felt her stomach twist.

"We've made every payment, right?" Denny asked.

"Right. Always on time."

"A simple yes, you have the money, or no, buzz off, would be fine. Why the appointment?"

Sighing, Stef said, "I don't know, but I don't like it. Something isn't right about this. Open the other envelope." She felt her hands trembling and balled them into fists in her lap.

Denny dutifully tore the envelope open and read. Her jaw dropped. "Sonofabitch."

"Read it." Stef responded on automatic.

"The bank is accelerating our loan. They want the entire amount of the first mortgage within thirty days or they will begin foreclosure proceedings, which, according to them, they can expedite."

Leaning across her desk, feeling sweat on her upper lip, Stef ground out, "Based on what?"

"Based on the fact that we didn't have written permission to engage in a second mortgage."

Exploding, Stef was on her feet. "What? The bank recommended the investment firm. Our loan officer made the introductory call."

Holding up both hands, Denny said, "I know, I know. That's what it says here, that's all."

The air went out of Stef and she landed in her chair with a pop. She and Denny stared at each other.

"Stef, how much money do we have left?"

Struggling to keep her voice calm, Stef said, "If we continue the way we are, about two months. I've spent too much on the infrastructure. Even with that designer delaying her fee, we don't have enough to finish all the floors, even minimally. We need more money, and when I requested it, that Trip rodent was happy as a clam. He said he didn't think it would be a problem." Stef was heartsick. "I'm sure they were sent a copy of this letter from the bank. They might accelerate, too."

"What are we going to do?" Denny looked daunted.

"Don't skimp on anything. Denny, make sure everyone is on schedule, help Jock secure the best prices, too. I need to meet with these people, to see what they want."

"We better talk with Mamaka."

"I'll do that." Stef wasn't looking forward to admitting their situation was even worse than a budget shortfall. "I have some things to work out, sooner than I thought, but these circumstances have forced our hand. Let's get to work and we'll talk later."

After Denny left, Stef scheduled an appointment with Boynton and once again found herself staring out the window. She felt an overwhelming need to see Laurel. Just to see her incredible eyes, listen to her talk about the project, the mystery of the Elysium Society, the passion she experienced doing her research. It felt so normal, contained. Perhaps she just needed to be in their room, since she didn't want to disturb Laurel.

She snorted at the thought. A dank and musty place that was scheduled to be gutted soon, and still, she'd come to think of it as a small, private universe that was solely hers and Laurel's.

Unable to help herself, she visited the room briefly, content to see the files, ledgers, room diaries. The pad of paper that was always close by. She was suddenly clammy, fear skittering up and down her spine. What if Laurel went back to Rochelle? It happened all the time. Women made excuses for violent partners and returned to terrible situations.

She made a full 360-degree sweep of the room, then backed out, closing the door behind her. She felt like running to her bedroom, as though Laurel's presence there would prove something. Stef held herself back, reasoning that she had no need to panic. Laurel wasn't going anywhere. She might be battered, but she wasn't crazy.

She went through the small living room and crept to the bedroom door and quickly pushed it open. A pair of frightened eyes instantly found hers, and before Stef could think of anything to say, she was stumbling toward the bed, reaching for the woman beneath the covers.

"Are you okay?" she blurted.

After a few seconds, she could tell Laurel recognized her. "Yes, of course. You just startled me. I was dozing and when you opened the door, for a moment I thought you were…her."

Laurel was trembling and Stef took her hands and tried to rub warmth into them. "I apologize. I suddenly got nervous and needed to see you, just checking to make sure you were all right. So I barged in and scared you to death. I'm such a klutz sometimes."

Stef knew she couldn't gaze at Laurel's bruised face without her anger showing, so she concentrated on finding another blanket. She got the throw that was on the couch and brought it back to the bedroom and fussed with tucking her in. A cold hand on her arm made her finally look up. She felt the sting of tears as her heart ached for this beautiful woman. How could anyone ever harm her?

"It's okay, Stef, I'm going to heal. Would you do me a favor? Would you mind holding me?" She asked so sweetly, Stef was helpless to do more than nod. Kicking off her shoes, she started to settle on top of the covers.

"No," Laurel said. "Under the covers. Take off your clothes."

Complying, Stefanie shed her pants and shirt. Only her underclothes remained as she stood uncertainly before Laurel, knowing she would do anything for this woman. Anything.

"All of it," Laurel said. "And help me get out of my pants at least. I'm pretty sure I can't get the T-shirt off because of the pain, but I'm willing to try."

Stefanie felt no shyness at all, and discarded the rest of her clothes, then helped rid Laurel of hers, even freeing her of the T-shirt. Within moments she was under the covers holding Laurel gently in her arms. She gazed beyond the bruises and cuts and saw only welcome. She kissed Laurel's sweet lips lightly, so as not to hurt her. Laurel's hands ran over Stef's back, drawing her closer. She traced the line of Stef's jaw and outlined her lips with her finger, staring at her mouth in what seemed like wonder.

They continued their slow, delicate exploration for what seemed an eternity. Stef tenderly caressed Laurel's body, careful of places that might hurt, amazed at how familiar, how right every plane and soft curve felt to her. She allowed Laurel to do the same to her, and then they settled into each other's arms, never having spoken a word.

As Stef started to doze, she realized that she'd never been so intimate with another person and yet she and Laurel knew next to nothing about each other. But that wasn't important. She wondered if this was what it felt like to be in love.

If it wasn't, it should be.

CHAPTER THIRTEEN

The next morning found Stef marching into the Beresford building determined to make nice with Trip Boynton. She'd never known a hard money firm to turn its back on profit, and she was certain she could work out whatever problems their first mortgagee had. There were more people's livelihoods at stake than her own. He needed to understand.

The offices of the firm were on the tenth floor, with all the floors above them devoted to Beresford corporate concerns. The receptionist studied her with frank interest. Stef had experienced that kind of appraisal all of her life. People felt entitled to look over the rich kid and decide if she measured up. The woman told her to be seated, then walked into Boynton's office to announce her arrival. A few moments later she returned to tell Stef he'd be available soon. Stef understood the tactic. She was supposed to stew, to realize he had the power. It chafed, because whatever she was, she was a Beresford.

She took the aggravation for five minutes, then threw her magazine on the coffee table and marched into his office before the receptionist could block her. There, with their feet up on the desk, smoking cigars, were her brother George and Trip Boynton, the man who had been so eager to lend her money.

George grinned and checked his watch. "Four minutes and forty-five seconds. I win, pal. You owe me twenty bucks."

Trip and he high-fived each other and looked at her expectantly.

"You know each other?" It was all that came out of Stef's mouth. She was trying to make sense of the scene.

George removed his feet from the desk and put the cigar down, but not before he took another drag and blew it in her direction. "Know him? We were college roommates, sister dear."

"What's this all about? I don't want Beresford Hotels involved."

She was going to have a talk with her dad, and with Jason for blabbing. But in some ways, she was relieved. Maybe her father would see the merit in lending them more money.

George stopped her in her tracks. "Dad has nothing to do with this. You, sweet sister, belong to us. Only to us. And your hotel will be perfect for our plans."

Stef toyed with the idea of lunging at him and beating the smug look off of his face. Fighting to control the adrenaline racing through her veins, she asked, "What the hell are you talking about?" To Boynton she said, "We've met all the terms of the loan." Her voice was thin, but steady to her ears.

Boynton shot a grin to George. "George is one of the investors in this firm. And we've decided against additional funds for your project."

George stuck his cigar back in his mouth, talking around it as he delivered the next blow. "Yeah, about that. Can't see the profit in it. Women don't need or want a hotel that excludes men. They want hotels where they can pick guys up."

"What in the hell are you talking about?" Stef's eyes were burning but she held back any tears. She wouldn't give him the satisfaction.

Letting out a stream of smoke, George said, "Remember the men's club down the way from you? The one where the big boys in the world meet and mingle and entertain each other? The one where they pick the next president. That one?"

"Yes." She knew it well. The proprietors also owned the Bohemian Grove, an enclave in northern California where they gathered on weekends all summer long and did God knows what. They were the richest and most powerful men in the world.

"Well, seems their building needs complete renovation, too. Has to be retrofitted, et cetera, that type of thing. They also want all that security that you're building into your little establishment. Got to protect your peeps, you know?" Her brother's eyes, like hers in color only, were hard and brittle with malice.

"Get to the point, George." She had to get out of here before she threw up in front of both men.

"Well, not only are they offering a shitload of money to lease your hotel as their temporary premises for a year or whatever it takes, they're offering *us* a membership. Do you know how long the wait list is to be a member? At least ten years. Me, a member of the Bohemian Club. You should be proud of your brother." He took another puff.

"You forget, I still own the hotel."

"Only for a few weeks. The acceleration clause has been activated, though, so it'll be in our hands soon enough."

Wheeling her attention to Trip Boynton for the first time, she caught a sly grin on his face. "You knew this would happen. You purposely didn't ask for written permission."

"Relax, sis. You're getting all worked up. Guess you should have made that little detail your business, huh?"

"But the bank gave me your name. Made the phone call. That's tacit approval, and you never said a word."

Blowing a smoke ring, George chimed in. "Yeah, Trip, what did your attorney say?"

"My attorney is the best in the business. He assures me all is in order on our end."

Stef had never felt more alone. "Does Dad know about this?"

"I don't report in to our father about my own investment activities," George pompously intoned.

Relief fluttered through Stef's chest, lifting the dead weight from it a little. If she couldn't find her own way out of this financial jam, she would have to ask for her dad's help. It was good to know he hadn't betrayed her, too. "You can both go fuck yourselves."

George laughed and stroked the cigar. "No, sister dearest, I believe we just fucked *you*."

She felt her eyes narrow as she spoke. "Really, George, I thought you preferred to play with your cigarillo. At least that's what I recall from childhood. You're deluding yourself with that big cigar."

Boynton was choking on the smoke and George sputtering vile epithets when she slammed out of the office. On her way out of the reception area she ran into Agnes Brady, who looked down and blushed intensely.

"I'm, I'm so sorry, Ms. Beresford."

Stef finally blew out the breath she'd been holding since walking in. "You knew about this?"

The assistant stared at the floor, her silence providing the answer.

"Well, I feel sorry for you, wasting your time with scum like Boynton and my brother."

With that, she left the building and walked out into the bleakest beautiful day in San Francisco she'd ever known.

❖

Laurel was horrified. "Have you told Denny and Sika?"

"They know." Stef still had trouble believing George could sink so low. He'd managed to squeeze her out of the Beresford family business. Wasn't that enough? "Denny offered to break kneecaps and Sika is working on some kind of plan. They're my real family."

Laurel found her hand and held it. "Stef, what about your father and your other brother? Do you think they're involved in this?"

"George says Dad had nothing to do with it." Stef paused, still bewildered by George. "I don't know why he hates me, but he does."

"So the first mortgage holder is the one accelerating, and you think your brother and his friend duped you into not notifying them in writing about the second mortgage."

"That's about it. We were desperate for the money, we needed it immediately to keep on schedule. I was too hasty. I assumed something I shouldn't have."

"Don't be too hard on yourself. You did the best you could."

They entered the café area where the others were gathered. Denny signaled for a private word as Stef poured a glass of wine for Laurel and opened a bottle of beer for herself. Leaving Sika, Jock, and Irina Castic to care for Laurel, Stef ambled over to Denny. Her friend's eyes were dead serious.

"We have another problem, Stef."

"What now?"

"Our attorney dropped us as clients. He stated conflict of interest. Seems he'd rather make bucks from the rich dudes who own our second mortgage than us. Thinks we're 'iffy,' at best."

"Charming. And all the other attorneys I know work for my family. Therefore, they work for George."

Glancing over her shoulder at the group around the table, Denny said, "Look, we'll find out more tomorrow. I just needed to give you a heads up. Let's go join the others. Laurel's already looking around for you."

Stef cast a quick look at Laurel. She seemed to be enjoying herself, listening to Jock telling a humorous story about the day. Stef appreciated the way her friends had rallied around Laurel, helping without fawning, doing for her without making a big deal out of it.

Softly, Denny asked, "You okay? You seem a little out of it. How's Laurel?"

"What? Oh, I'm fine. Laurel's sore, but I admire that she has the courage to face everyone. I'd want to stay in our hole." She must have sounded disappointed that they didn't stay there.

"Stef, what happened? And don't evade."

Damn, Denny always knew when something was up. After a few seconds of intense scrutiny, she muttered, "We kissed." She didn't mention holding Laurel. It was too personal, too intimate.

Denny frowned, as though she could barely hear, then her eyes became much wider. She sagged against the sidebar Stef was leaning on. "Be careful, my friend. She's probably not in a very good place right now."

There was no judgment in her tone. Knowing that Denny really liked Laurel, Stef was sure the concern was for both of them, and she had a point. The timing could not have been worse. "I know. I didn't mean for it to happen. It just…did."

"I'm dying to lecture you right now, you realize that, right?"

"Uh-huh. Thanks for not doing that." Sneaking another glance toward the women a few yards away, Stef asked, "Are you going to tell Mamaka?"

Shaking her head and grinning, Denny said, "Do you think I need to? Look at her."

Dismayed, Stef watched Sika say something to Laurel. Her expression was patient and knowing, suggesting that not only had she guessed, she had an opinion about it. Stef got the sinking feeling she was soon going to get that lecture anyway. She took a few steps toward the group, Denny at her side, and tuned into the conversation.

"I've been searching for a month," Laurel said. "But I can't find a direct reference to the Elysium Society. The Internet, library, journals, archives. There are some indirect ones, though, and those make it seem like a myth. But when I go through the room diaries of the hotel, the references are everywhere."

"Perhaps it was just an informal group." Sika's casual tone seemed to belie her laser focus on Laurel.

"Maybe, but I think there was more to it. Didn't you say the club you were involved with wasn't just a reading group, Mrs. Castic?"

Mrs. C gave a noncommittal shrug. "The hotel guests all had different interests."

Laurel nodded. "From what I can tell, there were some very powerful women, some straight, some probably gay, who came to this hotel. I suspect most of them were connected to the Society. Some traveled a very long way, considering the transportation available at the time. I've checked a few of the big names against newspapers of the period. There was no mention of their visits."

Shrugging, Jock said, "Well, that's not surprising. They didn't have the media we do now. No paparazzi."

Denny agreed. "Without extensive research, maybe biographies, it's difficult to confirm details like that."

Laurel nodded, but pressed her argument. "I think there was

more to the Society. If I can discover what it was, it might be a real find in the field of women's rights."

It occurred to Stef that this arena was where Laurel felt confident and in command. Her mind, her research. Stef moved so that she was standing behind Mrs. C and could see Laurel's face. As marred as it was by the beating, she was still a striking woman. Stef could get lost in those beautiful eyes, so alive with enthusiasm. She let herself absorb Laurel's animated features and the expressive movements of her hands, delighting in her obvious comfort with the people around her. Though muted by her injuries, her passion shone through with crystal clarity.

Despite her appearance and the self-consciousness she must feel, she seemed so engaged in her subject, Stef couldn't help but feel an irrational optimism. Whatever the obstacles, Stef was determined not to be defeated. She wanted to see that expression on Laurel's face every day. She wanted to give her everything Rochelle had denied her. Affirmation. Support. A safe place. The encouragement to become the terrific woman she was.

The strength of her feelings startled her. And there was more. She wanted to give Laurel the care and affection she deserved. Stef's heart started to pound. She wanted to hold Laurel, and kiss her, and feel her respond. She wanted to be naked and feel their bodies slide together. Unnerved, she pulled out a chair. She really needed to sit down.

"What will you do with the information?" Mrs. C's voice cut quietly into Stef's tangled thoughts. "If you uncover the purpose of the Elysium Society, I mean."

There was more than anticipation in the room as Laurel considered her reply, there was tension.

Stef thought the answer was obvious and said so. "She'll publish, of course. If it's really juicy, she could turn it into a book, then she could name the university she would go to, as a full professor. That was why you started the project in the first place, right? To publish."

That statement only served to heighten the tension.

"What am I missing here?" Stef asked.

Laurel's gaze never broke from Mrs. C's. "I think Mrs. Castic is asking about some of the entries that suggest love relationships between women who were previously thought straight. There could be evidence that confirms long-held suspicions or rumors about these women."

"Well, that's good, right?" Stef wasn't sure why Mrs. C would be worried about facts coming to light, especially if the women were deceased.

Sika interjected, "It depends on who you are talking about. Some of these women must have gone to great lengths to ensure their privacy. I think that raises some ethical questions about respecting their wishes, doesn't it?"

Laurel said, "Historian and biographers always face such questions. There aren't any simple answers. Besides that, I think there was more to the hotel than providing a secret place for trysts that were not allowed in society at the time." Looking directly at Mrs. C, she continued, "The majority of these women were wealthy and influential in their own right, through family or marriage. They seemed to have formed an organization that, on the surface, was acceptably concerned with fashion and literature. But notes left in the diaries have far more depth than one would expect from women in their positions."

She paused to sip water and Stef thought she was choosing her words carefully. "They spoke of wars, of jobs, of the poor, of politics. All in relation to the status of women. Some alluded to directing their influence to issues. I can't tell for sure if the Elysium Society adopted an organized approach to wielding its members' power unless I can find minutes of meetings, or perhaps talk in detail to someone who was involved."

Everyone at the table followed Laurel's gaze to Irina Castic. The silence made the air in the room feel heavy.

Eventually Sika said, "Your theory is fascinating, but why would they base their society at this hotel? Surely these wealthy women could meet anywhere they chose."

"I think it was patterned after the Bohemian Club." Laurel hesitated as though expecting skepticism. "That's an all-male private club made up of the wealthiest and most influential men in the world. They direct domestic policy and make decisions on global matters, all from behind their closed and very private doors. And they've marginalized women from the very beginning. Their building is down the street from this hotel."

"You're saying the Elysium Society was the female antidote to the Bohos?" Jock concluded.

"Possibly. That would explain the need for secrecy. Women are expert at flying under the radar, and I think that's what they did, right here at this hotel."

"So what happened?" Stef frowned. "This is exactly the kind of club that could have kept going for generations, with all the social change we've seen."

After a pregnant hush, Mrs. C said, "We probably would have." She seemed to be deliberating over her every word. "They got control of the hotel. No one saw it coming."

"What do you mean?" Laurel had to be exhausted but she was riveted to Mrs. C, as was every woman in the room.

"The Bohemian Club was responsible. They gave their orders and their members acted individually. Remember, some of the women who belonged to the Elysium Society were married to members of that organization. Others were daughters, sisters, and such."

"I see," Laurel mused aloud. "They were threatened?"

Mrs. C took a sip of wine and rested a moment. "Women who were from wealthy families were told they would be disinherited if they came to the hotel. Married women were forbidden, sometimes by force. Those who made money themselves, such as artists, actresses, or writers, were told they would never work again if they so much as set foot in the building."

Stef's mouth had gone dry as soon as Mrs. C started talking. A feeling of dread began to form in her gut. "So the men in their lives just went along with it, even the decent ones?"

"They were vulnerable, too," Mrs. C replied. "Their businesses and reputations could have been ruined. Contracts awarded to someone else. False accusations made. I know a few of them agonized over it, but they were in the minority. Most were outraged that their woman would be involved with something so reprehensible as seeking rights for themselves and networking to have influence."

"It's incredible that these women just allowed this to happen." Stef couldn't help but think about herself as soon as the words were out. Her brother and his cronies had all but checkmated her, and this was the twenty-first century.

"You have to remember that back then even if a woman was the source of her husband's wealth, she had no rights once she was married. And if women insisted they didn't want to marry, their families could choose to have them declared incompetent. There were plenty of judges willing to sign the orders."

"That's why it seemed to happen overnight," Laurel said. "The hotel went downhill very fast. I've been wondering why."

"They systematically destroyed it." Mrs. C sighed. "They gained control and designated it for cheap, pay-as-you-go occupancy. Drug dealers and disreputable people immediately took it over, but not until the finer amenities had been stripped by those bastards."

Laurel was insistent. "But how did they actually get the hotel? Who owned it?"

Mrs. C smiled and looked to the window, as though seeing a memory. "Seraphina Drake inherited the hotel. She was a delightful and determined woman, a dear friend. She had to marry—her father insisted, and chose one Clayton B. Holloway II. Holloway was decent enough in the beginning and ignored Sera and the hotel while he managed their other holdings. I think he thought the hotel would keep her occupied so he could do as he pleased with her wealth." Her voice took on a bitter edge. "He became quite accustomed to money and power, and my vibrant friend began to vanish right before my eyes. Holloway had affairs, and flaunted them. It was worse after he joined the Bohemian Club. And, of course, he served this hotel up to them like the faithful flunky he was."

Stef might as well have been kicked. She turned to Denny and then to Sika and saw the same realization on their faces. To the group she said, "I think those men are trying to sabotage this hotel again."

CHAPTER FOURTEEN

The room was dark when they returned. Laurel needed more help walking along the hallways and getting ready for bed than she would have liked. She was incredibly stiff and sore even though two days had passed since Rochelle attacked her. But Stef offered without asking and it felt amazingly good to be in contact with another body, especially Stef's body. Laurel kept telling herself that Stef was her friend, her close friend. But even she, so accustomed to denial of reality, couldn't keep up that pretense.

Stef was her rock, she had been there for her, offering shelter and friendship, but so had the others. Laurel frowned, feeling dizzy and fearful suddenly. Two days had passed without her going to work. As usual Rochelle would have made excuses for her, but by now she had to be wondering where Laurel was and waiting for her to walk back in the door full of apologies. Without her realizing it, her breathing must have changed or her body slackened, because suddenly Stef was holding her close, crooning reassurances as if to a child.

"I've got you," she whispered sweetly. "I won't let her hurt you anymore. You're safe, you're safe."

They were on Stef's bed and Laurel hardly remembered getting there. But Stef's tone, and the certainty of her words, broke the dam that had been crumbling for some time. Laurel lost what self-control she had. Ignoring her painful ribs and sore face, she sobbed into Stef's shoulder, burrowing into her chest, trying to hide and be safe from the monster that was her life.

Rochelle wasn't the monster, *she* was. She had allowed their dysfunctional relationship to continue. She had let her life be ruled by an out-of-control narcissist who thought nothing of sacrificing Laurel to her own wishes and desires. She was so pitiful, she had even started to believe all the hateful things Rochelle had said over the years. It was her own fault that she was in this mess. Between racking sobs, she confessed it all to Stef, knowing that, in the end, Stef would be repulsed by her weakness, but not able to stop herself.

Stef held Laurel, brave and steadfast, letting her cry. She heard the self-loathing, the blame she had taken on, the shame for allowing it. When Laurel's body softened into a deep slumber, purged of the venom that had ruled her life for so long, Stef gently extricated herself, slipped out of the bed, and left the room, sure that Laurel wouldn't wake for some time.

After locking her door, she walked to the service elevator, deciding at the last minute to ignore it and take the stairs instead. Running up seven flights seemed like nothing, and she propelled herself into the room Jock and her crew would start demolishing in the morning.

She plugged in one of the portable lights and found the sledgehammer Jock liked to use. Without hesitation, she hefted it as though it were a baseball bat and started swinging, all the while screaming at Rochelle Jacobs, her brother George, her family, the Bohos, and anyone else she could think of. The plaster was reluctant to give at first but the rotten backing and boards didn't last long against the onslaught. Again and again she swung, until her arms hung unresponsive at her sides. Then she kicked the wall repeatedly and when one foot ceased cooperating, she tried the other one, ending up in a heap on the floor, almost howling in frustration that she couldn't force her body to work well enough to keep attacking the wall.

Then she listed onto her side and lay in the midst of her destruction, chest heaving.

"Having fun, Squirt?"

Jock's voice made her start. The gentle tease was at least better than "Stump," and her tone bore no trace of mockery. She hauled Stef to a sitting position and supported her while she righted herself.

"How did you know I was here?"

"You mean aside from the yelling and crashing?"

"I guess I got a little…absorbed in what I was doing." Stef couldn't quite hide her embarrassment.

Shaking her head, Jock said, "Poor Ember left her backpack up here and came to retrieve it. She got about ten feet from the door and came running back to tell us."

"Oh." Stef was lucky to give that much of a response. She was spent.

"I have to admire your work. Took a sizeable chunk out of the wall. Always looking for ways to cut costs, eh?"

The gentle teasing paid off. Stef had to laugh at the comment. Jock was turning out to be a good person, nothing like the woman who tormented her in college. "Got to save those pennies. Wouldn't want to mess up George's new hotel. Prick."

Sitting back on her heels, Jock said, "I presume that's George's nickname and not mine."

Stef regarded her for a moment. "It used to be yours. You're so different than the sports star I remember from school. What happened?"

"That woman was an ass," Jock said with a thoughtful expression. "I guess I realized it was time to grow up. I may have realized it too late to save you from my thoughtless words, but at least you had the good sense not to date me."

"I don't recall being asked."

Giving her a look full of contrition, Jock quietly said, "Denny made it clear that she'd shoot me if I hurt you. I would never go against Den. Anyway, count yourself lucky."

"Why?"

"I think we both know I'm not good partner material."

"Is that what you really think?"

Jock reacted to Stef's soft challenge with an offhand shrug and an evasive half-smile. "Come on, let's get you out of here. I'm sure Laurel won't want to wake up alone, and you're covered in plaster and sweat. You need a shower."

"I need a few aspirin, too." More like a bottle. Stef was beginning to hurt.

Jock picked up Ember's backpack and they strolled to the elevator.

As they rode down, Stef said, "Would you handle the explanations to the troops? I don't feel like facing them right now."

"No problem. And any time you need help kicking her partner, pardon me, her *ex*-partner's ass, don't leave me out of the fun." Jock walked her to her door, adding, "I'm not kidding. I don't like bullies."

"I'll keep it in mind." Stef touched her arm. "Thank you. For everything. You're really a friend."

Jock smiled. "Glad you noticed."

Before the elevator door closed on her floor, leaving Jock to return to the dining room, Stef faced Jock and said, "Maybe the college kid wasn't good partner material, but you would make any woman proud."

A few minutes later, as the warm water sluiced over her aching muscles, Stef found her thoughts wandering to Laurel and the magic of being with her. Although theirs seemed to be a shared attraction, she wondered if Laurel was just reacting to the events of the past few days.

Jock's comment about Laurel's ex played in her mind. She seemed to assume Laurel was actually going to follow through and leave Rochelle permanently. Only time would tell if Laurel had broken free. The thought made her try to shutter her heart to protect herself, and that hurt her soul. It was no use, she'd fallen for the beautiful professor, and she was willing to wait for Laurel to make the decisions she would have to make. But if she returned to Rochelle, Stef would not, could not, stand by and repeatedly pick up the pieces.

❖

The next morning Laurel awoke with a clear head and a body that, although painful, was on the road to healing. As she looked around the dingy room, she was content. Hearing a soft snore to her right, she realized that Stefanie was asleep beside her. Against the tightness of her lip, she smiled, inordinately pleased. Then, despite her better judgment, she reached over and gently brushed Stef's hair from her face, so she could gaze at her.

She studied the rich brown hair, the soft sensuous mouth she kept wanting to kiss, the pale flawless complexion, the slightly crooked nose. Imagining exploring Stef's beautiful body, tracing her ears with her tongue and touching her spectacular breasts, made her wet, aroused. The reaction was almost foreign to her, it had been so long. Had she ever felt that way?

Her face tingled with a blush as she tried not to react to her thoughts. Her struggle was interrupted by a deep, gravelly, voice.

"Mornin'." Stef stretched, and the covers came down low enough to show that she was wearing a loose-fitting tank that revealed the curve of a breast and the border of a pink nipple.

Laurel's body paid no attention to her mind's desperate plea to stop reacting. She was so wet now that she was uncomfortable. She fought for control. Her own nipples were getting harder by the second, so she pulled her covers up to under her arms.

"You're red. Are you okay?" Stef's voice seemed more like a croak.

When she laid a hand on Laurel's forehead, the warmth of it was almost Laurel's undoing. She stayed perfectly still and tried to relax.

"I don't think you have a fever." Stef had raised up to support herself on one elbow, revealing even more cleavage.

It took a monumental effort for Laurel to tear her eyes away, since they seemed to be locked on Stef's body. She managed, "A fever? I...don't know."

"You're blushing."

Laurel met the chocolate brown eyes she had been fantasizing about since the first day they met. "Yes." She could not deny the truth.

"Why?"

The question was so innocent, the answer so simple. "Would you mind, please, covering your breasts? They're... distracting."

Laurel desperately wished she could have made something up, but her brain had finally disconnected completely from her body. It was receiving signals farther south. Loud and clear. The realization of what she'd confessed must have sunk in, because Stef complied, at first rather shyly, but then a sly grin spread over her face.

"Do you like them?" Now the gravel tone, though still there, had been replaced by a husky quality that only made Laurel's resolve more precarious.

"Oh, for God's sake. Yes, yes, yes. They're magnificent, beautiful, I could never imagine anything so lovely as your breasts." Her exasperation must have been evident, because the grin was replaced by something more somber.

"I don't mean to tease you. If it helps, everything about you feels that way to me."

Laurel bolted upright and just as quickly fell back, pain stabbing her into stillness. Once her breath came back to her she said, "God. I'm so sorry. I didn't mean to say that I only admired your breasts, as...special as they are." She hesitated. "Don't you see? I'm completely entranced by everything about you. I have been since we first met. I have no right, no right at all. I should have left Rochelle long ago, but I didn't. I should have stayed with Sika and Denny, but I didn't. I wanted to be with you because I feel safe with you. Damn, even *that* is a lie." She searched the room for the door, the urge to escape almost overwhelming her.

Stef gently squeezed her arm, bringing Laurel's attention back to her. "Why is it a lie?"

Unable to skirt the truth any longer, Laurel sank back on the bed. "That isn't why I wanted to stay with you." Rolling carefully to face Stef, she said, "I think I've fallen in love with you. Bad timing, unrequited and all." Tears seeped out of her eyes at the truth of her confession, the final nail in the coffin.

After a moment, Stef asked, "What makes you think it's unrequited?"

"Because who could love a pathetic, miserable... Wait." Studying the warm inviting eyes and the shy smile, she said, "What did you say?"

"I said, 'what makes you think it's unrequited?'"

Laurel started to reply only to find those fantastic lips meeting hers. Stef confirmed what had only been a wish, a whisper, and probably a prayer. She pulled Stef on top of her and they both yelped in pain and flew apart.

"God, my ribs." Laurel tried to calm her panting, because it hurt, then noticed that Stef was grimacing, too. "What's wrong?"

With a huff, Stef sat up. "I was working in one of the upstairs rooms last night and I'm sore today, that's all."

Thinking about that, Laurel said, "I've been leaning on you a lot, too. I'm sorry."

Placing a hand on her shoulder, Stef smiled sweetly. "I went up to the remodel last night after you were asleep. I pretty much took down a wall. I'm sore, that's all. It's nothing."

Looking deeply into her eyes, Laurel understood. "Did the wall have a name?"

"Yes. Fuckface."

A chuckle started deep in her belly but mushroomed into full guffaws. At the same time, Stef collapsed back on the bed and they both alternated between wheezes and groans because of all the sore and damaged muscles they were using. When they calmed down, they lay side by side on their backs, staring at the stained ceiling.

Laurel asked, "Is it unrequited?"

"What?"

"You know what."

"Do you love me?" Stef's voice shook slightly.

Sighing, Laurel said, "Yes. I tried to be honorable, to control myself, to ignore my emotions, but I lost. I've fallen in love with you. I should apologize, but I won't. But I hope for the courtesy of your honesty when you tell me if you return my love. I hope not to lose your friendship. That means so much to me." Talking to the ceiling was so much easier than face-to-face. Almost like rehearsing her rather long speech.

"Well, you're no longer my friend, if that's what you're asking."

Laurel's heart stood still, she was sure of it. She'd blown it and didn't know how to recover.

"Because now you'll be my lover."

Laurel could barely hear what Stef had said, her own recriminations were so loud in her head. "What?" She sat up abruptly, ignoring her protesting ribs.

"I said, now you'll be my lover. I'm in love with you, Laurel. Bad timing and all."

Gazing into the brown eyes that revealed the truth of Stef's words, Laurel asked, "Now what?"

CHAPTER FIFTEEN

Irina Castic was poring over papers spread on the kitchen table. When the nice young man from the delivery service had knocked on her door the other day, she was surprised to see him. It had been such a long time since anyone had needed to see her identification and passport, and he was evidently quite taken with the importance of his task. It was probably a novelty to him.

She was uneasy, though, because her memories of producing passports and proof of identity were many times filled with dread. She was often amazed at how cavalier Americans were about the freedoms they possessed. As though they would have them forever. She'd read a quote once from an American statesman, she couldn't remember who it was. "The price of freedom is eternal vigilance." How true that was. If people only knew how much their lives were controlled and decided upon by a few powerful men, they might understand that they could take nothing for granted.

The Elysium Society had learned that lesson brutally. But arrogance might just get their enemies yet. Irina couldn't help but laugh to herself at the irony. It would be wonderful if a group of women could teach those Bohos a lesson.

"What's so funny, Mrs. C?" Ember was busy loading her pack and tidying up her sleeping area, which doubled as the living room sofa, so she could take the train to school. Irina had never been on it, this Bay Area Rapid Transit train. She wouldn't go under the bay to get to Berkeley. A tube underwater! There was no way, even with Ember's gentle teasing and offer to hold her hand.

She regarded her young friend. Ember was a beautiful woman by any measure. She never spoke of her past, but Irina knew she came from a life of privilege. It took one to know one. Slowly she'd come to think of Ember as the grandchild she'd never had. She was a special child, intelligent, strong, and brave, and full of compassion. And she needed to attend university as a full-time student. If filling out all of these papers from hell could assist, Irina would gladly do it. After all, Ember had done all of the research and kept the matter alive. Now it looked like something might actually come of it. Irina hoped the desired resolution would come about sooner than later. Ember needed to get on with her life. She shouldn't be stuck in a cheap set of rooms with one old lady.

"Mrs. C?" Ember was still waiting for her answer.

"My dear, do you have a moment before you leave?"

Smiling, Ember said, "Sure." She sat in a chair across from Irina. "What's up?"

"I was wondering if your family knows where you are. If they know you are safe."

From the look on Ember's face, Irina had caught her off of her guard.

"I…wrote a note to say I was okay. You won't call them, though, right?"

"Goodness, no. I wouldn't know how and I wouldn't betray you like that. We are friends. But…" Irina didn't know how to ask.

"Why did I run away?" Ember did her the favor of reading her mind. Lovely child.

"Yes. I don't believe you were abused, you seem to have too much self-confidence for that. But something pushed you out that door. What was it?"

Ember studied Irina's face for a moment, perhaps deciding whether to trust her with her secret. "My mom died when I was ten. My father always plied me with everything I could ever want. It wasn't anything more than all of my friends had, we were spoiled brats. He was gone all the time. That's pretty normal. Their parents were never there, either. I had a series of nannies. Not just one nanny at a time, I mean, they took shifts. I could literally drop a soda in the middle of the living room at two a.m. and someone would be there to clean it up. It was pathetic."

Nodding, Irina said, "Yes, I understand. But if you knew no differently, and you weren't beaten or molested, how did you come to run away?"

"Heather."

"Ah. The famous Heather. You've mentioned her before. You fell in love and your father forbade it?"

Shaking her head, Ember said, "Well, I fell in love, but I don't think Heather noticed. She was a sophomore in college and became one of my many nannies. The pay was good and the hours could work with her classes. She talked to me like I was human, she actually liked me." Giving Irina a sad smile, she added, "And she worried about me."

"Why, my dear? You had your life before you with no financial worries."

"I was surprised, too. She worried *because* of that. I didn't know how to take care of myself, I was lucky I could get dressed without help. Talk about shallow. I had no idea about poverty, about human suffering, about kindness. That's what worried Heather."

Sitting back in her chair, Ember stared at the ceiling. "She became my friend. I was only fourteen when she started working for us. I looked forward to every minute with her. She taught me to at least not treat my other nannies like slaves, she demanded that I make really good grades, even though I could have skated."

"What did your friends think of her?"

"They ignored her. She was 'the help.' It kind of became Heather's and my private joke, with lots of eye rolls when they did some vacuous thing and expected Heather to wait on them. I got so that I didn't have anyone over if she was going to be there. Then they accused me of having an affair with her. Bitches." The hurt in Ember's voice was raw.

"You said you were in love with her. Did you have an affair?"

"No. I mean, I would have, in a second, but Heather would

never betray my trust like that. She told me she loved me like a sister, and maybe someday we might be more, but we both had growing up to do. She quit as my nanny after she graduated from college."

Irina was struck by the pain so evident in Ember's eyes. "What happened then? You must have missed her terribly." She wanted to reach across the papers scattered on the table and take Ember's hand, but she resisted. Ember was talking and she didn't want to interrupt.

Tears rolled down the planes of Ember's face. "She was determined to do some good in the world. She was a teacher and got a job in New York City, working with inner-city youth. We e-mailed every day and she was full of stories about how the kids were responding, how great they were. She was really happy and I was happy for her."

Sniffing loudly, her voice was halting as she spoke. "I promised her I'd keep up my grades and I did. I kind of fell back into my old ways, though. It was easy enough to do. I could never talk Dad into just getting rid of the damned nannies, so, what the hell?" She hugged herself, perhaps against the memory.

"What happened, Ember? Please, tell me." She braced for the answer.

Staring into the distance, she said, "Heather was killed in a drive-by shooting. An innocent bystander, on her way to work with kids who loved her and needed her. Just…dead."

Ember started sobbing, and Irina opened her arms and said, "Come here, child. Right now."

Ember fell on her knees and clung to Irina, her body racked with the agony of a loss she had neither grieved nor told anyone else about. After a few moments she quieted, then found her chair and scrubbed her face with her hands to get rid of the tears. Her eyes were red and swollen, but she somehow looked lighter.

"Do you feel better now?"

"Yeah, I do. Thanks, Mrs. C, you always know what to do." Her voice reflected the mutual warmth and love they had developed and it made Irina's heart sing. But there were two questions left unanswered, and now was the opportunity.

"Ember, I'm sorry for your tragic loss, but why, exactly, did you leave your home?"

Anger suffused Ember's features. "I told my dad about Heather, and he barely remembered her. He said he was sorry and went back to his newspaper. Then I said I was going to get a job and he laughed at me. He told me I wouldn't have a clue about how to actually *do* anything. I was better off going to a good university and marrying a rich man. He hadn't even noticed I didn't date boys."

Irina hesitated. "Did you date girls? Did your friends know you thought of yourself as a lesbian?"

Blushing, Ember studied her nails. "No. Heather was the only one who knew. She was, too. It was another secret we shared."

Deciding to leave the subject alone, Irina asked her last question. "Ember, what is your family name? I know it isn't Jones, because when we first met, you mentioned a different one."

A look of suspicion crossed Ember's face but then her shoulders relaxed. "Lanier. My last name is Lanier. I paid for fake ID papers. Spent a bunch of my money on it, too. I don't know where I thought more money was coming from."

"You've done well for yourself. You have a job, a place to stay, you go to school, and you have good friends. I should think you have proved your father incorrect about your ability to survive. Why not call him? He must be worried about you."

Shaking her head, she said, "I doubt he's paid too much attention."

"Then why change your name? I think you knew he would look for you."

Shrugging, Ember stood and hefted her backpack onto a shoulder. "I guess that's true. But I'm not ready to go back. I like my new life. Oh, I wanted to tell you. Remember that kid who stole your purse when we first met?"

Nonplussed as to where this question was going, Irina only nodded.

"Well, his name is Joey G and he's all clean and sober now and goes to Cal. I'm going to go to his place after class and play computer games. He's a caretaker for a warehouse south of Market Street and lives there, too. See you later."

Still a little teary, Ember sailed out the door, the very picture of vibrant youth. Irina could see that she blamed her father for Heather's death, but she suspected it wouldn't be long before she saw the error in that logic and forgave him enough to contact him. She fervently hoped he had tried to find her, for Ember's sake.

She would miss her young companion when the time came for her to leave, but for now, in case she needed her and because of the others, she would finish this bureaucratic nightmare and hope that the end was near. Forty years was long enough to wait. And after that?

"Seraphina and I will have a talk because I think it is safe. I wonder how the years have changed her. I wonder if she's remembered our promise."

All of the activity and sense of purpose had reinvigorated Irina. She felt better than she had in years. She rarely used her walker now and woke up excited for each day. It was good to be of service, to repay kindness shown so long ago. She no longer had to wait for the moment, it had arrived. And she was ready.

Stef was deep in an erotic fantasy involving Laurel and her and a tub full of whipped cream when she heard a soft knock and looked up to see Agnes Brady shuffling nervously in the doorway. She was expected, as she always came by to pick up the payment each month. The envelope was on the reception desk, and it was unusual for her to peek in Stef's office. Under the present circumstances, Stef thought she had some nerve.

Fighting to be civil, she said, "Ms. Brady, how may I help you? The check should be on the corner of the desk out there."

She pretended to become engrossed in her computer screen in hopes the woman would go away. She really didn't want to start screaming this early in the day, especially since her body was still reacting to that damned fantasy. Stupid whipped cream. She was wet.

This idea that she and Laurel had concocted, about not being physically intimate until Laurel had moved all her possessions out of that woman's house, was so dumb she couldn't believe it. She had to sleep next to the most beautiful woman she'd ever met, one she'd already fallen in love with and *declared* that love to, and they weren't going to have sex? How stupid was that? A loud sneeze and congested cough pulled her back to Agnes Brady. Why was she still here?

Agnes dragged a very old and wet tissue from her pocket to mop up where she had sprayed when she sneezed. *Ew.* Stef passed a box of tissues to her and kept a sensible distance while she noisily blew her nose from what sounded like the bottom of one of her lungs.

Agnes wheezed, "Oh, thank you. I hope you don't catch this stuff, it's no fun." She grabbed another tissue and dabbed ineffectually at the globules of sputum she'd deposited on the desk.

Note to self: boil desk.

"Oh, don't worry. I never get sick," Stef declared with a phony smile.

"I had to come by to...to apologize to you. I didn't know, when they were talking about the acceleration clause, that they were referring to this hotel." Her watery eyes pleaded for understanding.

Stef felt her own eyes narrow in response. "Is that why you looked so guilty every time you came by to get the check? Because you didn't even suspect?"

Looking even more miserable, Agnes admitted, "I did suspect, but I was too cowardly to ask. I've worked for them for a few years and it hasn't been a good experience. They're not good people. But I wanted to be a lawyer someday, and I help support my family so I need the money. My mom isn't well."

Stef relented. It was hard to stay angry in the face of such a heartfelt apology. Besides, now she was curious. That, and she wanted to return to her musings. "Okay. Is there anything else, Agnes?"

"Well, yes." Agnes shuffled some more and her pale skin turned pink. "I was wondering if you could put in a good word for me with Lefty." She sneezed again, but this time caught most of it. From the look of her she was quite communicable.

"Lefty who?" The name sounded familiar.

"Lefty Petrovsky." The expectant way she said it suggested Stef should not only recognize the name but be seeking an autograph as well.

"She's part of Jock Reynolds's crew, right?" Was this distraction really necessary?

Agnes's sickly pallor colored again. "Yes, I met her a few months ago when I took a tour of the remodel. She's been ignoring me since this whole thing happened." She sounded completely dejected.

"Have you talked to her about it? Maybe she doesn't understand." Stef wasn't sure *she* understood, either. *Could someone please get rid of this walking flu bug and let me get back to, um, business?*

"I tried, but she won't listen. She worships Jock and Ms. Phelps and thinks I personally am trying to dismantle the hotel. I tried to explain I'm just an assistant, but she won't take my calls."

"I really don't see how I can help. I'm not trying to be mean, I assure you." *I'm thinking I should whip the cream myself. Yes, organic cream with vanilla and a touch of sugar. That way when I lick it off Laurel...*

"I quit my job." Agnes lapsed into another coughing spell.

"And you want me to tell Lefty for you?"

Agnes nodded with feverish gratitude. "And I want to apply for a job with you."

Stef rid herself of the vision of Laurel's breasts covered in organic whipped cream with just her nipples peeking out. It wasn't easy. "Why would you do that? We have no money, which, I think you know."

"Yes, I know. You're going to need a good attorney and someone to assist in the litigation. I'm very good and very thorough. I can save you money."

Something felt a little off. "Wait, back up. What do you mean, I'll need a good attorney? I thought that was obvious."

"You probably know this already, but the Bohemian Club plans to have the original sale of the hotel to you voided. They're trying to declare Seraphina Drake Holloway incompetent. Then any action she took as trustee of the Holloway family trust will be null. Including the sale of the hotel. That's why I quit."

Stunned, Stef could only stare. "Agnes, I'm pretty sure that anything you've overheard is confidential. If those guys find out you've warned us and they decide to pursue it, your chances of getting into a good law school will disappear. Consider carefully."

Agnes's set her jaw. "I don't care. You and the women who work for you are so nice, and those people are so scummy. I know the rules, but sometimes you just have to do the right thing. If you can use a secretary or anything at all, I'll take it."

Stef stared at her. "Is this all about Lefty?"

Agnes shook her head, then wiped her nose again. "Of course not. But between your urging and my noble deed, maybe she'll find me irresistible. Can't hurt, right?"

❖

Stef walked numbly down the hall toward Irina Castic's rooms. She gazed longingly at her own door, not yet able to rid herself of the vision of a naked Laurel covered discreetly in whipped cream.

Mrs. C seemed to be expecting her. She had a pot of tea prepared and served them both before a word was spoken. When Stef was through with her explanations, she sat back in her chair and stared at a place over Stef's shoulder. "Well, we must discover if there is any substance to this claim. What else did Miss Brady say?"

"That Seraphina's son, Clayton B. Holloway the Third, has put her in a private facility for the very wealthy. We can't get to her easily, I'm afraid. They have a lot of security at those places." Stef felt weary. It seemed like no matter where she turned, there was someone there to block her.

"Perhaps I could visit my dear old friend," Mrs. C said.

"You know Mrs. Holloway?"

"Very well, although we haven't seen each other for many years."

"Agnes says she can't have any visitors unless they check with her son first."

They sipped tea in silence for a moment.

Mrs. C asked, "How old are you, dear?"

Her bright blue eyes were full of intention, and Stef answered immediately. "Thirty-four. Why?"

"I'll need a child or a grandchild. One who, like Seraphina's son, is shopping for a place to dump off dear, rich Granny while she spends her money. I think you'll do very well." Her smile was full of mischief.

"Nice. But don't they check your portfolio?"

"Give me another day, and then you can make the call. They'll see us."

Stef had no idea what Mrs. C, who had lived in the hotel for so many years and was penniless, was going to do, but she felt better immediately.

"Now go and check on Laurel. I think she needs you." Mrs. C's smile made Stef blush. She could feel her cheeks tingle. "Oh, please take those two bags of papers to her. I believe she will find them useful."

Stef nodded and hefted the bags, thankful that she had an excuse to see Laurel at last. It had been at least four hours. So much had happened that she wanted to share with her. She fought the urge to check and see if Sika had any whipping cream in the refrigerator.

❖

Laurel was restless.

She was going to go back to class tomorrow, not at all sure

how she would be received. Ember had reported concern among the students for her absence and absolutely not one word of explanation from the faculty. There'd been a notice on her office door that classes were cancelled for one week. She assumed Rochelle had made up an excuse, because she hadn't called. No more covering up for Rochelle; that was her new promise to herself.

Sighing, Laurel knew she would have to face Rochelle soon. She needed her clothes, her things. She was grateful that she had forgotten her laptop in her car and therefore had it, but her class notes and a lot of other student information were on her desktop computer at the house. Stef had been more than generous, and had even converted the room where the project was housed into a temporary office for her. She'd offered to have a bed put there as well, but they dismissed that idea almost immediately, agreeing that they at least needed to sleep in the same bed.

That was the main reason she had to face Rochelle. She wanted to keep her agreement that she would end her relationship with Rochelle before starting a new one with Stef. But really, hadn't she already done that? Wasn't moving her things out just a formality? Rochelle had already accused her of sleeping with Stef, screamed it at her when she was attacking her. As far as Laurel was concerned, there was little left to be said, but she wanted to do whatever would make Stef comfortable.

She could understand Stef's doubts, and her desire to see complete closure. Women often went back and forth as they were trying to leave a relationship. Obviously Stef didn't trust Laurel enough to accept that it was over, and there was no chance that she would change her mind, unless she made the "divorce" final in every possible way. That meant getting her stuff out of that house. The day couldn't come soon enough, as far as Laurel was concerned.

A knock on the door brought her back to the present and Stef peeked in, her expression warm and inviting. She plopped two heavy and somewhat bedraggled-looking shopping bags on the floor by the couch. "Mrs. C asked me to bring these to you. Said you might want them."

Laurel elbowed herself upright and made room on the couch for

Stef. Smiling up at her, she said, "I wonder if those are the minutes of the Elysium Society meetings."

Stef took the notepad from her lap and put it aside, scooting to sit next to her. Touching her face gently, she asked, "How are you feeling?" She continued to fuss, pushing some of Laurel's hair away from her cheeks.

"Much better. My lip is almost healed. Thanks to you." Laurel pulled Stef to her and they shared a sweet, soft and lingering kiss. Laurel felt her heartbeat pick up and could tell from Stef's breathing that the same was happening to her.

"Stefanie?"

"I'm sorry." Stef looked at her guiltily. "I know we have an—"

Laurel put her fingers on Stef's lips to shush her. "About that agreement." She searched Stef's apprehensive face, hoping she wouldn't disappoint her. "It's not going to work."

A chill passed across Stef's features like a cloud obscuring the sun. "You're going back to her?"

"No, absolutely not." As Stef's shoulders dropped in relief, Laurel said, "There's something I want you to know. In my heart, I left Rochelle a long time ago. The day she did this to me, she screamed at me that I was...fucking you. What I should have screamed right back at her was that I wanted to. With all my heart, and *not* just to have an affair."

Stef's eyes shone. "What are you saying?"

"I should have told her I loved you, and I would give anything to make love with you. Instead, I denied it. I was relieved that we hadn't done anything." Laurel sighed. "I'm making a mess out of this, aren't I? Some professor I am. Can't even beg for sex without confusing the one person in the world I want to have sex with." The thought crossed her mind that she'd ended a phrase with a preposition. She had even screwed that up.

Stef took her hands. "Are you saying we can chuck that idiotic agreement? Think about this, because you're going back to school tomorrow. You might see Rochelle, and if I have anything to say about it, you'll look different."

Laurel mused aloud, "Look different? What are you talking about, are you planning on covering me with hickeys?"

Smiling, Stef checked her watch. "We have four hours before I'm supposed to be in a meeting with Sika. Then we have all night. I've been fantasizing about making love to you ever since the first time I saw you."

Taking Stef's face between her hands, Laurel looked directly in her eyes. "So have I." She kissed her softly, then deeply, pulling her close.

Stef responded carefully at first, but Laurel knew she was holding back, trying not to hurt her. She helped her to her feet and led her to the bedroom. It was obvious that because of her injuries, Stef would let her lead. That would be a change, but Laurel was exhilarated and equally concerned that she'd do everything right.

That concern dissolved when Stef stood before her and pulled her pale yellow sweater over her head, revealing a lovely bra that Laurel wanted to tear off and toss into a shredder. Then, before Laurel's eyes, she unfastened the bra and let it slide off her shoulders to reveal the most exquisite full breasts she had ever seen or could imagine. For the first time, Laurel let herself drink in the sight for as long as she wanted. Tears came to her eyes, and she licked her lips, mesmerized as Stef's nipples tightened.

Somewhere she registered Stef's voice. "If you don't touch me soon, I'm going to disintegrate. Please, I need you."

"My God. You are so..." She realized her hands were trembling when she reached for Stef and heard her moan.

Stef's body felt exquisite, the toned muscles of her abdomen a sharp contrast to the soft heaven of her breasts. When she ran into the texture of cloth, Laurel fumbled and pulled ineffectually, almost whimpering in frustration.

Stef stilled her hands and stood back, stepping out of the remainder of her clothes. "Now you. Do you need help?"

Laurel was wearing a front zip sweatshirt and tie sweatpants. Yet even those seemed welded closed. "Yes, hurry."

She was pretty sure she would pass out soon unless Stef made love to her. She'd never felt this way about anyone—everything was brand new, so new there was no time to be shy, be polite, she couldn't *think*, for God's sake. Her clothes were too tight and Stef's naked body wasn't helping. Stef started on the zipper, pulling it slowly down. Laurel couldn't stand it. Night after night she'd lain next to Stef, ending up in her arms or wrapped around her by the morning. Despite the distraction of her injuries, she'd been swollen for every minute. Even her attempt at relieving the pressure herself was a miserable failure. She only wanted Stef and she wanted her now.

She tore the zipper from Stef's hand and finished the job herself. Then she pulled the drawstring on her pants to let them drop unceremoniously to the floor and stomped to get out of them, kicking them off. Thankfully, she hadn't worn anything else. Without a moment's hesitation she took Stef's hand and placed it where she had dreamt of it being for so long. Long before Rochelle, long before any woman she had ever been with, she realized she'd longed for Stefanie.

"This is what you do to me," she said. "Don't leave me."

Stef's eyes widened in recognition. Her pupils, already so large, almost completely filled her irises. "On the bed."

They almost leapt from where they were, Laurel ignoring her protesting ribs as they landed in the middle of the covers. For a moment, they searched each other's faces.

"I love you, Laurel, I think I always will."

Stef returned to Laurel's center and stroked her, pushing inside, giving her so much pleasure Laurel burst into a strong orgasm within seconds. She called out Stef's name and begged her not to stop, coming to another, stronger orgasm on the heels of the first.

They lay for a moment, both trying to catch their breath. Laurel had felt Stef ride her thigh and was sure Stef had come, too. But not like she was going to.

"I was selfish." She skimmed the side of one of Stef's breasts. "I couldn't stand it, you drive me insane."

Stef gasped, "It's okay, I couldn't help but come with you. Just to be naked with you…to make love to you, see your face. I've wanted you for so long."

"I must be selfish again, I have to."

"What can I do? Be as selfish as you want." Her eyes told Laurel all she needed to know.

"Lie back, I need to have my way with you."

As Stef collapsed onto the bed, she flung her arms over her head and opened her legs wide. Laurel could see how swollen she was. How wet.

"I'm a pig. Thinking only of myself." She reached down and ran the pad of her thumb the length of Stef's need, then leaned in to suck her clit to a hard prominence.

Stef groaned, and her hips rose to push hard into Laurel's mouth. Laurel flicked her clit with her tongue, then gently bit down and felt Stef jackknife almost to a sitting position before collapsing back on the bed. She entered Stef, using her tongue to stroke her.

"More," Stef implored. "Oh God, more. I'm…almost…there."

Laurel concentrated on Stef's clitoris, making the movements sharp and quick until Stef became still, her legs trembling. When her body rolled with the shocks of her orgasm Laurel, didn't stop until she'd driven her relentlessly to two more.

Stef finally begged for mercy, and Laurel, completely drunk with power, granted it.

Chapter Sixteen

Uh, Dr. Hoffman? I think you missed the exit." Ember's voice dragged Laurel back to reality.

"What? Oh, I was just…thinking." Laurel's life was upside down and her concentration was shot. She should have insisted that Ember drive, but she needed to drop her off a few blocks before the campus so no one knew of their friendship. The precaution protected both of them.

"You sure you'll be okay until class? I can come with you to your office. It's no problem."

She was so innocent in her offer; Laurel hoped she never lost that innocence. Ember had no idea of the political ramifications of a stunningly beautiful young woman escorting an instructor to her office. The gossip would be in full swing the moment they exited the car. With phone cameras, their picture together would be on the university intranet before class started. She probably should have dropped her at the BART station.

"No, it's better this way," Laurel said. Rochelle would never do anything on campus. "After I drop you off, please call and tell Stef I'm okay."

Ember nodded, staring out the windshield. She extracted the new cell phone Jock had given her and said, "I've got her on speed dial."

Laurel would call, too, of course. It was all she could do to get

Stef to agree to Ember as her sole bodyguard. She'd almost had all of Jock's crew following her in a convoy. Her heart swelled at the recognition that so many wanted to help.

After leaving Ember, she drove into the faculty parking lot. She was nervous, despite her brave words, because Rochelle had been so unpredictable lately. But she wasn't scheduled to be on campus today, so Laurel clung to the hope she would stick to her routine.

As she walked across the expansive lawns of the university, she was aware that the new clothes she'd purchased in a quick shopping trip fit differently. She'd chosen brighter colors, and her style was less constrained, more active and in charge. She had even picked out a tank that revealed her figure and some cleavage, something she wouldn't have dreamt of doing before.

She knew exactly why, too. Stefanie Beresford. Stef made her feel special. She admired her mind and worshipped her body. She loved her soul. From the moment they touched, Laurel was forever and irrevocably a new woman. She returned every molecule of love to the woman who'd brought about the change. It didn't matter what Rochelle or anyone else said or did, there was no going back. That knowledge gave her courage she didn't know she possessed, and the vision of Stef's eyes shining with love lifted her spirits and filled her with resolve.

So, yes, Stef was right about her being changed when she saw Rochelle again. But it wasn't her clothes, or the fact that she bore some marks of their lovemaking. Those were not visible anyway. She'd thoughtfully chosen a shirt to wear over her tank top, since every time she thought of Stef, which was constantly, her nipples hardened.

Rochelle would notice a confidence in her that was completely new. She would no doubt tell Laurel that her glow was only because she was fucking Stef. Rochelle wouldn't recognize the real basis of the change, that Laurel felt loved and could give love in return. Rochelle didn't even know what that meant.

"So, you've decided to grace us with your presence."

Laurel stopped, her chest tightening at the sound of Rochelle's voice. She was behind her and Laurel wondered how long she'd been there. She whirled to meet her former partner's glare, wondering if she'd even notice the fading bruises or the slight scar on her lip.

"I had to let the bruises fade. You know the drill."

"Keep your voice down. Someone might hear you."

In the past she would have instantly complied, but no more. "That's your problem, Rochelle. And even if I were completely silent, no one's blind and the facial bruising is still rather obvious, wouldn't you say."

Rochelle studied her and a knowing sneer settled on her features. "I knew it. You're fucking her."

Shrugging, Laurel said, "Well, I wasn't when you kicked the crap out of me, dearest. But now? You bet I am."

Rochelle's face darkened with fury. "We'll talk about this at home. I'll be waiting after class." Her jaw muscles were working overtime.

"No, Rochelle, we won't. I've moved out. I won't be alone with you because I don't trust you."

"I can break you, Laurel, so watch your mouth. I can get you dismissed and make sure you never work in a university again."

"Perhaps. But understand one thing. I. Don't. Care." Laurel turned on her heel and strode toward the classroom building. She'd only taken several steps when her arm was in a vise, forcing her to face Rochelle.

"How dare you talk to me that way. I ought to—"

"Dr. Hoffman? Dr. Hoffman?" They both looked sideways to see Ember running toward them and skidding to a halt. Her smile faded as she spied Rochelle's grip on Laurel's arm, and Rochelle immediately dropped her hand. "Oh, I'm sorry, am I interrupting?"

Rochelle forced a terse smile. "Why no, we were just discussing…a project."

"Oh, great." Ember dripped innocence. "I was hoping to talk to Dr. Hoffman about my term paper. You're Professor Jacobs, aren't you? Wow, what an honor." She stuck her hand out and pumped vigorously, the picture of admiration.

Rochelle preened. "Yes, I am. And you are—"

"Oh, just a freshman. But I hope to be a student here for a long time and be in your class someday. I can't believe I got to meet you."

Before Ember piled it on a bit too thickly, Laurel said, "Well, we have a few minutes before class, so why don't we talk about your paper on the way."

"Sure, so nice to have met you, Professor Jacobs." Ember stood back, all smiles and beautiful cluelessness, waiting for Laurel.

Rochelle gave them a thin smile. "Very well, see you after class, Dr. Hoffman."

As they walked briskly across campus, Laurel ventured a glance over her shoulder to see Rochelle engaged with another student. "Thank you, Ember. I'm pretty sure you would get an A in my class, if you were enrolled."

Breathlessly, Ember said, "Hey, I really, really, want to run. Guess that wouldn't be, you know, cool, right?"

"Right. Let's do it anyway." They broke into a run that didn't slow down until they were through the building's glass doors.

❖

Stef had enough energy to pull Laurel on top of her, after recovering from the last session of lovemaking. It took a bit of strength, too, because Laurel was unable to help. How she got that way brought a satisfied smirk to Stef's lips.

"You're gloating." Laurel regarded her with those disconcerting green eyes.

The passion in her gaze caused a reaction in Stef that, although she couldn't do much about it for a bit, she didn't bother to suppress. "Yes, I am. You are so wondrous when you come. And I'm improving my technique."

Resting her chin on Stef's chest, Laurel let a hand wander, enjoying the hitch in Stef's breath when she found a sensitive spot.

"So, tell me, how did Ember do as a bodyguard? I apologize for not asking until now, but I hadn't seen you in forever and needed to feel you close to me."

Actually, they'd practically ripped each other's clothes off the moment they were alone. The first round was fast and desperate, each seeking reassurance from the other. The second and third were much more leisurely.

Laurel explained Ember's escort to class, then added, "When class was over, Rochelle was lurking outside the door and, to tell the truth, I was jumpy. All of a sudden I was surrounded by at least half my students, Ember leading the way, and we walked, like a Roman phalanx, to my car, everyone chatting and asking questions. Rochelle couldn't get near me without causing a huge stir. It was great." She grinned.

"Way to go, Ember."

"You know what else? I'm going to start playing racquetball again. My sister and I always loved it and I played in college with friends, but I stopped because Rochelle was so miserable to play with. Ember's agreed to be my practice partner. What do you think of that?" Laurel's eyes threw off more sparks of gold as she spoke. She looked happy.

Stef was thinking about a raise for Ember, perhaps a bonus. "Racquetball, that's great."

"What happened with Mrs. Castic?" Laurel asked. "Did the place they're housing Mrs. Holloway fall for the story?"

"We'll know soon. Mrs. C said to pass on the information she had given me, some Serbian attaché number in New York City, to the institution. To say they were snooty is to understate it."

"If they go for the bait, what then?"

"According to Mrs. C, we march in there, she plays a doddering fool, and we tour until we find Seraphina Drake Holloway. Mrs. C says she'll recognize her, no problem. Then we'll ask her what's going on, assuming she really isn't demented."

Stef felt her body begin to heat as Laurel continued her teasing exploration. She relieved some pressure by allowing her pelvis to rock in rhythm with Laurel's. It was a temporary fix.

Laurel said, "Oh, my. That's…nice. What were we saying?" She sat up to straddle Stef, fondling her breasts, gently teasing her nipples with her thumbs as she continued rocking. She slid her clit against Stef's pubic hair and gasped.

"Christ." Stef moaned. "You're making me so excited, I can barely…talk."

"Talking is the last thing I want you to do with your tongue, the very last thing." Laurel raised up and turned so they could have access to each other. Feasting with their fingers and tongues brought them to thundering climaxes within minutes.

When they were once again in each other's arms, Stef mumbled, "I want you again."

That was the last thing she remembered until the next morning, when she got her wish.

CHAPTER SEVENTEEN

The building Mrs. Holloway was housed in was across the Golden Gate Bridge in Marin County, about fifteen minutes up Highway 101 and then into wooded hills. Set in a small hollow, with surrounding outbuildings, it reminded Stef more of Wuthering Heights than a posh retirement facility. Behind the stone walls were beautifully tended grounds. Nothing moved, not even a stray leaf. The place was so quiet it gave her the creeps.

The tall, imposing security gates slowly swung open after she rang the bell and identified Countess Irina Castic and her granddaughter Stefanie. She was still reeling over that one, too. Mrs. C seemed to have the role down pat. Stef wondered if she had been an actress at some point. She walked regally to the chauffeur-driven car they'd arranged for the trip, wearing her finest clothes—dated but elegant. She'd insisted that Stef tart herself up, including exposing cleavage in a skimpy dress. Stef's face warmed at the thought, because Laurel had really liked her new look and they were lucky the dress was still in one piece after she demonstrated just how much it turned her on. Her professor was full of surprises.

When the chauffeur opened the car door at the Heath Retirement Center, Mrs. C required much more help than before and seemed a bit addled. Impressed, Stef hoped she could play her own part as well.

The woman who greeted them was fortyish, rail thin, and had an icy demeanor. Her clothes were obviously expensive and her dark hair well tended. Her smile revealed capped teeth and her eyes remained distant, as though calculating net worth and the chances of getting some of it. She identified herself as Mrs. Juanita Stonewell, the executive director of the facility. While she was solicitous to the point of fawning to Stef, she virtually ignored Mrs. C, who made a show of looking bewildered.

Trying to separate from Mrs. C's clinging fingers, Stef said, "Yeah, Gram, this is the place I told you about. As soon as you sign those papers you can live here."

She turned to Juanita Stonewell and said, "Grammy's losing it and I want to protect her, you know? I need her power of attorney so someone doesn't take advantage of her. Gram was royalty in her country." She made this announcement with sarcasm and rolled her eyes, giving Mrs. Stonewell a knowing look.

"Well, perhaps we can help. We can do a psychiatric evaluation here, to assess mental capacity, and we've often been called upon to testify on competency cases."

"So I've heard. How much does that cost? You know, the testing and testifying part." Stef picked Mrs. C's hands off her arm again.

Warming to the topic, Mrs. Stonewell said, "Oh, it is rather expensive, but we can add that into her residency payments. The countess can more than afford it." She offered a conspiratorial wink. Stef fought to not slap her.

"Um, yeah, that's good. Listen, do you have any other old ladies here that you've, er, helped? Maybe we can park my Gram with them and you and I can discuss the details." She lowered her voice to a whisper. "She's driving me crazy."

Stonewell nodded. "Let's walk down to the TV room, there are lots of interesting things there and she can visit with the residents."

Raising her voice, Stef yelled, "Gram, let's go watch TV."

Mrs. C looked at her in surprise. "Stefanie, is this the place?"

"Yeah, Gram, let's go."

They slowly made their way, following Mrs. Stonewell down a dark hallway that smelled of disinfectant and decay. Stef stole a glance at Mrs. C and thought she saw anger sharpen her eyes, then the dull sheen of confusion was back. No wonder Mrs. C was glad to stay in the hotel. As shabby as it was, it was better than this. And these people had money.

The "TV room" featured three televisions positioned in their own areas, each tuned to a different channel. Seemed like news, sports, and soap operas at first glance. Most residents were gathered in the soap opera pod. There was only one somnolent woman propped up on a couch in front of the television with the news on. She appeared to be sleeping.

The sole attendant in the room looked more like a guard than a nurse or aide. As they stood just inside the door, he nodded to Mrs. Stonewell and left, as though he was on rounds, checking on the inmates. Stef thought he should be slapping a baton against his thigh.

"Oh, can I watch the news? You know I love the news." Mrs. C released her grip on Stef and tottered over to the couch, where she plopped down and seemed engrossed in the program.

If the woman on the couch with her was Holloway, Stef wished her luck. She looked heavily sedated. "Gram looks happy here for a while," she told Mrs. Stonewell. "Show me the rest of the place. She won't remember it anyway and it would take all day. I gotta get back to work."

She needed to keep Mrs. Stonewell distracted for at least thirty minutes for Mrs. C to try to talk to Mrs. Holloway, so she asked a lot of dumb questions as they toured the facility. The Heath Retirement Center wasn't bad considering how old the building was, but for the enormous price they were charging they could have sunk a few hundred thousand into renovation and made it much better. These people were raking in the money. Given Mrs. Stonewell's willingness to practically guarantee a diagnosis of incompetence, and the hefty price tag that went with that diagnosis, it was clear that most of the residents were in the same boat as Mrs. Holloway. Their families weren't willing to wait for the relative to die before getting their hands on the money.

Toward the end of the tour, a thought occurred to Stef. "Mrs. Stonewell, what if one of the residents tries to escape? You know, since they're incompetent."

A smile of pride softened the woman's severe features. "Well, we have excellent security. The property is completely surrounded by stone walls and the front gates are operated from our security room. You probably noticed that you had to announce yourself before they would open."

"Yeah, that's good. But what if one of them falls or tries to hide somewhere?" Stef had noticed security cameras in the halls but wanted to see if they were active and monitored. Thanks to her research for the hotel, she was familiar enough with security systems to be able to make a reasonable evaluation of the one in this facility. She suspected security was where they spent their money.

"You might have noticed the security cameras in the halls. They are also in the common areas and the rooms. Not only can they call us if they need something, we can monitor them. Just to make sure they are okay, of course."

"Whoa. That seems a little, you know, over the top, don't you think? What if they're naked or something?"

Stonewell gave her a pitying look. Then she spoke as if talking to one of the residents, slowly and with simple words. "It's for their own good. We take their safety very seriously. Besides, we only turn on the video portion if need be."

Impressed and repulsed, Stef asked the most important question. "Sounds like a huge job. But I guess you only check in every now and then."

Mrs. Stonewell looked mildly affronted. "As a matter of fact, we have a security room staffed around the clock."

When Stef produced a dubious look, that seemed to be all the prompting Stonewell needed. She directed them down a hall that had been completely remodeled, and luxuriously so. The administration wing, she called it. Using a key card, she opened a room marked "Telemetry," revealing a large control desk and numerous monitors. A husky man minded the switches, his fingers moving slowly over the board, turning screens on or off, watching. He had headphones on and was evidently listening, as well.

Stef felt queasy just thinking about Mrs. C trying to make herself understood to a sedated elderly woman, probably shouting.

Anxiously, she asked, "Can you hear the residents talk to each other?"

"Yes, if we wish. But only if we think it's for their safety."

"So, if someone's attorney visits them, say, to fight a competency hearing, you could overhear it, right?"

"We can't monitor those, of course. Client confidentiality."

"But you could, right? Not that you would, but you *could*." Stef tried to look conspiratorial instead of disgusted.

She must have succeeded because Stonewell said, "Yes, we *could*." Stef could almost hear the cash register sound going off in the woman's head. Another service with a hefty price tag.

After she'd stalled for a few more minutes, they ambled back to the TV room and looked around for Mrs. C. Stef almost panicked when she didn't spot her immediately. Upon closer inspection, though, she seemed to have fallen asleep on the other couch occupant's shoulder. The two were holding hands.

Stef prodded Mrs. C gently. "Hey, Gram, wake up."

Mrs. C started and looked around in fright at her surroundings. "Stefanie. Where have you been?" She reached up and grabbed Stef's hand for help in standing.

Red-faced, Mrs. Stonewell immediately demanded, "Did you talk to Mrs. Holloway?"

"Who?"

Stonewell pointed. "That woman right there."

As if noticing her for the first time, Mrs. C smiled. "Oh, why she's asleep. What a pretty woman. Stefanie, can we go out to lunch? You promised me." She placed her arm through Stef's as if ready to leave.

"Okay, Gram, but we have to hurry. I have an appointment later. Say good-bye to the nice lady."

It wasn't until they were on the highway back to San Francisco that they relaxed and Mrs. C was suddenly her old self again.

Relieved, Stef asked, "Did you get anything out of Mrs. Holloway? She looked pretty drugged to me."

"She's virtually catatonic," Mrs. C said, obviously upset. "They're keeping her that way intentionally. She's being held against her will, and her worthless son wants her declared incompetent. The hearing is in two weeks. That was all I could find out, but I told her we would help her. I told her to try to not take the medication. It's difficult for her. They watch very closely."

"I hope you were whispering, because the place is bugged up the wazoo."

"I noticed."

Stef grinned at her. "You did a great job. Want to go to lunch?"

Smiling broadly, Mrs. C said, "Do we have enough money in the budget?"

"Well, we can't go to the best place in town, but I think we could find a nice one, maybe in Chinatown."

"I think that would be lovely. You did very well, too, my dear. We deserve a reward. But after that, we need to call an all parts meeting. We have much to do. And our new ally, Miss Brady, must be present."

"All parts? I think you mean all hands. Everyone there, correct?"

"Of course, that's what I said." Mrs. C winked and settled back for the ride.

❖

"Hey, sis, have you been waiting long?" Jason's voice was right next to her ear.

Jerking sideways, Stef yelped, "Jesus, you scared the hell out of me, Jase. Why are you sneaking up on me?"

"I wasn't. You were just daydreaming."

Still smiling, Jason sat down opposite her at their window table at Sam's Café in Tiburon. Stef had called and found him up in the wine country. They'd agreed to lunch at Sam's, halfway between the two. She felt okay about being away for a few hours, knowing Laurel would be playing racquetball with Ember.

"Why didn't you get us a table on the deck?" Jason asked. "It's a gorgeous day." That was true; the sailboats were out in full force and the San Francisco skyline was gleaming in the background.

"Because those damned seagulls are so fat and brazen from being fed nonstop by the tourists, I can't eat in peace." The seagulls here were not shy about landing on the tables and helping themselves to fries, burger buns, you name it. They were huge.

"I left a beautiful woman asleep in the room," her brother said. "Hope she's there when I return. What's up?"

"Let's order, I'm hungry." Stef was trying to figure out how to assess what Jason knew without tipping her hand. At this point, she didn't trust anyone but the inner circle.

She stirred her coffee and added a dollop of cream, staring blankly at the lunch menu as she mulled over her situation. She was being attacked on three fronts. If Seraphina Holloway was ruled incompetent, her son, Clayton B. Holloway III, would take over the Holloway family trust and void the sale of the hotel. She had to repay the first mortgage because the bank hadn't formally approved the second mortgage. The second mortgage holders hadn't asked for written permission either, but that didn't change anything. Trip Boynton and George were rubbing their hands at the prospect of her defaulting. George no doubt planned to piggyback onto the acceleration of the first mortgage, or buy the hotel for himself for pennies on the dollar.

In other words, her dream was in deep trouble. It was hard to imagine so much subterfuge over one small hotel. Stef had a strange feeling that she was caught up in something that predated her project. The Elysium Society must have been a real threat if the thought of a women-only hotel could still get the Boho boys fired up. Stef was puzzled that it mattered so much to them. Why would they even care? She could understand George looking for a way to grind her down, to prove her unfit just in case their father ever considered taking her seriously. But he couldn't do this alone. The impetus had come from the Bohemian Club.

Evidently, the wrath of these men hadn't dissipated over time. The Elysium Society had disappeared from the face of the earth, but that wasn't enough for them. They wanted the building that had housed it all those years ago. Why?

Jason ordered a Bloody Mary to drink before his burger arrived. Stef got a refill of coffee. "Hey, Jase, are you on vacation? I never asked."

Shrugging, he said, "I guess. George wanted me here and then told me to take a week off. You know, he can be weird."

A tumbler clicked in Stef's mind. "Jason, remember the last time we were together? We went for Swedish pancakes."

He squirmed a bit in his chair and wouldn't look at her. "Those were good." The squirm had always been Jason's tell. He was a terrible liar.

"Did you mention our breakfast to Dad or George? We talked about the hotel and you gave me money. Did you mention it, Jase?"

The waiter placed the drink in front of Jason and he sucked at least half of it down with his straw, still not looking at her. Then he picked the celery out of the glass and bit off a large piece, crunching loudly.

Stef said, "Jason, you told them I needed money, didn't you?"

His eyes, so like hers, revealed the truth. "I was worried. I told them because I was sure they would help. George said he could. He said you wouldn't even have to know. He told me he was trying to heal the rift between you two."

"And do you know what he did?"

Jason's reply mattered so much to Stef, she could barely breathe. If he knew and it was okay with him, that was it for her relationship with her entire family. She loved Jase, a betrayal would kill her.

"Well, yeah. He got a company he's an investor in to give you a second mortgage. That way you could finish the hotel." He looked at her hopefully, but his face started to fall when he met her eyes. "That's not what he did, is it? I shouldn't have trusted him. All his talk about his dear friends and investors, how they were going to get him into the Boho club, just like Dad. Why would he want to belong to that old fart club anyway?"

Stef almost dropped her cup of coffee. "Dad is a member of the Bohemian Club?"

Jason looked like he had just swallowed an egg, shell and all. He started perspiring and seemed like he might hyperventilate. "God, sis, you can't tell anyone. I'll be in big trouble. I was never supposed to breathe a word."

"Jason, I'm your sister. I'm the only one who has always looked out for you. Now you tell me, how long have you known Dad was a member of that club?"

Jason's Adam's apple bobbed as he fought to control his emotions. "Since we were kids. Remember when he would take George and me hunting and leave you and mom behind?"

"Yes, that important bonding time a man needs with his sons?" Stef said cynically.

"He would take us up to the farm the Bohos own. The one up by Healdsburg. It was all men and their sons. We'd have a great time, but we weren't allowed to tell anyone where we'd been."

In shock, Stef managed, "Jase, are you a member of the Bohos?"

"No, I've never had any interest in it. But George would jump through his own asshole to get an invitation. It's the final part in his quest to be ruler of the universe. You know George."

"God, does he have to do it at my expense?"

A sad expression crossed Jason's face. Stef was reminded of the many times as kids that George would side with his cohorts instead of protecting his brother or his sister. She had toughened up, but Jason never did. "Yeah. He did it at my expense, too. He knows how close we are."

They were silent for a moment. Searching to change the subject, Stef said, "Jase? Guess what? I'm in love."

Jason broke into a surprised grin. "Did you just say what I think you did?"

She knew she was blushing. "I did, and her name is Laurel. She's a professor."

"Does she love you, too? For real?"

She and Jason had both been through love affairs and been disappointed.

"I think so. She seems to love me as much as I love her. And it feels very real, in a dreamy, doofus way."

Jason took her hand and squeezed it. "I'm so happy for you. How did you meet?"

A warning bell went off in Stef's head. She had to protect the Elysium Society papers from George and his ambition. Carefully, she replied, "One of the construction crew is a young woman who bats for my team. She introduced us."

That was as close to the truth as she could afford to get. Jason was too easily manipulated. She loved him, but she had to be careful.

"Wow. That's very cool. When do I meet her?"

"Soon. But first, I need to figure some things out about the hotel."

"Can I help?" He seemed desperate to make amends and maybe she could use that guilt.

"Jase, how secret is the Boho group? Are the members really not supposed to say it exists?"

"Yup, it's top secret, in a hiding in plain sight way. Ostensibly, it's like the Moose Lodge, but according to George, it's really a big deal. They even have different divisions you can join without the full membership."

"Like associate members?" That would certainly extend their influence.

Jason nodded. "Yes, they have a section of world-class musicians who are also very successful businessmen. They play for the others, network, share information. But other than seeing some of the big guys at the conclaves, they aren't privy to exactly who belongs. It's, like, compartmentalized. Real cloak and dagger stuff."

Interesting. "Is Dad one of the big honchos?" Stef asked. "The cloak and dagger kind?" She wanted to know if he was behind George and his takeover bid.

"I don't think so. He's kind of lost interest. He didn't even push George about getting an invitation. He asked him why he wanted to belong. I don't know why, but George is doing it despite Dad, if anything."

"Jase, is there any way you know of to get a membership list?"

Munching on his burger, Jason shook his head. "I doubt it. I'd bet a master list would be like trying to get a state secret out of the Pentagon. To the point where it might even be dangerous. I wonder if there even is one."

"Oh, you can bet there's a list. But, yeah, you're right. I was just curious."

They finished their meal with Jason bragging about his latest hot woman conquest and Stef deflecting questions about Laurel. She headed back to San Francisco on the three o'clock ferry.

All that fresh air didn't help the cold feeling Stef had in her gut. She was freezing by the time she set off for the hotel.

Chapter Eighteen

When Stef got back to the hotel she found Agnes examining the legal documents, looking for loopholes. "They're saying that selling the hotel to you at below market rates proves incompetence. It's evidence of Mrs. Holloway's inability to properly manage the trust and could place other assets of the trust in jeopardy."

"What a load of garbage." Stef took a seat across from Agnes. "That woman was so smart and astute. She was delighted that we were buying the hotel. Thrilled to see it come back to its former glory."

For a moment the only sound was Agnes's pen scratching on the pad of paper. She must have realized there was a void because she looked up. "Stefanie? Are you okay? Can I get you some aspirin or something?"

Jerked awake, Stef said, "What? Oh, must have dozed off there. Now, where were we?" She made a mental note to try to stay away from Laurel's exquisite body long enough to remain awake during the day.

Agnes closed her notebook. "I'll talk to the attorney and see if there's something else she needs. Are you sure she's qualified to argue this case? She looks young."

Stef had never seen Agnes so forceful. She thought maybe this was a glimpse of what she'd be like as a lawyer, if she ever got that far. "She's the best we could do, given that all the big-time attorneys seem to be busy. That's odd, too. George and Boynton aren't big fish. But they seem to be wielding a lot of power."

Without looking up, Agnes said, "The power is probably from the other investors. Trip would almost kiss their feet when they arrived for a meeting."

"Could you get me a list of those investors?"

"Sure. I had to prepare minutes and agendas for the board meetings, and sometimes I worked from home when I had to take care of Mom. I think I still have the list. They'd croak if they knew. It's supposed to be confidential, but none of them would deign to type out anything or be a lowly secretary." Agnes was smiling slyly and then gave Stef a hard look. "Okay, meeting's over. I'll find the list and get it to you. You look tired. Go to bed early tonight."

"Agnes, we still need to—"

"Can you tell me two things I've said to you in the past ten minutes?"

"What was the question?" Stef squeaked.

"I rest my case. It will take a day to get the information, then we can talk."

"Okay, okay. But one thing: Why do you call Boynton by the name Trip? Is that a real first name or a nickname?"

"I'm not sure." Agnes angled her head as though wracking her brains. "I don't know if I ever saw a document with his full name on it. Everything was always made out under the company name."

"Something else." Stef came back to Boynton's sloppy approach to paperwork. "The second mortgage broker didn't even request a note from the first. That seems like an amazing amount of stupidity, including my own."

"I brought that to Trip's attention and he said it wasn't necessary." Agnes had that guilty expression again. "I asked twice and he told me it wasn't my concern. So I stopped asking. That was another reason I quit, the whole thing felt slimy to me."

"Anything associated with my brother George is slimy."

Agnes studied her a moment, then snapped her fingers. "I did see his name once. He's Clayton Boynton Holloway the Third."

"Seraphina's son?" Stef could hardly take it in. Now she knew she wasn't being paranoid. George and Boynton weren't just greedy opportunists trying to swindle her, there really was some kind of conspiracy, and if she didn't come up with a plan soon, she wouldn't be the only woman facing a total loss.

❖

Laurel circled the block a few times, trying to screw up enough courage to enter the house she and Rochelle had shared for three years. Rochelle's car wasn't there, but Laurel found herself seriously considering returning to San Francisco and asking Jock to accompany her. Then she scoffed at her own cowardice. As it was, she was skulking in and sneaking her stuff out; the least she could do was manage that on her own.

She wanted to be gone from this house, this life. Whatever future she might have with Stef, she wanted it to be as clean as possible. She needed to hurry, to get back to Stef so she wouldn't worry.

She had enough to think about with the stress of getting the hotel completed. Laurel wanted to nurture her and support her. This was a new world of emotion and she wanted to absorb all the feelings and enjoy them. Ending Rochelle's influence once and for all was a big part of that process.

She used her key to open the door and called to see if Rochelle was there. She never got home after work this early. When she met only silence, she entered and took a moment to look around, doing a quick inventory of items that were hers. Other than clothes and office records, there was surprisingly little of Laurel in the house. A few pots and pans, but she didn't care about them.

She began clearing the closets of her clothes and loading her car. She carted boxes of books and records, student and personal papers. There was one antique oak filing cabinet that she loved and had purchased years before meeting Rochelle, but she couldn't lift it and had no room in her car. She'd been in the house for about an hour and was starting to get nervous to be gone.

Giving the place one more look, she removed the key from her ring to leave on the table in the hall. She was just about free.

"Hello, Laurel." Rochelle stood in the kitchen doorway, having come in through the back door.

Laurel's heart rate skyrocketed. She quickly looked for signs of drunkenness but found none of the usual swaying or slightly unfocused eyes. She didn't know if that was good or bad. Rochelle was absolutely unpredictable when she was sober. Drunk, she was uniformly nasty. Laurel decided not to wait to see which way this would be played. It was her job to say the truth and be the woman Stef thought she was.

Hoping her voice wouldn't betray her fear, she said, "Hello, Rochelle. I came by to get my things. I've left the key."

"So, that's it? You're just throwing everything we have away?"

"Anything we had has been gone for a long time and you know it. If you were so in love with me, why have all those affairs?"

Rochelle's eyes widened in surprise, then narrowed. "They meant nothing, you know that." Her voice was flat, uninflected.

"They meant you had no respect for me, or for us. They meant you thought of no one but yourself." Laurel knew her voice was shaking, but she said the words. That counted for something.

"You're out of your mind leaving me for that hotel bitch. She's using you. Probably has a dozen pathetic losers like you hanging on her every word. She has no class."

"If I'm so pathetic, why do you still want me around?" Warning sirens were going off in each lobe of her brain, but Laurel ignored them. She'd remained silent far too often. "No, it isn't that you want me or love me, it's that you don't want her to have me. Guess what? No one *has* me. Especially you."

Sneering, Rochelle took a step to a kitchen drawer and pulled out a small filleting knife. Laurel was so astonished, she stood stock-still. This had to be a joke.

"Put the knife down," she said calmly. "There are some things you can't control with bullying, and this is one of them."

Ignoring her, Rochelle taunted. "Do you really think that woman cares for you? You believed me, and I was lying through my teeth." She laughed when she realized she'd landed an emotional punch to Laurel's midsection. Taking a few steps toward Laurel, she said, "We aren't through until I say we're though."

Laurel knew she should be afraid, but her anger overrode her instinct to flee. "You are welcome to say whatever you wish to your toadies, Rochelle. But it's over. Nothing you threaten me with can change that."

Rochelle stopped, her eyes like stone. "You can't leave." Her grip on the knife tightened and Laurel balanced her weight, getting ready to dodge and run.

The door burst open, and Stef lurched inside. "Hey, get away from her! Laurel, are you okay?"

Rochelle yelled, "Tell her to leave." The knife had disappeared behind her back.

Stef was immediately by Laurel's side. Laurel looked from one to the other. Her past and her future.

Stef focused on Rochelle and got in her face. "Did you hurt her? I'll kick your ass."

At that moment Jock and Denny tumbled through the door, looking like they were ready for action.

"Hello, girls. You're just in time." Laurel was starting to enjoy this. She had a posse.

Rochelle's expression was changing moment by moment. "Who are you? Get out of my house."

Jock held out her hand and said, "I'm Jock Reynolds, and you?"

Rochelle automatically brought her hand forward and the knife clattered to the floor. She wouldn't meet Jock's hard stare. Jock kicked the knife in the direction of the kitchen.

Checking the room, Denny asked, "Anything else you want?"

Laurel reminded herself that she was entitled to take her possessions. "That oak file cabinet. Do you have room for it?"

The two women toted the cabinet out to Jock's truck. When

they came back, Jock and Denny stood by the door, arms folded across their chests, looking larger and taller than Laurel could ever remember. She caught a glimpse of Ember, wearing a sweatshirt with the hood pulled over her head, waiting outside.

Rochelle hadn't moved from her spot. "Please leave."

They looked to Laurel for direction and she nodded. Denny said, "After you, Laurel. If you'll take Stef with you, our helper can drive her car."

It dawned on Laurel that they were being careful to not identify Ember. Good move.

❖

It took three hours to drive back and unload the truck, then celebrate with pizza and beer. They stored Laurel's clothes in Stef's room, and the rest of her records and furniture in the project room. By the time they bade the last woman good night and tumbled into bed, they were exhausted but exhilarated by the events of the day.

They reached for each other to make sweet love for a time, each bringing the other to a thundering climax, and then were content to gently hold and touch. Stef was astounded at how quickly Laurel had become the most important person in the world to her. It all felt so right.

"Stef, what do you think will happen to the hotel?" Laurel murmured, resting her head on Stef's shoulder.

Stroking Laurel's soft blond hair, Stef said, "Well, assuming we figure a way out of this mess we're currently facing, I want it to be astoundingly successful. Beyond our wildest dreams. What do you think will happen to your research project?"

Laurel hugged her tightly. "I don't know just yet. But I think this hotel could become a destination for women of influence from all over the world. I have a feeling that if we can get Seraphina Holloway out of that institution, she and Irina could provide all the structure we needed to construct a fairly accurate version of the Elysium Society again. Only, with technology, it could be a worldwide effort."

Burying her nose in her lover's hair, Stef snorted, "Is that all? Well, I guess we'd better come up with a plan to get the hotel up and running."

"Does it have to be legal?"

Staring into the dark, Stef whispered, "As much as possible."

CHAPTER NINETEEN

Ember and Joey G had been loitering for a few days, taking turns keeping an eye on a guy named Glenn R. Bach, and they watched as he exited the Boho building. According to Jason, he was the president of the local San Francisco contingent of the Bohos. No one could have been more surprised than Ember, because she knew what he looked like from having met him at parties at her house when she was a child. The connection made her wonder if her father was a Bohemian, too.

These days Bach had more gray hair than she remembered and more pounds around the middle, but he still carried the same ancient leather briefcase she recalled him bragging about when she was a kid, saying how old it was and how much it held. Guys like him put everything in that kind of case. It was their purse. She just hoped he had his computer in it, too.

"Are you sure about this?" Joey G shifted his weight around nervously.

"We need the computer for the membership list. Nothing else. It's the only way I can think of to get it, but I can do this myself, if you don't want to. I mean it."

"No way." They followed Bach, keeping a safe distance. "Hey, I'm trained for this, right? I even know how to dress for the occasion. Homeless 101."

"Joey, if you get caught it'll ruin everything for you." When she'd talked it over with him, she was looking for pointers more than anything else but he'd immediately offered to make the grab himself. Said he owed her and she'd never be able to disappear into the crowd like he could.

"If I get caught, I'm just a relapsed junkie." He grinned but they both knew the risks.

"You are an awesome friend," she told him.

He cocked his head to the side. "Besides, I won't get caught because you'll provide the distraction." Tipping his head toward their mark, he said, "Look at him, not a care in the world. Probably figures no one would dare come near him this time of day in crowded streets. I can't tell you how many fixes I got off of guys like him. A lot of them put their wallets in the case, too. Don't want to ruin the line of their hand-made Italian suit."

"Are you sure Ben is okay with this?" Ember had only met Joey's boyfriend a couple of times. He seemed to like her but she doubted he would want to be involved in a crime. "What if Bach's computer is, like, tied to the Pentagon or something?" She was going forward no matter what, but she didn't want to drag her friends down with her.

"Then we'll back out. We're only looking for the list, nothing else. If it's encrypted, we might have a problem, but let's at least try."

They increased their pace as Bach turned a corner, catching up with him. Ember's heart thumped hard against her ribs. Part of their brilliant plan involved her identifying herself to Bach. She hoped he wouldn't tell her father, but she knew the chances of that were not good. She was willing to deal with the consequences. This was history and she was going to do her part. *Don't pass out or giggle insanely. Do it.*

❖

"Mr. Bach?" The man kept walking, evidently oblivious to anyone else. Forcing her voice louder, Ember hailed, "Mr. Bach, is that you?"

She ran up to him and tapped his shoulder. He whirled with

a scowl on his face, perhaps thinking he needed to fend off a panhandler. His expression turned to confusion for a moment, then the dawn of faint recognition.

"May I help you, young lady? Do I know you?" He had the handle of his briefcase in both hands as he faced her.

"Hi, Mr. Bach. I'm Ember Lanier. Remember me? Lawrence Lanier's daughter." She stuck her hand out and he hesitated only a moment before he released his grip on the case and took hers.

"My God, Ember, I haven't seen you or your father for years. How are you? You've grown into a beautiful woman."

Ember ignored the half leer he gave her when he complimented her. Why was it these old codgers thought a younger woman would be interested in them? Gross. He didn't seem to know that she'd been missing. Stung by the thought that maybe her father hadn't searched for her at all, she said, "Thanks. I thought I recognized you. It sure has been a long time." *Talk about chitchat, how inane.*

He shifted his weight to one hip, briefcase dangling from his hand, the other one in his pants pocket. He was settling in for a conversation. Where was Joey G? As if he'd heard her, a scraggly looking man whipped past them and took off at a dead run. There was another moment of confusion before Bach looked down at his empty hand and paled. "My case! He took my case."

Ember tried to look befuddled instead of delighted to take up a second or two, then she squealed, "Oh, my gawd." Although Joey G was long gone down an alley, she pointed and cried, "There he goes. Wait here, I'll get him."

But Bach was already in pursuit, and she had to run to catch up with him. The alley looked empty, but Ember knew Joey G was probably on the other side of a Dumpster against the wall midway down, waiting for her. She caught Bach's arm.

"Wait, Mr. Bach. What if he has a gun?" She was sweating, scared to death.

Bach stopped abruptly. His face was almost purple with rage and what looked like fear. "He has my wallet. My laptop. Fuck. Do you have a cell? We have to call the police." A loud thud signaled something landing in the Dumpster and Joey G scurried down the alley and disappeared around a corner. "I think he dumped the briefcase," Ember said. "I'll chase him, you look."

"No, you're right, he might be armed. Let's see if it was my bag."

They made their way down the alley, disturbing a few rats. The garbage container stank of old food and stale booze and other stuff she didn't want to think about. Peeking in, they saw the satchel in a pile of garbage toward the back of the container.

"There. Can you reach it?" Bach obviously thought Ember, with her youth and height, would retrieve it for him. She reached in and made a few ineffective swipes, but came back and tried to look female and helpless.

Shaking his head and muttering, "Women," he angrily tossed his suit jacket at her and tried to find a foothold on one of the sides of the Dumpster. His loafers slid a few times and he grunted and strained to make it up to the lip of the yellow box.

"Here, let me help." Ember gave his rear end a healthy push and he yelped as he fell headfirst into the pile of garbage. She quickly wiped the grin from her face as he popped up, spitting and swearing. "Sorry, Mr. Bach. Your bag is right behind you. Why don't you hand it to me so you can climb out?"

Without a word, he passed the satchel over and Ember put it on the ground and stood back, praying the computer would be missing when he opened it.

Bach looked like he was on the verge of a heart attack as he knelt and flipped the flap of the old leather bag open and peered inside. "My computer. It's gone." He looked around furtively, as if he expected to be struck down for this admission.

"Do you have your wallet?" Ember asked, hoping she sounded suitably horrified.

Distractedly, he pulled out his wallet and thumbed through it. "Money's gone, but everything else seems to be here."

"Well, that's good, right?" Ember sighed loudly. "You can't even walk around here in the middle of the day without getting robbed. It's just terrible. How much did he take?"

"Only about five hundred or so. He'll spend it on drugs, of

course." With a frown of confusion, he said, "But my computer, why steal that?"

Trying not to let her voice shake, Ember said, "I guess they take anything they think they can sell."

"Well, everything in it is encrypted. Good luck trying to open it." Bach rose to his feet, his suit and shoes ruined.

Ember helpfully picked a piece of wilted lettuce from his hair. "He'll probably realize that and dump it. Why don't I go look for it and you call the police? Do you have a card? If I find it I'll call you, but otherwise I have to catch a bus to class."

"All right. I'd better report this." He handed her a business card. "Thanks, Ember. Good to see you."

As soon as he was out of sight Ember forced herself to look carefully around, just in case anyone noticed. After a block or so she picked up her pace and speedwalked to Ben and Joey's warehouse. She waved at the security camera and the door lock released.

Joey called from the second floor. "Up here, Ember, Ben's working on the laptop."

She clambered up the stairs and gave Joey a hug. "We did it. What a rush. I thought I was going to lose it a few times and just start babbling."

Joey laughed, his clear blue eyes dancing. "I was watching when you shoved him into the Dumpster. I almost cheered. You rock, Ember."

Ben's deep baritone intruded in their celebration. "Don't get too excited yet. This encryption is pretty good."

Joey and Ember fell silent and peered over Ben's shoulder as his hands flew across the keyboard.

Joey squeezed his shoulder in encouragement. "You can do it, Ben. Piece of cake."

The toothpick that Ben was chewing on wobbled as he talked. "Trouble is, I might have to tap into the company software to decode this stuff. I think I can cover my tracks, but I'm not sure. We need to do this quickly so we can dump the laptop."

The next few hours were tense, filled with coffee, swearing and pacing. Ben did have to use company computers to decrypt, but eventually he was successful, much to their relief. He scrolled through the various files, finally finding the Boho membership list.

Ben said, "Wow. This reads like a Who's Who of developed countries. Man, a lot of these folks would not want anyone to find out they belonged to a secret men's club, or even knew each other. Let me quickly copy this and get out, then cover my tracks."

Joey and Ember high-fived each other behind him and Ember pulled out her cell to text Stef when the front door buzzed as someone let themselves in.

Ben's only utterance was, "Shit."

Filling the doorway was a tall woman with perfect features, auburn hair, and intense blue eyes. She stepped inside, walked up to Ben's desk, slipped her hands into the pockets of her perfectly tailored trousers, and stared at the data on the screen.

Addressing Ben, she said, "What the fuck do you think you're doing?"

❖

The limo once again wound around the streets and hills of Marin County, after crossing the Golden Gate Bridge. Stef was even more tarted up than she had been the first time, the better to complete her assignment. Mrs. C was looking dowdier and dizzier by the minute, probably preparing for her mental competence examination.

Stef hadn't intended to break Seraphina Drake Holloway out of the Heath Center, but Agnes was sure that if they tried a writ of habeas corpus, it would only give Seraphina's son time to tighten security and make sure she was so drugged she couldn't put a sentence together.

Agnes had been putting in long hours, digging her way to the truth. From searching public records, she found out that Seraphina had been placed at the Heath Retirement Center without a court order. If they could spirit her out of there and get her cleaned up, she could testify on her own behalf about what had happened to her. The plan was to file a writ as her advocates, as soon as they rescued her.

Sika had made arrangements to place her in a facility that specialized in drug detox and discretion. The bills were mounting but, so what? Stef couldn't worry about cost overruns anymore. They were making a stand, and it was all or nothing at this late stage of the game.

The second phase of their plan was to get their hands on the complete membership roster of the Bohos. Laurel had assumed the task of researching the group, enlisting Ember's help. The most powerful white men in the world had belonged or did belong, although they passed themselves off as just a fraternity of men who liked to get together with their peers and play. The ultimate good old boy network. Good old *rich* boys.

They were able to obtain the directory of the board of directors of the bank that held the first mortgage to the hotel because it was public knowledge, and Agnes located the list of private investors in the second firm. There were no common names. They were betting everything that many of them knew each other through the Bohos. The car slowed and arrived at the gate. Denny was about five minutes behind them in her own car, a beater that she'd had since college. She had to look like "the help" because she had the most important task, stealing Mrs. Holloway. She was strong enough to handle an almost comatose woman if she needed to, and she could be invisible or formidable if someone challenged her.

Everyone else had also volunteered to help, but Laurel couldn't handle the physical demands, and Jock was needed at the job site too much to risk a night in jail. Stef thought she detected more than a little friendly worry on Jock's part that Denny might be caught. Ember was on her mission to obtain the Bohemian Club membership list and Sika was down at the courthouse, filing the writ so they could obtain an order to show cause today, after they sprang Seraphina.

They had their plan timed to the minute, with very little room for screwups. Stef had talked to Mrs. Stonewell and scheduled the evaluation on a day she wouldn't be there, saying it was the only day she could bring her grandmother. Mrs. Stonewell wasn't about to give up a day off, so didn't argue.

The gate swung open and they glided in and drove to the front of the old building. Stef yanked her bodice down a little lower and said, "It's showtime. Let's do this."

The chauffeur opened the door, and Stef eyed the security camera before turning to help "Grammy" out of the limo. To the driver, an old acquaintance she could trust, she said, "Pull over there and wait for the signal."

Once Mrs. Castic was in the room with the psychologist, Stef insisted she be allowed in the security room to observe the testing. The assistant director refused at first, but Stef told her Mrs. Stonewell had okayed it and she could call her to verify. Her gamble paid off when the woman immediately gave in and escorted her to the security room. No one disturbed the director on her day off.

The guard operating the console was the same one as before and smiled at Stef's chest in welcome. Feeling like a complete idiot, Stef flounced her way to the console and looked around at all the monitors, trying to seem impressed instead of terrified. She found the outside camera screen and was relieved to see the limo had moved out of range.

Then she located the TV room and tried to find Seraphina. There she was, in the same location. Stef wondered if she had come there every day to wait for Mrs. C. Stef would have. They had purposely scheduled the evaluation at the same time as their last visit. Seraphina's tinted red hair was visible on the monitor. That was how Denny would recognize her.

Stef introduced herself to the security guard and started peppering him with questions about his important job. *Boobs, don't fail me now.* Denny's beater rolled up and the gate buzzed. She claimed she was here to pick up a Mrs. Smith to take her to her daughter's for lunch. Stef pretended to study the monitor trained on Mrs. C's testing procedure but was holding her breath, praying for Denny. If this didn't work, she wasn't sure what to do next.

The security guard asked which Mrs. Smith. He was still checking out Stef's chest.

Denny acted harried and put out. "Lemme check. Hold on." She rattled some papers and muttered, "Shit. I didn't write it down. Who you got there? I'll recognize it."

Without hesitation or care, the guard checked his manifest and said, "We have Hazel, Sarah, or Elizabeth."

Scrunching up her face for the camera, Denny said, "I think it's Sarah. I have a description so I'll know her. Look, I gotta hurry and deliver this one and go get another one up in Novato, so could you move it along? I get in trouble if I'm late."

He hit a button Stef memorized and Denny drove in. She hurried out of the car, then was inside, asking directions for the TV room. A secretary pointed and Denny commandeered a wheelchair from beside the front desk and disappeared.

Stef distracted the guard again, asking about this and that, allowing ample time for him to ogle her breasts. She was going to have to scrub them with pumice to get his eyeball energy off her. *Ew.*

Denny had made it to the TV room and was looking around. Stef slid her hand into her pocket and pressed a button that would vibrate a phone in Mrs. C's jacket. Mrs. C suddenly made startled movements, waving her hands around.

Stef pointed to the screen. "Gram's upset. Maybe I should go to her. What do you think?"

While the guard seemed to be assessing the situation, Stef watched covertly as Denny marched over to where Mrs. Holloway was sitting and lifted her into the wheelchair before whisking her out of the room. Stef buzzed Mrs. C again and she got even more animated, standing and appearing to yell at the psychologist.

Stef leaned forward, her chest almost in the guard's face and studied the screen. "Oh, God. I think she's having a fit."

"You better go calm her down," the guard sputtered, obviously torn between staring down her front and trying to see the monitors. "We can't give her a shot without a doctor's order because she's not a resident yet."

Having seen Denny load Mrs. Drake into her car, Stef said, "Okay, I'll deal with her, otherwise she'll need an ambulance. Will you help me?"

The gate button sounded because Denny was trying to leave. "Hey, lemme out. I'm ten minutes late already."

The guard distractedly slapped the button to open the gate while explaining to Stef that he couldn't leave the security room. Mrs. C continued her machinations and the psychologist was looking decidedly uncomfortable, trying to calm her down.

Stef said, "Damn. I have to get her. We'll reschedule."

The gate buzzer sounded again and Stef saw the very clear markings of a sheriff's cruiser waiting to enter. Offering one more cleavage shot, she marched out the door, heading toward the test room as fast as she could. Her freaking high heels were killing her.

The psychologist was thrilled to have the out-of-control patient taken off his hands. Mrs. C calmed down right away and clutched her purse to her chest.

"My dear child. Where have you been? You promised me lunch at the Top of the Mark."

"See what I mean?" Stef informed the man conducting the tests. "She's crazy. Write that down."

By the time they reached the front steps, the limo was there and they managed to fall into the backseat and squeal out of the gate just as it was closing after the cruiser. Hopefully, the notice would be served by the time they arrived at their rendezvous point. Three blocks later they pulled over and Denny assisted a very wobbly Seraphina into the limo, where she collapsed into Irina Castic's waiting arms. Mrs. C held her tightly and crooned words of love and safety to her.

Denny said, "Wow. What a rush. I'm shaking like a leaf. I hope Mrs. Holloway will be okay."

"Let's give them a moment," Stef said. "I think we just scored a point for team Elysium."

Denny smiled. "It's about time."

❖

"Who the hell are you?" Stef focused on the stunningly attractive woman who, along with a bashful-looking Ember and a couple of young men, had just interrupted her meeting.

The woman cast an impatient look at Ember. "Want to explain?"

"We couldn't decrypt the file," Ember mumbled. Pointing to the men, she added, "This is Joey G, the guy I told you about. And this is his partner Ben. He was helping us."

"Using the resources of my company," the auburn-haired woman inserted. "Which triggered our alarms, and here I am. Looking for one good reason why I shouldn't file a police report."

Stef kept her cool, especially since the woman standing before them hadn't offered any more information. "That still doesn't explain who you are."

Ember winced. "She's Ben's boss."

"I see." The knot in Stef's stomach had grown to a fist.

"I own the systems he used to break the encryption program."

"Oh. Well, I'm sorry if he used your resources. We'll pay you for the time." She just wanted this woman to go away, and it didn't look like that would be happening anytime soon. She hadn't budged.

"Not good enough. Do you have any idea what was on that hard drive? In addition to the list you were trying to steal?"

Stef had a terrible sinking feeling. She said a silent prayer that this woman wouldn't turn them in to the authorities. "What's it to you?" she said boldly. Her father had always taught her to try to stay on offense if she found herself in a bad situation. "I said I'd pay for the time he used."

"Still not good enough. There are some highly classified files on the hard drive. Even the complete list that you wanted has names that could get you killed. I'm not joking here. Do you get that?"

Stef deliberated for a moment, then took a gamble based on nothing more than a gleam she detected in the eyes of this compelling stranger. "I'm Stefanie Beresford and this is my hotel. The men whose names you want to protect are trying to shut us down. They don't like the idea of a women-only hotel and club."

The woman studied her for several long, intense seconds, then said, "How is it going to help you to have the membership list?"

"I need some proof of conspiracy," Stef replied. "I'm trying to match some of the names to the board of directors of the bank and private investor firm who hold our paper, so that I can prove conflict of interest. That's the truth. I don't care about anything else on that hard drive."

This time, the pause was infinitesimal and Stef understood that she was looking at a woman accustomed to making her decisions quickly. "It's going to take some time to erase the footprint on the laptop as well as the traces to Ben and to my company. Meantime no one, and I mean *no one* in this room will ever say anything about this. Using the information will be up to you, but they cannot know how you got it. Understood?"

Stef nodded. She felt almost giddy. "Who are you?" She asked again, aware that the question sounded clumsy.

"Conn Stryker." A firm hand met Stef's. "Stryker Software."

Stef returned the handshake. She wasn't sure what to say, exactly. Pathetic gratitude seemed in order, but with her team watching she opted for a display of dignity. "I appreciate your help. We're planning to leave the laptop where it can be found and returned to the owner."

Ember's idea seemed reasonable. Jock was going to turn in the computer to the police, claiming one of her crew had found it on the way to work.

Conn Stryker shook her head. "I've got the hard drive. Dump it in the bay."

"You said the other files are sensitive?" Stef said. "So you've seen them. What are you going to do with the information?"

"It's of no interest to me, at the moment." Conn reached in her pocket and placed a flash drive in front of Stef. "Here's your list. Use it wisely. Oh, and one more thing. I want to be considered for membership. I'll help you design your secure floors."

Stef cast a sharp look at Ember. How much had the young woman given away to try to save their skins? It sounded like Conn Stryker knew everything about the hotel.

The woman glanced at the laptop and moved toward the door.

After a quick, pointed look at Ben, she told Stef, "I'll be in touch, and good luck." Then she and the men were gone.

There was a group sigh as the door closed. Gazing dreamily into thin air, Ember said, "I think I'm in love."

Stef snapped her fingers, finally realizing why the name seemed familiar. "Of course, now I remember. She's the woman who was held prisoner in Pakistan last year. She's famous and she's an out lesbian. Wow."

Everyone stared at the closed door as if she were still there.

"What did she mean, 'considered for membership'?" Ember asked.

"She must think we're starting the Elysium Society again," Stef murmured. She was instantly gripped by a thrill of excitement and anticipation. "And perhaps we are."

CHAPTER TWENTY

Stef finished dressing and took the stairs to her office. It wouldn't be long before she and Laurel and Mrs. C would have to move out to let Jock start on their floor. Things were moving along quickly and the money was almost gone. First things first. They had to get rid of the threat that the Bohos and George posed. Part of that was dealing with Seraphina Drake Holloway's competency hearing. She hoped to dispose of all three items with one meeting.

When she opened the door to the waiting room she found Seraphina, Mrs. C, and Agnes huddled around the computer monitor.

"Good morning, everyone." Stef smiled. "What's up?"

Clayton Holloway III aka Trip Boynton must have ordered some heavy sedation for his mother, because without the drugs her eyes were as clear as a thirty-year-old's. From the looks on their faces, she and Mrs. C were determined to deal with any obstacle in their way.

Agnes, who seemed equally joyful, said, "I just finished a motion for summary judgment to dismiss the petition to remove Mrs. Holloway as the trustee of her husband's estate. We have her sworn affidavit setting forth all the facts that will warrant the dismissal. We'll have it ready for you in the next hour."

"That's wonderful, dear Agnes. You are my friend, and I want you to call me Sera. You, too, Stefanie. Irina has told me everything. Those old fools will not get their hands on this hotel if I have a say in it." She squeezed Mrs. C's hand and got a delighted smile as her reward.

Mrs. Holloway had no desire to pursue criminal charges against her son, no matter how much of an ass he'd been, and Stef had assured her that wouldn't be necessary. The collusion they could document was actionable on a number of levels, and she intended to take full advantage of the fact.

"Is it just me or is love in the air today?" Stef winked at Mrs. C, who blushed a rosy pink.

That was so cool, Stef thought. It was nice to imagine that she and Laurel would be just as much in love when they were eighty as they were now. That thought made Stef stumble and almost smack into her office door. She righted herself and escaped inside, smiling foolishly.

For the first time in weeks she felt as though she could breathe again. They weren't out of the woods yet, but once she'd downloaded the list from the flash drive Conn Stryker had given her, it didn't take long for her to grasp the lengths their enemies had gone to in order to secure the hotel. There were Bohemians on the board of directors for the bank that held the first mortgage, and several members were among the private investors in the group that held the second mortgage.

Working feverishly, Agnes had not only written the motion, but all the complaints they could file against them, both individually and collectively. Because of the list they had stolen, they also knew which members of the club were judges. There was no way one of their members could sit on the case without exposing his conflict of interest. Stef decided that if they had any money left when they got out of this mess, she'd figure out a way to help Agnes with school. She'd been invaluable.

For the first time since she could remember, she was looking forward to talking with her brother George. She placed a call and left a message with his assistant, requesting a meeting with him, Trip Boynton, and two others who she guessed were most involved. George and Trip would be sweating bullets at this point, because they were no doubt well aware of Seraphina Holloway's escape.

Just as she reached for the phone to let Laurel know she'd be right down, it rang, and her brother didn't bother to exchange courtesies. "Be here at two o'clock if you want Trip and the others to attend. And you'd better have a check in hand, too, you bitch. I'm in no mood to waste more time on you."

The loud click in her ear told her George had disconnected, probably by slamming the receiver down. "Nice to talk to you, too, bro."

She quickly called Laurel.

"Darling, I'm sorry. George told me the meeting is today and I need to get this over with so they can remove the lien on the property and arrange more money to finish the renovations."

"Of course. I have to leave for class soon, but I'll avoid Rochelle. I should see Ember there, too, and I'll have her walk with me to my car. Now, I want a moment-by-moment recounting of the whole thing when I see you later. Go get 'em, Stef. Remember I love you."

"Are you sure you don't want to cancel class today? You could come with me." As confident as Laurel sounded, Stef still felt uneasy.

She had successfully avoided Rochelle since the day they removed her possessions from the house, but the situation couldn't continue. They worked together, and Laurel needed to discuss publishing her work on the Elysium Society.

"No, darling, I'd feel awkward tagging along to your meeting," Laurel said. "And I'm not going to let Rochelle think I'm still intimidated by her. We'll do our things and see each other later. Perhaps a bottle of good champagne and another sleepless night will be called for."

Stef smiled. "I think we've both earned that."

"If I have time I might even go practice racquetball at the sport center," Laurel said. "I'm getting back to playing form, like I used to be when my sis and I enjoyed it, and Ember's pretty good. That's another thing I let Rochelle take away. She played dirty and I hated it. I'll call and if you're still unavailable, I'll decide then. Love you, and good luck, not that you need it."

"Love you, too. See you tonight."

Staring at the phone after they rang off, Stef told herself she was being ridiculous. She had a lot of details to attend to and only had a few hours in which to do it. Ember would be with Laurel and nothing was going to go wrong now. Rochelle was trying to avoid extra gossip, that was obvious.

Feeling marginally better, Stef started assembling her arsenal. She intended to score an important victory today, and she would make sure her private celebration with Laurel tonight would be something to be remembered.

❖

"You can tell Mr. Beresford I'll see him and his colleagues in court," Stef informed the receptionist. She, Denny, and Sika had been waiting for ten minutes and she was out of patience with the power game.

The woman who had been so uninterested stood abruptly and asked them to wait, perhaps she could slip her boss a note. In under thirty seconds they were shown in the office, where George, Trip and two others were present, looking bored.

Barely waiting for them to be seated, George snapped, "Do you have the money? Otherwise, we're scheduling a court date to take over the property, so you can start packing."

Stef returned his glare with complete calm. She took her time opening her briefcase and pulled out several packets of paper. "Fine. Be sure to line up a few extra attorneys, because we'll be filing complaints alleging fraud and misrepresentation against each of you, and every man on the boards of both the bank and this firm that are also members of the Bohemian Club. Oh, and Trip, or should I say Clayton Boynton Holloway the Third? Your mother sends her regards. This is for you."

Stef slid a particularly thick sheaf of paper to him. To the group she announced, "His mother, Seraphina Drake Holloway, is filing a motion for summary judgment. Attached to it is a copy of her sworn affidavit setting forth the facts."

They stared at her as if she had spoken in a rare foreign language.

"Feel free to peruse the complaints," Stef invited them. "Obviously you'll all need to confer with your attorneys."

Fifteen minutes later the men looked up with shocked expressions. First at her and then at each other. James Pickle, president of the bank where their first mortgage was held and a major honcho in the Bohos, spoke first.

"Have you filed these?"

His already florid complexion was coloring even more and Stef briefly hoped he was on blood pressure medication. All that rich food and power must be curdling in his fat gut. George pointed a finger at her, his jaw rigid with fury. He opened his mouth only to have Pickle command, "Silence!"

George slammed his mouth closed so quickly Stef heard his teeth clatter. Looking around she paused one more second, to prolong the moment, then said, "No." She heard their collective breath let go with a whoosh. "As you no doubt realize, Trip here, by drugging his mother and having her held in a facility against her wishes, opens himself to criminal charges. As does anyone else who conspired to help him."

The look James Pickle gave Trip was frightening. "You told us your mother had Alzheimer's. You had her held against her will? Are you insane?"

Sputtering, Trip said, "But you said—"

"I said nothing, Mr. Holloway, nothing."

Trip's eyes bulged and his Adam's apple bobbed, but he remained silent.

"Seraphina Drake Holloway has no wish to see her only child in prison, gentlemen. If he voluntarily withdraws the petition to have her declared unfit to administer the family trust, this all goes away. Her husband left her in charge because of his son's lack of good judgment, as he has more than demonstrated to you."

Pickle immediately said, "I'll see that the petition is withdrawn before end of business tomorrow, Ms. Beresford."

Both George and Trip started to protest but stopped when

Charles Teller, the member who had so far not spoken one word, merely lifted a finger off the table. Stef was impressed.

She continued, "Now, in reference to the complaints—some with multiple counts—we're seeking damages, punitive damages, an injunction to stop foreclosure on the hotel against both the lending institutions and the individuals involved, and we plan to report these irregularities to federal regulating agencies as well. We charge conflict of interest. Comments?" She prayed that Agnes's research and writing had been good enough. They'd had to let go of their only attorney because they had no money, and Agnes seemed better anyway. If they didn't go along with this, they would have to try to find another attorney, and there was no money to do that.

Pickle and Teller looked at each other for perhaps two seconds, evidently long enough to reach a decision. Pickle said, "Most judges would throw out the charges as spurious. There isn't one member of the bank's board who is also on the private investor board."

"I disagree, but I'm willing to test that, as long as any judge trying the case is not also a member of the Bohos. And we'll be checking."

Another long silence ensued.

Teller spoke for the first time. "And if we rescind the foreclosure?"

Keeping her face neutral, and not daring to look at either Denny or Sika, Stef replied, "Then we won't file these charges. All of the papers, you have your copies, will be held in a secure place and never used. Unless you decide to come after the hotel again, of course."

"How can we be sure you'll keep your agreement?"

"Mr. Pickle, Mr. Teller, you will have my word."

Pickle leaned back and folded his arms across his chest. "Out of curiosity, how did you get your hands on the Bohemian Club membership list?"

Stef smiled politely and gave an evasive reply. "Nothing is confidential anymore, gentlemen. Don't you just love the Internet?"

Pickle gave her a thin smile. "I have a question. How do you propose to finish the hotel? You'll need more funding, and although your mortgages are safe as long as you make your payments, there isn't a lending institution in this country who will give you more. I can guarantee that."

Stef kept her gaze and her tone steady. She was a Beresford, after all. "Then it isn't your concern, is it?"

His mouth formed a straight line. "You wanted the hotel just for women, then perhaps it can be funded just by women. You could have a bake sale."

George snickered.

Pickle said, "Shut up." George did.

"Perhaps we will." Stef rose and the others followed. "Gentlemen." Then, "George."

Stef held the door for Sika and Denny and was almost through it when Teller spoke once more. "Wellington was right, you are the smartest one in your family."

Whirling on him, Stef asked, "He knew about this?" Her father was against her buying the hotel, but this?

Teller regarded her thoughtfully. "No. I just asked him about you and that's what he told me. I thought you'd want to know." His gaze was impenetrable.

Stunned, she could only manage, "Good day."

❖

Laurel finished class and checked her cell phone. She had one voicemail. She'd been in such a hurry to get to school on time she hadn't noticed the message. It was from Ember, asking if she was still going to cancel class, because Jock needed her to work. That explained her absence.

Gathering her notes, Laurel thought about calling Stef but didn't want to disturb her focus. The meeting was probably still underway. She was sorry Ember couldn't join her for a game of racquetball, but there was no reason to miss the practice she was looking forward to. She could put in an hour and still be home to celebrate with Stef. It was wonderful to have the love of the game back in her life.

Walking across campus to the gym, she marveled at the new pronouns and nouns in her life. Their *home*, two small rooms that were only adequate at best. Yet she thought of it as home in a way that she had never experienced before. She only lived in Rochelle's house, and she paid half the mortgage. Even the spare bedroom never felt like hers. Living with Stef had been completely different from the first night. Although they hadn't talked about what would happen when they had to vacate to allow for the remodel, she knew that whatever they decided, it would work out best for them.

The certainty of that surprised her. She'd always had so many fears, needed reassurance, almost needing to belong to someone. That was probably the reason she'd fallen for Rochelle. She mistook control and possession for safety and solidity. She knew now that the only way to true safety lay within her.

She was grinning by the time she had changed clothes and grabbed her eye guards, racquet and balls, wallet, and cell phone. These new courts were great and she enjoyed watching others play as well as playing on them. The back walls were shatterproof glass and observers could look down from above, too. She waved to some students who were leaving, and put her things down to do some stretches before entering the play area. Walking to her court, she jumped when a ball slammed loudly into the back wall of one of the courts she was passing. Checking out the action, she froze when she saw Rochelle on the other side of the glass, smiling at her.

Breathe, don't let her scare you away. Straightening, she realized that she was almost as tall as Rochelle. Odd, she'd always thought Rochelle was much taller. She nodded neutrally and Rochelle cocked her head in question, then swept her hand to indicate she was inviting Laurel to play. Invite was not the right word. Challenge. That was the word.

Laurel studied her impassively. She looked bloated and unhealthy and this was not new. Rochelle had always won by cheating and intimidation, so much so that Laurel had refused to play with her. She shouldn't play now, but something in her ex's insolent expression, in the way that she expected Laurel to run away yet again, propelled her through the door.

Surprise evident on her face, Rochelle said, "My, my, look who's not afraid to play racquetball. Did you finally grow a spine?"

"Can you say anything without trying to bait someone? You invited, I'm accepting. Any other questions?" She strode over to the wallet-lock on the wall and stored her phone, keys, and money. "Your serve."

With an exaggerated shrug, Rochelle said, "Your funeral," and waited for Laurel to get ready. She served a rocket that was not only in bounds but managed to just miss Laurel's head. Smirking, she said, "Gotta be faster than that, m'dear."

The rest of the game was similar, with Laurel barely able to return service, let alone get a serve in. Game: Rochelle.

"Want to quit? This is usually where you decide you don't like this game and go off to lick your wounds."

Laurel was quiet for a moment, seething. Seething instead of quaking. Buoyed by her anger, she whirled on Rochelle. "My serve."

With no effort to disguise her disdain, Rochelle ambled to the back of the court to take her place and receive.

At the service line, Laurel bounced the ball a few times, then swung and hit a winner that sent Rochelle into the wall to try and stop herself after she whiffed the return.

Recovering, Rochelle patronized her with, "Not bad. But that's all you're getting."

The battle was on, with each point being hard-won. When the second game was tied at eight, with sweat trickling between her breasts, Laurel noticed that they'd attracted a crowd. A strangely silent crowd, almost as if they were holding their collective breath.

Laurel won the second game at 15-12, and a cheer erupted, then the crowd fell silent when Rochelle glared at them. Whipping to face Laurel, she accused, "You've been practicing. What, does your rich bitch play?"

Meeting her glare steadily, Laurel said, "No, I've been playing. It helped me recover from the beating you gave me."

Stepping menacingly toward her, Rochelle snarled, "Keep your voice down."

"What's the matter, Rochelle? Afraid of a little truth? Relax, there are no microphones in here and I wasn't shouting, so unless someone can read lips, you're safe. But here's another truth. If you ever try to hurt me again, you'll regret it. Care to serve for the match?"

Rochelle's face was mottled with anger as she grabbed the ball. She stepped up to the service line and promptly double-faulted because she was so erratic, trying to hit Laurel more than to score a point. Laurel merely sidestepped the first serve and caught the next after the second bounce.

"Temper, temper. You really must learn to control yourself. My serve." Laurel couldn't help the teasing singsong tone of her voice, especially when she saw Rochelle's face darken even more.

She nailed three points in a row before Rochelle was able to return and then win service after a long and heated rally. As she walked to the back of the court so Rochelle could serve she noticed that there were more onlookers. Just as she turned, the ball came sailing past her.

"My point." Rochelle was chasing the errant ball down to get ready for her next serve.

"I wasn't set, Rochelle. You could see that." So, this is how it would be. Rochelle couldn't stand to lose, and if the score wasn't in her favor she often resorted to cheating.

"Pay attention next time." Rochelle served again and struck a clean winner.

The next one Laurel was able to return and Rochelle couldn't reach it. "Side out. My turn."

The score seesawed up to a tie at nine. The first one to score eleven would win the match.

Rochelle served hard and it bounced, then ricocheted off a side wall. Laurel anticipated the ball and slammed it back, sending Rochelle skidding to try and reach it and she landed on her ass when she missed. Some clapping from the gallery ensued.

She screamed, "Serve again. I hit a wet spot and slipped." She was panting and sweating profusely. One of the onlookers booed.

Laurel walked up and looked at the spot she said she'd slipped on. It appeared fine. Maybe she dried it with her butt. She shrugged and again went to the service line, hitting a clear winner. Rochelle shot her a murderous glare and stood to receive the ball. Laurel bounced it a few times and served hard, but Rochelle was able crush the return so that it caromed off of two walls before bouncing. Laurel returned the ball the only way she could, bringing the racquet behind her back and between her legs. She won the point and the match.

As whoops erupted from the crowd, Rochelle stood three feet from her, chest heaving and bitterness pouring out of her mouth. "You cheated."

"No, I don't play the way you do, Rochelle. I won, that's all. It's just a game."

"So, are you going back to your *owner*? To be her little play toy?"

The words stung, but only because of Laurel's realization that she had allowed herself to be dominated by this pathetic woman.

"No one owns me, Rochelle. She knows that and respects it. I am in love with her, forever, I hope. So, yes, I'm going to her. My choice, my life."

The hostility and rage that Rochelle had barely controlled erupted and Rochelle screamed, "Then take this with you!" She used her racquet and slapped the dense rubber ball as hard as she could, aimed straight at Laurel's face.

CHAPTER TWENTY-ONE

By the time Stef, Denny, Jock, and Ember approached the campus sports facility, Stef had tried many times to reach Laurel. She'd been stunned to find Ember at the hotel when she got back after the bloodless coup that had neutered her brother and his buddies. When Laurel didn't show up or answer her cell phone, she decided not to wait.

A tremor shook her spine as they turned into the parking lot and saw flashing lights. An ambulance and police cruisers were parked close to the front doors. Medics were guiding a gurney to the back of the vehicle. The occupant was waving her arms around and screaming for a doctor.

Stef fought her way through the crowd and skidded to a halt by the gurney to see Rochelle with an ice pack on her nose and her clothes covered in blood.

"Oh, my God." Her heart stopped and she frantically looked around for Laurel.

Ember touched her arm and Stef whirled on her, panic consuming her. "Where is she? I can't see her."

"There." Ember pointed to the police cruiser. "In the backseat. She's...her head is bandaged."

Shouting, "Laurel!" Stef rushed to the car and within seconds they were in each other's arms, tears streaming down their faces.

"Are you okay? I'm going to knock that bitch from here to..." When she was able to look into Laurel's eyes, she saw joy there.

"You don't have to, my love, I've already taken care of that." Laurel winked at her. Winked!

Stef asked, "What happened?"

Ember had hustled up to them and answered on Laurel's behalf. "She beat the wicked witch, and everyone's talking about it. Dr. Jacobs tried to attack her when she won at racquetball and ended up hurting herself. That is so cool."

Stef held Laurel at arm's length and said, "You beat her at racquetball? Really?"

Nodding, Laurel said, "Yup. And she got so upset she tried to serve the ball to my face." When she saw Stef react she quickly said, "I didn't have time to think, I must have instinctively flipped my racquet in front of my face and the ball hit the racquet. It rebounded into Rochelle's nose and I think she broke it. Talk about instant karma."

"But how did you get the bandage on your forehead?" Stef didn't care about Rochelle, she wanted to know about Laurel.

"I guess the recoil of the racquet when the ball hit it nailed me. It all happened so fast, then chaos ensued, as it were."

Stef stared at Laurel for a second, then smiled. "You're enjoying this. Congratulations. The wicked witch is dead."

"Or at least out of my life." Laurel was actually bouncing on the balls of her feet.

"What about school? She's still department chair."

"I'll think about that later. Let me finish here and then will you please take me home? We have all the time in the world to plan our next move."

Despite all the commotion, Laurel had managed to send a message that landed directly in Stef's heart and made the world a brighter place. They had all the time in the world.

An hour later they were back at the hotel, and much to Laurel's surprise, her friends had held up their celebration until she could be present. Her heart flooded with appreciation at that knowledge.

Denny and Jock took the champagne and sparkling cider and filled the delicate flutes that Sika and Mrs. C had set out.

Sika said, "To courage, then and now."

They all had a sip and sat down and were chatting excitedly when Seraphina Drake Holloway stood and held her glass up, tapping it gently.

In a voice that belied her age, she said, "Years ago, a member of the Elysium Society gave us what was to become a toast we often used. I think it is appropriate tonight. To celebrate all of you. Your courage, your history, and your future."

All stood and held their glasses to the air and waited.

"'When we do the best that we can, we never know what miracle is wrought in our life, or in the life of another.' Here is to the miracle of the women that have gone before us, and the miracles we have yet to perform for others. Here is to the future."

They drank and were silent. After a moment, Laurel said, "I know that quote. It's from Helen Keller. Was she a…"

Sika raised her glass again and said, "To the Elysium Society, as it rises again."

❖

Back in their room, Laurel and Stef were quiet, each absorbing the events of the day. Laurel glanced at Stef, so deep in thought, and went to her.

"Penny for your thoughts." She took Stef in her arms.

Cocking her head, Stef said, "Pre nineteen eighty or post?"

"Hmm?"

"Well, there was more copper in them pre nineteen eighty and so they weighed more and are worth more today, you know."

"Okay…pre nineteen eighty." Laurel wondered where this was going.

"Well, I was wondering what your reaction to your time with Rochelle was. I mean, I was hoping that…"

"Do you know that Rochelle once told me that her partner should tell her she's right, no matter what she says? And I didn't question that, I held my tongue."

Eyes round, Stef said, "Wow. That woman is such a…"

Hugging her tightly, Laurel said, "That is so nice of you to take my side and I love you for it. But *I* was wrong for not running as fast as I could out the door. She told me exactly the kind of person she was, and I was so insecure I couldn't leave her. Knowing that, how can you respect me?"

Stef could only answer from her heart. "Maybe I'm the same kind of person as Rochelle. I'm hot-tempered and always looking for betrayal. I can be arrogant, self-centered, egotistical…" A finger gently placed on her lips followed by a soft kiss shushed her.

"Not to mention redundant." Laurel deepened the kiss.

Pulling a millimeter away, Stef murmured, "That, too."

"For the record, Stef, you are nothing like Rochelle. You are strong and kind and sweet and honest, and I love you." A few more heated kisses and Laurel managed, "I'm a mess and I need a shower. I'd invite you in but it's so cramped I'm afraid we'd get stuck and the call for help would be really embarrassing. What about you?"

"I'll get in after you. All that stark terror has left me in similar shape."

Laurel backed away and squeezed Stef's hands. "I won't take long, and don't you either." She was stripping on her way to the bathroom and naked by the time she stood in the door, smiling seductively. "Be right back."

Stef wondered if perhaps she was in a dream, a fantasy of what love could be like if it was real. She drifted into the bedroom and removed her clothes, slipping into a short terry robe. She took the few steps to the bathroom door and pushed it open.

Laurel was easily visible through the clear shower curtain. She was soaping her body and Stef could only admire every move. After a moment, Laurel realized she was there and smiled, resoaping her breasts and using slow circular movements to rub them, then lightly pinch her nipples, her eyes never leaving Stef.

Stef stood transfixed as Laurel rinsed, then squeezed some gel in her hands and addressed her center, running the length of her sex and pulling slightly, until Stef could see her swollen clit, and she licked her lips, longing to taste. She let the front of her robe fall open and Laurel's eyes darkened with passion.

"God, Stef, come here." She separated her labia and let the water rush to cleanse the soap, moaning at the sensation.

Stef moved to be by her side, standing just outside of the enclosure. She pulled back the curtain and reached, feeling Laurel's need, all of the blood in her body rushing to the same place as Laurel's. She stroked Laurel as Laurel slowly sank to her knees.

Clinging to her, Laurel breathed, "Don't stop, darling, don't stop."

Stef concentrated on the sensation of her fingertips, the way she could feel every change in Laurel's body. She held her when she curled back, knowing her orgasm was imminent, and then shuddered as the spasms overtook her love as she came and it flowed over her hand. The hard pulsing in her clitoris told her she was close to her own orgasm.

Laurel said urgently, "Stand up, stand up."

Stef struggled to her feet and Laurel wrapped her arms around her waist and buried her face in her lover's core, sucking and stroking with her tongue until she felt Stef explode into a universe that was entirely their own.

When Stef came to her senses Laurel had switched positions on her and was outside the shower, dripping wet, washing her. She was leaning against the wall but was able to stand and still Laurel's hand as she began to address her throbbing center.

"Get dried off or you'll catch cold. I'll meet you in bed in five minutes." One corner of Laurel's mouth quirked up and she nodded, grabbing a towel and drying herself as Stef watched. She could barely wash her clit without coming again.

Stef turned off the faucets and grinned when a dry towel was tossed in her direction. She took her time, and when she crawled into bed next to Laurel, she turned off the lamp beside the bed and took Laurel in her arms. "Every time we're together it's different. It's always stronger, it always makes me love you more. But I worry."

Laurel was still, sensing something important was happening. "What about, darling? What worries you?"

"I think that I'll hurt you, that you'll think I'm like…that woman. That I'll be too rough with you. You're such a…so much a lady."

Laurel let out a sigh. "So that's why you always let me set the pace of our lovemaking, because you don't want to hurt me or remind me of *her*." She was grateful to Stef for talking about it.

"Yes. My feelings are so strong, so frighteningly strong sometimes. I…worry."

Reaching up to turn the lamp back on, Laurel said, "Darling, look at me."

Stef gazed at her, raw emotion there for her to see.

"I'm tougher than I look. I want you to take me any way you want me. And if you don't fuck my brains out for the rest of the night, you'll disappoint me. Because I definitely have plans for you."

When Laurel smiled slyly and reached for the lamp switch, Stef stopped her. "No, I want to see you." She rolled her on her back and pulled the covers off.

Laurel bent her knees and opened her legs wide. "Take me."

And Stef did, all night long.

CHAPTER TWENTY-TWO

One month later there was a tea at Seraphina's home in Pacific Heights. Stef and Laurel had moved into one of the many suites in the grand old mansion. Another two rooms held all of the material recovered from the hotel and the records that Irina Castic had secreted in her rooms for over forty years.

Stef felt like they were living in a fantasy with so many priceless antiques and modern touches, too. An elevator had been installed at some point, probably when Seraphina's husband had been ill. It wasn't used much because both of the older residents preferred the exercise of the stairs, but was kept in working order.

The work of the hotel had been halted two days before, there simply was no more money. Stef and the others were working on obtaining private funding from wealthy patrons but had found many doors closed to them. As promised, the Bohemians' tentacles were far reaching.

Seraphina and Irina had planned the tea, and Sika made sure all were in attendance from the hotel. Sika had been virtually absent from the hotel for the past month, over at the mansion working with Carolyn Flemons, the designer. She was in the hotel only to meet her friend from West Marin and plan the new kitchen. Stef felt so guilty about not having the money to realize Sika's dreams that she found herself avoiding that part of the hotel when Sika was there.

She kept herself busy making phone calls and running budget numbers, and when that became too tedious, joining Jock, Denny, and her crew and doing manual labor. The bones of the building were solid and set. Now all they needed was a few million more to complete rooms, and she had no idea how that would happen. Seraphina said if she hadn't already sold the property she'd make a gift of it to them, but it was out of her hands. Even selling more of her holdings to help would have Trip and his cronies on her all over again.

Irina kept patting her hand and told her not to worry, but Stef couldn't stand the insecurity. That morning she'd decided to contact her father and ask for financing help. As soon as this gathering was finished, she'd make the call. She'd told her partners, and Sika had insisted she wait until after the tea party. Stef was dreading the moment she would have to admit her father was right—she couldn't make it on her own.

Laurel had sent a letter to the university saying that she would complete her teaching obligations for the term and then was going on an extended leave. If they chose not to accept that, she would resign. A letter accepting her leave and signed by the university president as well as Rochelle Jacobs had been sent within the week. Evidently Rochelle was going to remain department chair, but the university was keeping tabs on her and was not going to rock the boat.

Laurel spent her days at the mansion with her precious find and she was in heaven, but she was also faced with a conundrum. Publishing her findings, especially about the Elysium Society, would no doubt make her career. But revealing the society's existence placed its future at risk and the accomplishments of its members in question. Revealing the names of some of its famous and illustrious members who were long dead would create repercussions over which she had no control.

The media could take the information and reduce all of the good works of these women into a quest for lesbian lust. The Bohos would most certainly do all they could to destroy their reputations, and their members included publishers and owners of huge media conglomerates. That knowledge helped her make her decision. The Elysium Society would stay secret.

When she and Stef finally fell into bed at night, they barely were awake long enough to make sure they were sharing the right bed with the right person. But the early mornings were very reassuring and started the day just right. It was good to be in love.

Stef watched the women file in and help themselves to sandwiches, tea, and coffee. Jock had even gone home and cleaned up, and Agnes had Lefty looking quite presentable, too. Agnes had become an invaluable executive assistant. Although Stef had yet to hear the sound of Lefty's voice, she knew that Jock trusted her, and that was good enough.

The doorbell rang again and Sika opened it to a lovely woman of about her age, whom she greeted warmly with a hug. Stef recognized her as the designer, Carolyn Flemons. She'd been so busy that other than a perfunctory introduction, she'd left her to Sika. It didn't matter that she'd forgone her fee, really, because even if her designs were award winning, eventually they would need to be paid for. Another brick on the load she carried. Carolyn introduced her daughter, Keri, and although she said the other woman, Dana, was her daughter, too, there was no familial resemblance and it looked very much like Keri and Dana were together.

Right behind them were some other women she didn't recognize, perhaps friends of Sera or Irina. It looked like they were bringing their daughters and/or granddaughters. *My, this really is a tea party.*

One face she did recognize belonged to the woman who had stormed her office that day and given them the membership list of the Bohos. Conn Stryker was accompanied by a lovely woman, and they were obviously a couple. Stef could feel their connection from across the room. Odd, why here and why now? Several more couples entered, too. She recognized Sika's friend who was helping design the kitchen, and the woman who was obviously her partner, known worldwide as a top journalist.

The last guest to arrive walked in quietly, came over to Laurel, and hugged her. Kate Hoffman looked like Laurel but definitely had the star quality about her. Stef stood and shook her hand politely, hoping Kate would like her and tell Laurel she approved. Kate grinned and hugged them both warmly and whispered something in her sister's ear. She then sat nearby and chatted with some of the other guests. Stef tried to catch Laurel's eye but couldn't.

Taking another look at all of the women around the room, she could feel a building excitement. Of all the ages, shapes, and sizes, the one thing that they seemed to have in common was a keen intelligence in their eyes. By the time the last guests arrived, Stef was sitting forward, sensing something more than tea would be happening.

Seraphina stood with the aid of a beautiful hand-carved cane and greeted everyone. She had only to clear her throat to silence the low-level hum in the room. "Today is a marvelous day in my life, one that I have waited and wished for, for over forty years. Today is the day that the Elysium Society rises from the ashes and begins again."

Stef felt Laurel beside her on the rolled arm of the chair, squeezing her shoulder. The current in the room almost crackled. Laurel had a tablet of paper and was taking notes.

"Our roots extend into the past, we aren't sure exactly how far. At least to the Civil War period, when we were active in the underground railway, supporting and hiding runaway slaves and finding jobs and training for them in their new lives. We had members who lived in Paris in the twenties and were part of the new intelligentsia. Our concerns were for women and the advancement of their rights and the rights of others. And always, always our purpose was secret. As far-flung as our membership was, the heart eventually rested here, in San Francisco, dating back before the great earthquake and fire in 1906. My contribution was the hotel, and although circumstances dictated that I marry, I was able to maintain control of it. Until we were discovered." Seraphina reached for Irina's hand and seemed buoyed.

"My husband, as much of a philanderer as he was, could not tolerate my love for Irina Castic. We fell in love before I had to marry him, and although I tried desperately to keep my vows, I could not bear to be apart from her. Someone discovered our relationship, I suspect my son. Trip was young but must have felt jealous of my obvious love of her and hers for me. More than that, whatever he said must have alerted Clayton that there was more going on at the hotel than just ladies having high tea and discussing books. Perhaps one of the guests of the hotel had been denied membership in the Society and alerted her husband out of spite. We might not ever know." Her voice trembled and her eyes shone as she remembered the betrayal.

"He seized control of the hotel, which was his legal right as my husband. He purposefully dismantled it, allowed it to turn into what it remained for all that time. The one condition he agreed to was to allow Irina, my lover, to live there. He only agreed to that to prevent a scandal and to get me to agree to never have contact with her again. He swore that if I did, he would not only evict her from the hotel, he would have her sent back to Serbia, where she most certainly would perish in jail. I had no choice, I had to protect her." Tears rolled down her cheeks, and Stef wiped her own eyes.

"The one thing he couldn't control was the fact that his son was too much like him. After many heated arguments, and many capricious and irresponsible episodes with Clayton the Third, he agreed to let me be executor of the estate. On his deathbed, he asked that I sell the hotel to the Bohemian Club.

"I will tell each and every one of you that I had no trouble ignoring that request. The hotel, and all of the holdings that he had not squandered, were mine. I was delighted when the opportunity to restore the hotel to women arose. Before I could offer more support, before I could once again unite with my beloved Irina, my son usurped me and I was incarcerated."

A pin dropping would have made every woman in the room jump. All were riveted to Seraphina Drake. She took the water that Sika offered and sipped thoughtfully, her hand trembling slightly.

"I must thank all of you for not only freeing me from that dreadful place, but for taking care of my Irina. We wish to begin the Elysium Society anew, with the women in this room. As you know, the Society is by invitation only, but the dues are commensurate with your ability to pay. It is character and dedication we seek, not wealth and exclusivity. This isn't a social club, it is an organization dedicated to women and the issues that affect us worldwide. And now I'm turning this over to Sika Phelps, who, with Laurel Hoffman, has developed the first membership list of the New Elysium."

Stef whipped her head around to look at Laurel, wondering why Laurel hadn't told her. But she thought of their busy lives over the past month and understood. Laurel was a natural choice, of course. Her researching capability and knowledge of the society would be invaluable assistance to Sika, Seraphina, and Irina. She hoped her eyes conveyed that she was proud of her.

A sinking feeling overcame her when she thought of what she had to report: that they couldn't go forward without further financing, that she would need to ask her father to help. Her stomach lurched at what she saw as failing not only her business partners and the women in this room, but giving up her dream of independence from her family.

Sika's voice, strong and calm, interrupted her thoughts. "There are several points of business to attend to. First, each one of you has been asked to pay an initiation fee that you will choose.

"Please stand and introduce yourself and tell us about your background and talents, education, or particular skills you wish to include in our master list of resources. You might be called upon to help with particular projects, based on this list. After you introduce yourself, give your envelope to Stefanie Beresford. Our first order of business, our first project, is to secure our home, the Hotel Liaison."

Laurel had to elbow Stef to snap her out of her daze as women started handing envelopes to her. Carolyn Flemons was first and a check for $100,000 was enclosed, along with a note canceling her design fee.

Ember looked her hot and babydyke-cute self when she stood and pledged whatever skills she developed in the future and volunteer labor when it was needed. Her envelope contained one hundred dollars in cash.

And so it went. Doctors, lawyers, scientists, technology experts, CEOs, chefs, students, politicians, executive assistants, actresses, plumbers, photographers, authors, artists, and so on. All had high levels of expertise in various subjects and connections to other women all over the world. The average check was similar to Carolyn Flemons's. But Conn Stryker and her partner, Leigh Grove, provided a check for one million dollars, along with all the planning and security equipment for the top two floors of the hotel. There was another stack of envelopes from those unable to attend. Stef's eyes must have been popping because there were a few chuckles from the audience. Kate Hoffman slipped Laurel a check that made Laurel give her a huge hug.

The top floors were designated to become a private club to house the Elysium Society, comprising some luxurious hotel rooms, meeting rooms, and a tech center. All with state-of-the-art security. Each and every service would be provided by women for women. Although there might be some rooms in the lower floors that would rent to men, the men would be unable to gain entrance to the Club.

Tears flowed freely down Stef's face as she realized what this meant. They would not only be able to finish the hotel the way it had been envisioned, they would be able to meet their mortgage payments each month without worry.

Irina Castic stood before her with her envelope in her hands. It was larger and thicker than the others. She grinned mischievously.

"Irina, you are automatically a lifetime member of the society, you know that. You have been…grandmothered in." Stef smiled to reassure her friend that she didn't have to feel she owed anything.

"Ah. How nice. But this is for you and Sika and Denny. And Laurel, of course."

Careful not to tear the envelope, Stef opened it and took out a fairly thick file of paper. She read and then reread the documents. "This can't be true. Irina? How could this be true?"

Denny piped up with, "Stefanie Beresford, if you don't tell us what you're looking at, I'm gonna get after you." From the background noise, Denny wasn't the only one.

"It is the first and second deed to the hotel. Paid in full. Our debt has been retired."

The cheer that went up from the members was so loud, no one could hear Stef asking Irina a question. When they calmed down, she repeated it.

"How did you do this? The debt is over twenty million dollars. Are these papers real?" She hated to insult Irina, but really, did she win the lottery? This was nothing to joke about.

"Oh, my dear, I assure you they are real. My mother country finally decided to join the twenty-first century and return the land stolen from my family by the Nazis and then the Communists. As it turns out, my property is worth quite a bit, so I sold some parcels and paid off the hotel." Turning around to face the others, she said, "The hotel is ours. No one can take it from us again. Our work can proceed unencumbered by outside detractors."

Stef was out of her chair and hugging Irina, Denny, Sika, and anyone she could get her hands on, ending with Laurel. "Did you know?"

"I knew something was going on and I helped Sika with the list, but I couldn't have imagined this. I think Ember might have had some idea. She helped Irina file the papers."

"That's why the people at the nursing home fell all over themselves trying to sign Irina up. I always wondered how she pulled that off. Wow."

Stef sat heavily on her chair and closed her eyes. She felt Laurel beside her and smiled. Surrounded by old friends and new, she started to absorb the full meaning of family. She was exactly where she belonged, with people who believed in her, and a partner who loved her. And the real work of building their future was just beginning.

As the afternoon drew to a close, she led Laurel to the small garden that consisted of well-established roses, canopies of flowering vines, and benches that brought privacy even in the midst of this beautiful city. They sat on a bench and stared at the bay and the Golden Gate Bridge before them. Fog was creeping over the Marin Headlands and through the towers of the bridge, giving everything around them a magical feel.

Stef slid her arm over Laurel's shoulder and kissed her slowly. "It's all coming true, Laurel. Every bit of it. Will you share it with me?"

Laurel leaned back and took in all of Stefanie Beresford. "My sister approves of you. She told me she's jealous because it looks like I've finally found the one. She's right. I'll share every bit of it with you, my love. Every minute. I love you."

"I love you, too," Stef said. "You complete my dreams, do you know that?"

Laurel held her tightly, emotions brimming. "And you've built brand-new dreams for me."

They kissed again and held hands, laying silent claim to one another and to the future they would build together. Stef smiled in contentment.

Their future. She couldn't wait.

About the Author

JLee Meyer utilizes her background in psychology and speech pathology in her work as an international communication consultant. Spending hours in airports, planes, and hotel rooms allows her the opportunity to pursue two of her favorite passions: reading and writing lesbian fiction. JLee's hobbies are photography, hiking, tennis, and skiing but she hasn't had time for them recently. Writing is her passion, and learning this new craft has been a joy. She and her partner CC live in Northern California with their two dogs. *Hotel Liaison* is her fourth novel.

Visit JLee at www.myspace.com/jleemeyer, or at her Web site, jleemeyer.com, or e-mail her at jlee@jleemeyer.com. You can also find her at www.boldstrokesbooks.com.

Books Available From Bold Strokes Books

Finding Home by Georgia Beers. Take two polar-opposite women with an attraction for one another they're trying desperately to ignore, throw in a far-too-observant dog, and then sit back and enjoy the romance. (978-1-60282-019-7)

Word of Honor by Radclyffe. All Secret Service Agent Cameron Roberts and First Daughter Blair Powell want is a small intimate wedding, but the paparazzi and a domestic terrorist have other plans. (978-1-60282-018-0)

Hotel Liaison by JLee Meyer. Two women searching through a secret past discover that their brief hotel liaison is only the beginning. Will they risk their careers—and their hearts—to follow through on their desires? (978-1-60282-017-3)

Love on Location by Lisa Girolami. Hollywood film producer Kate Nyland and artist Dawn Brock discover that love doesn't always follow the script. (978-1-60282-016-6)

Edge of Darkness by Jove Belle. Investigator Diana Collins charges at life with an irreverent comment and a right hook, but even those may not protect her heart from a charming villain. (978-1-60282-015-9)

Thirteen Hours by Meghan O'Brien. Workaholic Dana Watts's life takes a sudden turn when an unexpected interruption arrives in the form of the most beautiful breasts she has ever seen—stripper Laurel Stanley's. (978-1-60282-014-2)

In Deep Waters 2 by Radclyffe and Karin Kallmaker. All bets are off when two award winning-authors deal the cards of love and passion... and every hand is a winner. (978-1-60282-013-5)

Pink by Jennifer Harris. An irrepressible heroine frolics, frets, and navigates through the "what ifs" of her life: all the unexpected turns of fortune, fame, and karma. (978-1-60282-043-2)

Deal with the Devil by Ali Vali. New Orleans crime boss Cain Casey brings her fury down on the men who threatened her family, and blood and bullets fly. (978-1-60282-012-8)

Naked Heart by Jennifer Fulton. When a sexy ex-CIA agent sets out to seduce and entrap a powerful CEO, there's more to this plan than meets the eye…or the flogger. (978-1-60282-011-1)

Heart of the Matter by KI Thompson. TV newscaster Kate Foster is Professor Ellen Webster's dream girl, but Kate doesn't know Ellen exists…until an accident changes everything. (978-1-60282-010-4)

Heartland by Julie Cannon. When political strategist Rachel Stanton and dude ranch owner Shivley McCoy collide on an empty country road, fate intervenes. (978-1-60282-009-8)

Shadow of the Knife by Jane Fletcher. Militia Rookie Ellen Mittal has no idea just how complex and dangerous her life is about to become. A Celaeno series adventure romance. (978-1-60282-008-1)

To Protect and Serve by VK Powell. Lieutenant Alex Troy is caught in the paradox of her life—to hold steadfast to her professional oath or to protect the woman she loves. (978-1-60282-007-4)

Deeper by Ronica Black. Former homicide detective Erin McKenzie and her fiancée Elizabeth Adams couldn't be happier—until the not-so-distant past comes knocking at the door. (978-1-60282-006-7)

The Lonely Hearts Club by Radclyffe. Take three friends, add two ex-lovers and several new ones, and the result is a recipe for explosive rivalries and incendiary romance. (978-1-60282-005-0)

Venus Besieged by Andrews & Austin. Teague Richfield heads for Sedona and the sensual arms of psychic astrologer Callie Rivers for a much-needed romantic reunion. (978-1-60282-004-3)

Branded Ann by Merry Shannon. Pirate Branded Ann raids a merchant vessel to obtain a treasure map and gets more than she bargained for with the widow Violet. (978-1-60282-003-6)

American Goth by JD Glass. Trapped by an unsuspected inheritance and guided only by the guardian who holds the secret to her future, Samantha Cray fights to fulfill her destiny. (978-1-60282-002-9)

Learning Curve by Rachel Spangler. Ashton Clarke is perfectly content with her life until she meets the intriguing Professor Carrie Fletcher, who isn't looking for a relationship with anyone. (978-1-60282-001-2)

Place of Exile by Rose Beecham. Sheriff's detective Jude Devine struggles with ghosts of her past and an ex-lover who still haunts her dreams. (978-1-933110-98-1)

Fully Involved by Erin Dutton. A love that has smoldered for years ignites when two women and one little boy come together in the aftermath of tragedy. (978-1-933110-99-8)

Heart 2 Heart by Julie Cannon. Suffering from a devastating personal loss, Kyle Bain meets Lane Connor, and the chance for happiness suddenly seems possible. (978-1-60282-000-5)

Rising Storm by JLee Meyer. The sequel to *First Instinct* takes our heroines on a dangerous journey instead of the honeymoon they'd planned. (978-1-933110-86-8)

First Instinct by JLee Meyer. When high-stakes security fraud leads to murder, one woman flees for her life while another risks her heart to protect her. (1-933110-59-7)

Queens of Tristaine by Cate Culpepper. When a deadly plague stalks the Amazons of Tristaine, two warrior lovers must return to the place of their nightmares to find a cure. (978-1-933110-97-4)

The Crown of Valencia by Catherine Friend. Ex-lovers can really mess up your life…even, as Kate discovers, if they've traveled back to the eleventh century! (978-1-933110-96-7)

Mine by Georgia Beers. What happens when you've already given your heart and love finds you again? Courtney McAllister is about to find out. (978-1-933110-95-0)

House of Clouds by KI Thompson. A sweeping saga of an impassioned romance between a Northern spy and a Southern sympathizer, set amidst the upheaval of a nation under siege. (978-1-933110-94-3)

Forever Found by JLee Meyer. Can time, tragedy, and shattered trust destroy a love that seemed destined? When chance reunites two childhood friends separated by tragedy, the past resurfaces to determine the shape of their future. (1-933110-37-6)

Winds of Fortune by Radclyffe. Provincetown local Deo Camara agrees to rehab Dr. Bonita Burgoyne's historic home, but she never said anything about mending her heart. (978-1-933110-93-6)

Focus of Desire by Kim Baldwin. Isabel Sterling is surprised when she wins a photography contest, but no more than photographer Natasha Kashnikova. Their promo tour becomes a ticket to romance. (978-1-933110-92-9)

Blind Leap by Diane and Jacob Anderson-Minshall. A Golden Gate Bridge suicide becomes suspect when a filmmaker's camera shows a different story. Yoshi Yakamota and the Blind Eye Detective Agency uncover evidence that could be worth killing for. (978-1-933110-91-2)

Wall of Silence, 2nd ed. by Gabrielle Goldsby. Life takes a dangerous turn when jaded police detective Foster Everett meets Riley Medeiros, a woman who isn't afraid to discover the truth no matter the cost. (978-1-933110-90-5)

Mistress of the Runes by Andrews & Austin. Passion ignites between two women with ties to ancient secrets, contemporary mysteries, and a shared quest for the meaning of life. (978-1-933110-89-9)

Vulture's Kiss by Justine Saracen. Archeologist Valerie Foret, heir to a terrifying task, returns in a powerful desert adventure set in Egypt and Jerusalem. (978-1-933110-87-5)

Sheridan's Fate by Gun Brooke. A dynamic, erotic romance between physiotherapist Lark Mitchell and businesswoman Sheridan Ward set in the scorching hot days and humid, steamy nights of San Antonio. (978-1-933110-88-2)

Not Single Enough by Grace Lennox. A funny, sexy modern romance about two lonely women who bond over the unexpected and fall in love along the way. (978-1-933110-85-1)

Such a Pretty Face by Gabrielle Goldsby. A sexy, sometimes humorous, sometimes biting contemporary romance that gently exposes the damage to heart and soul when we fail to look beneath the surface for what truly matters. (978-1-933110-84-4)

Second Season by Ali Vali. A romance set in New Orleans amidst betrayal, Hurricane Katrina, and the new beginnings hardship and heartbreak sometimes make possible. (978-1-933110-83-7)

Hearts Aflame by Ronica Black. A poignant, erotic romance between a hard-driving businesswoman and a solitary vet. Packed with adventure and set in the harsh beauty of the Arizona countryside. (978-1-933110-82-0)

Red Light by JD Glass. Tori forges her path as an EMT in the New York City 911 system while discovering what matters most to herself and the woman she loves. (978-1-933110-81-3)

Honor Under Siege by Radclyffe. Secret Service agent Cameron Roberts struggles to protect her lover while searching for a traitor who just may be another woman with a claim on her heart. (978-1-933110-80-6)

Dark Valentine by Jennifer Fulton. Danger and desire fuel a high-stakes cat-and-mouse game when an attorney and an endangered witness team up to thwart a killer. (978-1-933110-79-0)

Sequestered Hearts by Erin Dutton. A popular artist suddenly goes into seclusion, a reluctant reporter wants to know why, and a heart locked away yearns to be set free. (978-1-933110-78-3)

Erotic Interludes 5: Road Games, ed. by Radclyffe and Stacia Seaman. Adventure, "sport," and sex on the road—hot stories of travel adventures and games of seduction. (978-1-933110-77-6)

The Spanish Pearl by Catherine Friend. On a trip to Spain, Kate Vincent is accidentally transported back in time—an epic saga spiced with humor, lust, and danger. (978-1-933110-76-9)

Lady Knight by L-J Baker. Loyalty and honor clash with love and ambition in a medieval world of magic when female knight Riannon meets Lady Eleanor. (978-1-933110-75-2)

Dark Dreamer by Jennifer Fulton. Best-selling horror author Rowe Devlin falls under the spell of psychic Phoebe Temple. A Dark Vista romance. (978-1-933110-74-5)

Come and Get Me by Julie Cannon. Elliott Foster isn't used to pursuing women, but alluring attorney Lauren Collier makes her change her mind. (978-1-933110-73-8)

Blind Curves by Diane and Jacob Anderson-Minshall. Private eye Yoshi Yakamota comes to the aid of her ex-lover Velvet Erickson in the first Blind Eye mystery. (978-1-933110-72-1)

Dynasty of Rogues by Jane Fletcher. It's hate at first sight for Ranger Riki Sadiq and her new patrol corporal, Tanya Coppelli—except for their undeniable attraction. (978-1-933110-71-4)

Running With the Wind by Nell Stark. Sailing instructor Corrie Marsten has signed off on love until she meets Quinn Davies—one woman she can't ignore. (978-1-933110-70-7)

More Than Paradise by Jennifer Fulton. Two women battle danger, risk all, and find in each other an unexpected ally and an unforgettable love. (978-1-933110-69-1)

Flight Risk by Kim Baldwin. For Blayne Keller, being in the wrong place at the wrong time just might turn out to be the best thing that ever happened to her. (978-1-933110-68-4)

Rebel's Quest: Supreme Constellations Book Two by Gun Brooke. On a world torn by war, two women discover a love that defies all boundaries. (978-1-933110-67-7)

Punk and Zen by JD Glass. Angst, sex, love, rock. Trace, Candace, Francesca…Samantha. Losing control—and finding the truth within. BSB Victory Editions. (1-933110-66-X)